Warrior Class
Blood Rain

Other Books by S. L. Kassidy

Warrior Class
Sky Cutter
Taming the Wind

Please Baby

Scarred Series
Scarred for Life - Book 1
New Cuts, Old Wounds – Book 2
Bandages – Book 3
First Degree Burns - Book 4
Learning to Walk Again – Book 5

Warrior Class
Blood Rain

S.L. Kassidy

Desert Palm Press

Blood Rain
(Warrior Class – Book 3)

By S.L. Kassidy

©2021 S.L. Kassidy

ISBN-(book): 9781954213036
ISBN-(epub): 9781954213043
ISBN (pdf): 9781954213050

Desert Palm Press
1961 Main Street, Suite 220
Watsonville, California 95076
www.desertpalmpress.com

Editor: Kellie Doherty
Cover Design: Jamani Hawkins-El

Printed in the United States of America
First Edition May 2021

Dedication

This book is dedicated to my family, who supported my writing long before I thought it was worth anything, and to my friends, who helped me believe in myself and my work. Thank you all.

Chapter One

THE SMELL OF THE library never failed to set Nakia Akshay at ease and she breathed it in like it gave her life. It was like walking through a forest, wafting with dried leaves and hints of fresh wood along with worn leather. It was only a recently acquired love and appreciation. *How did I not know how amazing books were until a couple of years ago?*

Being surrounded by so much knowledge made her giddy, footsteps transforming into skips, sandals tapping against the hard floor. She giggled in a way that was probably inappropriate for the royal consort of the ruler of the largest territory in the Roshan Empire, but she couldn't help herself. Her spouse would delight in knowing how much Nakia enjoyed the library. *It's her gift to me, after all.*

Sighing, Nakia made it to her spot, her chaise tucked into a quiet corner of the large library. She snuggled into the fluffy pillows, folding her crimson and teal robes in a way to keep them from bunching up. Her spot was just below one of the large windows around the space. The openings started halfway up the wall and went to the ceiling, spaced out by decorated columns. They allowed sunlight to pour in, making the library warm and bright. Any other time, she probably would've been outside, enjoying the gardens or markets, but she was in a reading mood. It was still a new feeling, and she made sure to nurture the desire whenever it popped up.

She had a stack of scrolls by her along with the book in her hands, currently craving Roshan history. Occasionally, she strayed to other subjects, but always came back to this one. It was a good thing she was interested in it. She needed to know as much as she could about the empire she married into. She wasn't sure if she'd ever know enough, especially to rule, but she did her best to learn.

"Why am I not surprised to find you here?" Saniyah Gyan, her spouse's chief weapons' engineer, asked as she stepped into view, moving around a tall shelf. She regarded Nakia with fond mahogany eyes and an amused smile on painted pink lips, but Nakia knew there was a plot behind the kind expression. Saniyah stood out in her vibrant colors, a radiant yellow that put the sun to shame and shimmering green against the library's shades of brown.

Nakia grinned, even though there was trouble afoot. "If my spouse has spent the last three years putting together this grand library for me, wouldn't it be rude of me not to spend time here?"

The library grew a little every day—books, scrolls, and other things finding their way to the shelves. The shelves were as high as three men, alive with knowledge. The rows seemed to go on and on, like a lazy maze with people wandering the landscape, feeding it with more information. There was no way Nakia would be able to enjoy the whole place in her lifetime, but she'd try.

Saniyah flipped her long blond hair over her shoulder, looking innocent enough. Her smile grew warmer, as it often was when she discovered Nakia in the library. Nakia had learned over time how much Saniyah respected knowledge and education. She didn't suffer fools, but a stupid fool was the worst.

Her gaze drifted around the library, focusing for a long moment out a window on the back wall. "Your spouse also gave you a grand city."

Nakia nodded. "She did, and I enjoy it as much as I do the library." *She's trying to get me out of here. What book do I have that she wants?* There were so many. Taking a glance, she had several histories in plain view. They probably had battle descriptions in them. Saniyah used old battles to inspire her. She might want them all. *So, don't let her distract you. Protect your hoard like the Roshan would.*

"When you're not locked away in the library."

"I do believe both our spouses lay the blame squarely at your feet."

Saniyah chuckled, a light, airy sound that settled Nakia when she first accepted Saniyah as part of her life. "What can I say, I'm a great role model."

Nakia didn't dispute that, eternally grateful from the moment Saniyah decided to help her understand what it meant to be the spouse of a powerful figure in the Roshan Empire.

Saniyah showed her how to be the spouse of a queen without losing herself or the things Ashni loved about her. Saniyah helped her understand issues she'd face being married to Ashni. One of the most whispered matters had to do with her being an outsider, and Saniyah helped her navigate that. Her spouse, General Adira Gyan, had also given some suggestions. People tried to trip her up with little things at dinners or festivals or the temple, trick her into false steps and embarrass the Court, but Saniyah and Adira prepared her. The education was necessary, and it was good Nakia didn't have to trouble Ashni over it. Ashni had enough to worry about with conquering the west.

Saniyah also introduced her to the library. Saniyah's estate back in Khenshu had a library, and she walked Nakia around it more than once as if it held secrets of the universe. Saniyah moved most of it with her across the sea, but she was often found in Nakia's library where there was a wider variety of knowledge.

"And because I'm a great role model and a great aunt, I'm here to remind you that you're supposed to have lunch with Bashira. She refuses to come searching for you again." Saniyah gave her a stern look.

Nakia winced. "I lost track of time." A bad habit. "I'm still trying to understand the early history of the Roshan nomads. It's still unclear how Ashni's great grandfather was able to rise in his clan and unite the others." She had read so much and still didn't understand how Ashni's family ended up in the position they did. Ashni was of little help since she didn't have the same questions.

Saniyah chuckled. "I'm sure you'll figure it out, but not in one sitting. Go to your lunch. Your sisters will be there."

Nakia leaped to her feet. *Thia and Saffi!* Just the thought of seeing them again made her giddy. "That's right! Has Ashni received Wicus and Thia yet?" If she missed that she'd never forgive herself, and the Court would whisper about it for days.

Saniyah waved her hand. "No. Adira told me they're going to formally receive your sisters tomorrow. Today is about relaxing and not worrying over all of the ceremony. They're taking Wicus to the arena to enjoy a spectacle. Apparently, those things are more important than decorum."

Nakia shrugged. "Wicus doesn't object if he's out there with them." Ashni and Adira were bad influences on him. Usually, Wicus would follow protocol for the visuals and to meet expectations. Wicus was a devoted ally, even though he didn't want to concede his territory was part of Ashni's territory when she continued her conquest. But his city-state of Valen was surrounded on all sides by Ashni's land. He liked to pretend he had autonomy—and Ashni allowed for the pretense—but Wicus couldn't make a move without Ashni's say-so.

Even so, Ashni treated him as family, something like a brother, so everything was civil anyway. There were even occasions when Wicus went on campaign with Ashni. He and Thia visited often, so the relationship only grew as time went on. It also allowed Nakia's relationship with Thia to mature. *I never would've thought that I'd be so close to my sisters.*

So Nakia had to leave. It was clear why Saniyah strolled into the library looking like mischief personified. She narrowed her gaze on Saniyah, whose eyes sparkled. *She wants my bounty.*

Nakia held up a finger. "Don't take my books." She didn't have time to have a servant pack the small mountain away and march them to the safety of her room, but she didn't want to lose them either.

Saniyah often let Nakia hunt for work and waited for her to become distracted, then Saniyah would walk off with many of the books, searching for inspiration on new weapon ideas from old battles or learning from old battles to see what her spouse might come up against in the field.

Saniyah pressed her palms together. "Considering this is your personal library, I can't help but take your books."

Nakia's face fell. Yes, it was her personal library, but she left it open to anyone close to her. "You know what I mean."

Saniyah grinned. "Do I?"

Nakia pointed to her pile of books and scrolls. "Those are off limits. Do not touch them."

Saniyah's eyebrows furrowed. "You can't possibly read them all at once. Would you even notice if I left with one?"

"No, but I'll notice if you leave with five, which would be if I'm lucky." She huffed. Her books would vanish with Saniyah the second she left them unguarded. *So don't leave them unguarded.*

Saniyah smiled at Nakia, bright and beautiful, a promise those books would be gone the second she left, but she needed to see her sisters and best friend.

Before Nakia left the library, she instructed a servant to go to her area and gather her books. If the servant moved fast enough, she wouldn't have to spend tomorrow finding new tomes. With that out of the way, she rushed through the palace, not wanting to be late for her own lunch date. *I have to get better at keeping track of these things.*

Nakia couldn't help taking in some of the art as she zipped by frescos and tapestries depicting a multitude of stories, a mix of religious stories from both Kairon and Roshan. Her favorite was the story of Ashni's parents, and it was told in several different mediums across areas.

Nakia patronized many different artists to tell her and Ashni's story. Nakia worked hard to normalize their relationship in Kairon, to get Westerners used to seeing two women together. There were plays, stories, and art showing, promoting, and embracing same sex relationships.

Beyond her own, Nakia patronized art throughout the territory depicting Roshan love stories and adventures of same sex couples. There were no shortages of such. She could see it in the markets, at public temples, and even at noble functions. Evidence of change never failed to fill her with hope and joy.

Nakia had to dodge many people in her mad dash. The palace was always a hive of activity. Ashni had a habit of attracting busy people, even the servants. There was always something to be done by someone somewhere. It didn't help that the palace was still under construction, as was the city. This western capital was home.

The city was once known as Phyllida, but Ashni changed the name once it fell under her control. It was now Nakian, a reminder to the people of why it was still standing after the way their former king had behaved toward the Roshan. Ashni could have destroyed the city, but she gave it to Nakia instead.

The gesture still made Nakia's heart flutter. It reminded her of what Ashni's mother told her when they met: Ashni would conquer the world and gift it to Nakia. Ashni tried to rename all of Kairon after her, but Nakia objected. That was too much.

Nakia halted just in time, almost colliding with Bashira. Her dearest friend was as bright and bubbly as always and somehow always managed to pop up out of nowhere. Her blond hair bounced and shone like the sun, like her personality. Sometimes, it was a surprise she didn't fall into more fluid movements since dancing was her passion. She giggled the moment Nakia stepped into the lush eastern garden.

"You made it," Bashira said, throwing her arm around Nakia's shoulders and pulling her into a hug. Nakia laughed, returning the embrace, and kissed Bashira's cheek. Bashira never failed to make her feel warm on the inside.

Nakia patted Bashira's arm as they pulled away. "Of course."

Bashira led Nakia into the garden with flowers as colorful as Bashira's robes. The smell of mint and mist greeted Nakia. Fountains kept the area cool, but also made the whole place sparkle when the sunlight hit it, like walking into a place for the gods or heroes.

Nakia smiled. "You didn't even have to send someone to find me this time."

Bashira scoffed. "Because my aunt was already headed to the library." She looped her arm around Nakia's and walked her to the lunch area.

"Nakia, we feared you forgot us!" Thia, Nakia's older sister, rose with all the elegance and grace of a queen. She never failed to remind Nakia what a true queen should look like, tall with brown hair that flowed like it had a mind of its own. Her face was fresh and full of wisdom.

"How could I? This is our first lunch with Saffi." Nakia's gaze fell to her other sister, Saffi, grinning so hard it hurt her face. Her heart filled at the sight of her older sister.

Saffi wasn't as graceful as Thia when she rose, and she didn't stand with the same posture as Thia and Nakia. Her brown eyes sparkled, but the light was new and helped display wrinkles on her pale face. She seemed older than Thia, even though Thia had a couple of years on her. Time with them should remedy that. *That's what people tell me.*

Much to Nakia's delight, Saffi wore Roshan attire, a long, light robes cascading around her like a rose-colored waterfall with streams of gold stitching. She wanted her sisters to embrace her and her adopted culture. Like Nakia, Saffi viewed the Roshan as her saviors. Ashni rescued her from her husband, Ferox, a wild king who foolishly stood against the Roshan.

Ferox put himself in Ashni's line of fire by aiding Dorian, Nakia's father, and standing against Ashni. He ran after she made a fool of him in battle. He probably thought he got away or she forgot about him as she conquered more of Kairon, but it was really that his kingdom was too far at first. That changed a year ago. Ashni's army made it close enough to his land and found a purpose for what most of Kairon thought was a wasteland. Rice fields. Ashni conquered it with glee and brought Saffi to Nakia, reuniting the sisters.

Saffi bowed her head to Nakia, but Nakia grabbed her into a hug. "Please, we're sisters. You have to stop bowing."

"I'm sorry. This is still so incredible. Never in my wildest dreams did I think I'd be able to see you both again," Saffi said, her voice low like always. It was like she had been trained to whisper, like her voice did not matter. She glanced between Nakia and Thia.

Thia smiled as she stroked Saffi's cheek. "I'm happy about it. I worried over you." She embraced Saffi and then pulled Nakia into the hug. "Our father didn't do right by either of you."

None of them could argue, though Saffi got the worst of it. Saffi's time with Ferox hadn't been kind and it turned out it wasn't even him. His other wives had tormented Saffi because she hadn't produced a child.

"Let's eat." Nakia motioned for them to sit.

Lunch was set up in Roshan style, pillows for them around food trays on low tables. An umbrella shaded them from the radiant sun. A mix of Roshan and Kairon foods lay before them, which Nakia always did. They settled on their pillows. Bashira sat by Nakia and Saffi sat on the other side of her. Thia was close to Saffi.

"How long will you be here, Thia?" Bashira asked.

She was familiar with Thia after moving west with Saniyah two years ago. Saniyah wanted to be close to her spouse and Bashira wanted to be with her aunts. Her father eventually followed to help develop towns, so Bashira had her whole family with her.

Thia studied the food. "I believe we'll be here for the rest of the month. Wicus wants to discuss the trade routes and Ashni had a matter to resolve."

"It's the tribes across the river," Nakia said.

Across the Great River Reve, the tribes up north were giving Ashni, Adira, and Layla fits. They raided towns and villages in Roshan territory, making pests of themselves. They needed to be stopped, but they were spread to the point where Ashni wanted as many soldiers at her disposal as possible to take them out.

"An invasion?" Thia arched an eyebrow.

Nakia shook her head. An invasion implied plans to stay. "Nothing of the sort. Just getting the tribes to stay on their side of the river."

Thia let loose a delicate snort. "We all know they won't. They want all of the new, shiny goods in Kairon."

Bashira waved her hands around. "Can you two save this for when you're sitting with your spouses and generals?"

Nakia laughed. "Sorry. That was rude." She glanced at Saffi, whose head was down. While this was annoying for Bashira, who simply had no desire to hear about military matters, it was foreign to Saffi, who didn't have a spouse who shared information with her as theirs did.

"Very. Forgive us." Thia bowed her head.

"You can sit in on meetings and discuss what the army is doing?" Saffi asked.

Nakia nodded. "We can bring you, too, if you like."

She recalled reigning had actually been an interest for Saffi. It was one of the biggest divides between her and their father. He always wanted Saffi to stay in a woman's place, and she never seemed to know where it was.

The color left Saffi's already ashen face, and Nakia hated to imagine what her life had to be like with the Tyrans. It would seem they broke Saffi. That wouldn't do.

"We should go shopping," Bashira said. Not the subtlest change of topic.

"Don't you have a show you're doing?" Nakia asked.

Bashira's face lit up and she clapped. "You can all come! It's a wonderful show."

"I still can't believe you're allowed to be in shows. And dancing of all things." Thia shook her head as her lips twitched, probably trying to hold in a frown.

"I still can't believe you refuse to come see me. Nakia will tell you. I'm quite good," Bashira replied, inclining her chin.

"She's not lying." Nakia reached for some dates. The fruit used to be considered a rare delicacy, but since trade opened up with the East, they were easier to get. "She's quite good. Her friends in her troupe are all nice as well."

Thia scoffed as she finally settled on having ginger cookies, also from the East. "They're obligated to be nice to you."

Nakia dismissed that with a wiggle of her fingers. "No one's obligated to be nice to me."

Thia leaned forward. "Everyone's obligated to be nice to you, dear sister."

Nakia laughed. "I've had diplomats sit across from me with Ashni three seconds away from burning their cities to the ground and they'll treat me like I'm lower than dirt." Or they treated her as if she didn't know what she was doing, like her father used to do. *He wasn't right, and they're not right.*

"And then you still talk them into an impossible deal and save their cities," Thia said.

Nakia smirked. Technically, her sister could be considered the first to fall victim to her. She had done that to Wicus and Thia. No, they didn't look down on her, but they had underestimated her early on when Ashni sent her to hammer out the details of their alliance. She swung the conversation back to Bashira, and they enjoyed the good food and beautiful weather.

***

Ashni typically didn't mind spending the day watching matches at the arena, but there was so much to do. The groans of animals, the grunts of warriors, and the shuffle of sand filtered through along with cheers, but they weren't as loud as they should've been. Half the seats were empty. Those sections of the building weren't done. *There's always something else going on.* She wasn't sure when she'd be able to really dig into finishing the infrastructure.

Even as she, Adira, and Wicus made their way back to the palace, all Ashni could see were the things that needed to be taken care of. Every temple they passed was under construction. Without a proper theater, shows were put on in tents. Some streets were unpaved. They cut through a small marketplace. There were people scattered about, buying and selling, but not in a hurry. *There needs to be more bustle.*

Ashni wanted Nakian to become Khenshu's sister city. Nakian had a long way to go. It would take time to become what she wanted, but it would take longer if she was out lazing about. A city named for her spouse needed to be as spectacular as her spouse.

We'll get it there. Of course, there was something else she had to do first. It would help make the city great.

"The city has become quite a crossroads. I see many Roshan influences," Wicus said as he weaved his broad shoulders about, cutting through the thin crowd. Hazel eyes scanned, cautious, questioning. His height gave him an advantage in that, even though his discomfort was written all over his smooth, sun-kissed face. He used to complain about walking among the commoners until he realized Ashni wouldn't stop to accommodate him.

"Things are coming along," Ashni replied, ignoring the eye roll from Adira. If it were up to Adira, they'd have shaped the city to look exactly like Khenshu. Even in ruins, the city was Roshan meets Kairon, East meets West, and Ashni wanted it to stay that way. She liked that both she and Wicus blended in, even though she was dressed in Roshan attire, solid colored, layered silk robes of teal and gold, while Wicus had on the Kairon robes complete with cloth draped over his shoulder and detailed designs of dragonflies against dark blue, yellow, and black linens.

Wicus made more of a show of looking around. "Then we'll be able to get more goods into Valen?"

Ashni sighed. "I thought we were waiting for tomorrow to discuss business. Our spouses would have our heads if we did this without them." Not to mention Layla wasn't there. Ashni would never hear the end of it if she discussed business without her sister.

Wicus nodded. Ashni liked that he respected Thia so much. She hadn't come across much of that in Kairon. The concept of men being above women wasn't new to her, but it never failed to set her on edge.

They continued on before Wicus cut into the silence again. It seemed he couldn't help himself but carry on a conversation. "That arena was a work of art. What were those matches we watched again?"

"We got lucky today. Those matches were for joining warrior guilds," Ashni replied. Those who won their matches today would end up in the military, helping her take more of the West when she was ready. For the moment, however, she needed to shore up her power in conquered territory.

Wicus pursed his full lips. "A warrior guild?"

Ashni took a breath. *How to explain this to someone not from the Empire?* "There are four warrior guilds in the Roshan society. You join one and those are your partners for life. We respect all warriors, but the members of your own guild are special to you."

"So, which are you?" Wicus asked.

Ashni was about to question his eyesight. Her guild was obvious to her and other Roshan. Her tattoos were prominent, but even the design of her braids broadcasted her guild. *There's no way he'd know, though.* "I'm of the Lion guild, as is Adira." She motioned to Adira; her single brown eye focused ahead as if she were above the conversation.

Wicus nodded. "So, to become a member of your guild, I'd have to kill a lion in the arena?"

Adira snorted and slapped Ashni against her shoulder. "If only it was so easy."

Ashni touched a lion's tooth around her neck. The trial to join a guild was much more ruthless than simply killing a beast. What it took to join her guild would always leave a mark, a stain on the soul. It was why all big cats were respected and treated well in her land. It was the least she could do.

"You don't think I could do it?" Wicus asked, a daring glint in his eyes.

Ashni spoke up before Adira insulted the man. "I'm not sure you'd want to. You noticed everyone we saw was a teenager, right?" When Wicus nodded, Ashni continued. "There's a reason. You're hungrier to prove yourself. When you're already an established warrior and commander, it's a little harder. It takes more of a toll on you." It took a toll no matter what, but if she did it now, it would come across as senseless. She couldn't even imagine how it felt when Adira did it, an older teen, but also a conquered person trying to fit in. "If it's really something you want, I'll arrange it."

The guilds helped Ashni's popularity. Social mobility gave her the masses. Joining a warrior guild for a person who had nothing was like suddenly gaining fame and fortune, just like joining the military. It gave people who had nothing something and that was worth fighting for. Ashni was worth fighting for, and so was the Empire.

Wicus squared his shoulders. "I have to discuss it with Thia."

Ashni and Adira laughed. Ashni patted him on the shoulder. "And this is why you're our ally."

"You're definitely one of us," Adira said.

Wicus smiled, his eyes twinkling. "Not a bad place to be."

The trio made their way back to the palace. Wicus went to check on his children, which Ashni admired. It reminded her of her father.

"Why aren't there more of him around here?" Ashni asked as she and Adira made their way to the throne room.

Adira shrugged. "Would make things too easy?"

"Probably." Ashni hadn't expected to like Wicus as much as she did, but it was a pleasant surprise. "Should we try to get some work done before officially welcoming Wicus and Thia with tonight's feast?"

With a smile, Adira threw her arm around Ashni and gave her a squeeze. "I really like how responsible you've become. There are some reports we could go over." That settled it.

The next morning, there was the proper meeting with Wicus and Thia. Ashni settled on a pillow with Nakia pressed to her. A small, sparse meeting room held everyone necessary. Pillows to sit on, trays with breakfast foods, some maps, and documents for everyone involved. To Ashni's right, Layla and Naren sat. To her left, Adira and her now second-in-command Hafiz Vivek, sitting up tall and proud, towering over all of them. He had matured in the three years he had worked more closely with them. Ashni had to admit Adira picked well when she picked Hafiz.

"So, we want to discuss getting more trade into Valen," Wicus said, sitting across from Ashni and Nakia. He motioned to Thia, next to him, as she helped herself to some fruit.

Ashni gave a shrug. "What's the issue? You have merchants coming into the city. You're getting goods from all over the Empire." Apples called to her as always and she ate a couple of slices dipped in honey.

Thia spoke up. "We get goods well after other cities. It's all leftover goods, if there's anything at all. Our nobles expected better, expected more. Where is the luxury? Where is the beauty? Where is the ease? We made promises, as you made promises."

Ashni rubbed her chin. "And I'm supposed to get merchants to you faster?" The fact that their nobles were up in arms over this was a waste of time. "You could easily remind your nobles where they'd be without this trade deal."

Nakia patted her thigh. "Not helping."

"So, you want the merchants to come to you first?" Layla asked.

"It would calm down our nobles who think we made a mistake allying ourselves to you. We don't want them to have an excuse to start trouble," Wicus replied.

"We were thinking we could build a direct road to the eastern ports to Valen," Thia said.

Ashni shoved several apples in her mouth to avoid laughing. *Do they think I have endless resources and time?* At no point in time would that road benefit her territory.

Adira smirked. "You mean, you want us to build the road."

Wicus' eyes glinted. "You do have the money, manpower, and it's through your territory."

"That benefits us in no way," Ashni replied. She could use the money and manpower to continue working on Nakian. Why waste it on them?

"What about your canal idea?" Nakia asked.

Ashni looked at her spouse. Water was the fastest way to move things and her territory was quite vast now. If she wanted to remain connected to the rest of the Empire, she needed to make sure she could move people and goods around quickly. A canal that connected to the rivers running through Kairon had been a plan long before she took the West.

"A canal would be good if it's going to come to Valen," Thia said.

"When would construction begin?" Wicus asked.

Ashni looked to Adira, who shrugged. "I've had my hands tied with our military. Ask Nakia."

"I've spoken to some engineers, but most of their attention is on the city and the palace," Nakia said.

"So, no canal?" Thia asked.

Ashni took a breath. She needed to start something soon or it would never get done. "We'll start the canal. Find or pull some engineers."

"I'll also need people to work on it," Nakia replied. She was technically in charge of the canal system anyway, as she handled most of their non-military infrastructure. It was a job she gave herself, and Ashni didn't argue. If Nakia could find manpower that didn't pull the military, Ashni would give her the world.

Ashni gave Wicus a look. "She's on it. Problem solved."

Wicus glanced at Thia, whose eyes were on Nakia. The sisters exchanged smiles and Wicus tilted his head in acceptance.

"Now, onto our business," Layla said, pressing her palms together.

Wicus nodded. "The northern barbarians."

"They've been coming across the river and terrorizing towns. We're going to march on them. I merely need to know you'll support us, as allies do," Ashni replied.

"Of course, yet I feel you want more than that," Wicus said.

Ashni waved the comment away. She needed the verbal assurance in front of witnesses. Allies had betrayed her on occasion and then claimed ignorance when confronted over it.

"Your support is fine, but we'll work out the numbers now, if you like," Adira said.

"Proceed." Wicus motioned to Adira.

Relief coursed through Ashni. That was really all she needed. Wicus would honor their agreement, but Ashni could let Adira entice him with why he should fully commit to their cause. Fighting the tribes across the river wouldn't be the open warfare he was accustomed to. Her new troops would have problems, too. They had not done anything beyond open field combat. She frowned. What if she had expanded too far? Even if that was so, she wouldn't be stopped. *This is a mere bump in the long road to glory.*

Chapter Two

NAKIA CUDDLED CLOSER TO Ashni while trying to fight off consciousness for a little while longer. If she could stay asleep, the day would never begin and if the day didn't begin, it wouldn't end with Ashni leaving to face the northern barbarians. Her stomach trembled at the thought of being left to handle everything on her own. It wouldn't be the first time, but it never failed to eat at her insides. She didn't want to think about it. She wanted to enjoy her spouse a little longer.

So Nakia held onto sleep as if it was precious, even though she was obviously awake. Sweet kisses to her neck and caresses to her bare abdomen from rough callused hands startled her. *Oh, this is worth getting up for.*

"Are you with me, kitten?" Ashni whispered.

Nakia purred. "Always." She pressed herself closer to Ashni.

"I love you more than anything, you know?" The words were low, as if a secret, but the world knew.

The expression of love made her strong, like she could capture the sun. She could do anything with Ashni by her side. *What about when she's not?* It was an old thought, but she wouldn't let the dark whispers from her soul spoil her limited time with Ashni.

Nakia stroked Ashni's muscular arm with her thumb. Her soft skin made Nakia want to feel her beloved's body against hers forever. "Do you want something, my love?"

Ashni placed a particularly wet kiss on her neck, just the way Nakia liked it. "Oh, I want a lot of things, kitten. Most of those, I want to hand over to you."

"I know." Nakia took hold of Ashni's thick, soft mane of brown hair, tugging her up until they locked eyes.

She couldn't help getting lost in Ashni's amber gaze. There was a hunger there, and it filled Nakia to the brim. *But it'll empty when she's away.*

Nakia smiled. "Sometimes, I swear you're a lion, staring me down."

Wild and carefree, Ashni grinned. "They are my brothers."

"I know." And if Nakia hadn't met other members of the Lion guild, she would've thought Ashni's look was part of the requirements. Beyond the hair and eyes, Ashni's thick muscles made her similar to her so-called brothers.

Ashni didn't seem to care for the discussion, coming in for a kiss. Nakia pulled Ashni closer. She moaned as their bodies pressed together, igniting passion.

"I love you," Nakia said when they broke apart. It came easily, freely, and never failed to be the truth.

Ashni caressed her cheek. "I love you, too."

"Then stay with me." It was impossible, but she pouted, just in case it worked. Sometimes, her smallest twitches could bring Ashni to her knees. It was probably too much power for one person, but Nakia didn't care. Ashni loved her, wanted to give her the world. Who wouldn't want that kind of affection?

Ashni gave her a sweet peck on the mouth. "For now."

"Forever."

"Kitten, even if I'm not here, I'm always here." Ashni pressed her fingers to the center of Nakia's bare chest.

Nakia clutched Ashni tighter as her heart fluttered. "But I want you here. Don't you want to give me everything I want?"

Ashni wiggled in between her legs. "That's my deepest desire."

Nakia never doubted that was the truth. *How did I become so fortunate?* It was like Ashni had descended from the sky and was presented to her as essential treasure. She caressed Ashni's biceps and got lost in golden eyes that gazed upon her as if she were the most precious thing in all of creation. A divine being looked at her as if she were a goddess.

"While you're away, I'll make many sacrifices for your victory," Nakia said. It was the only way she could help when there was a military campaign. She trusted the gods delighted in her prayers and protected her beloved.

Ashni flashed her teeth. "So, now I have your blessing to go?"

"You're going to go regardless," Nakia scoffed.

Ashni gave her a look. "You know I don't want to upset you, kitten."

"I know, I know." Nakia sighed. "Forgive me, love. I'm being selfish and spoiled. I'll miss you terribly, as I always do when you're away, and worry until you're back at my side."

Ashni gave her another kiss, and they lost themselves in the hot embrace. Ashni ground against her. A mutual moan echoed through their room. As they broke for air, sharing a breath, Ashni pressed her forehead to Nakia's. Nakia smiled at her favorite gesture.

"What am I thinking, beloved?" Nakia asked.

Had the Roshan who invented this gesture actually been able to read the minds of people they cared about? She'd bet her life on it. Ashni could always tell what she thought or needed. Maybe it didn't come through as a loud, clear message, but there was always a feeling.

Ashni hummed, like she had to think on it. "How much you love me."

"Always."

"You want me to stay."

"I already told you that."

"How you'll let me go because you understand why I have to lead my soldiers."

Nakia sighed. "I will." Ashni didn't have it in her to ask people to fight and not fight herself, to ask people to risk their lives and not risk her own. Nakia respected that. "I just want you with me."

"We've gone through this, kitten." Ashni gave her a peck on the lips, as if that would magically make things better. And for a moment, it did. "I'm here now."

"Let's make the most of it." Nakia took Ashni by the shoulders and pushed her. "Let me make my mark on your memory this morning."

Ashni laughed as she flipped onto her back, making sure to be as dramatic as she could be. "You're so strong now, hellcat."

Nakia straddled Ashni. "Yeah, I'm so strong I've subdued the most powerful force on the planet." *You only can do it because she lets you.*

"You're not wrong." She ran her hands along Nakia's sides, spending sparks through her that had little to do with Ashni's command of lightning.

Nakia smirked. "Oh, I know. Now, lie back and let me treat you."

"You sure?" Ashni combed her fingers through Nakia's hair.

"Yes. Sometimes, things can be all about you," Nakia replied. Ashni was the only person to ever spoil her, and it made her feel special. Ashni deserved to experience that, too.

Ashni's eyes twinkled. "Oh, when I have you at my mercy, it's all about me. I delight in giving you pleasure."

Nakia chuckled, thinking about the hours in bed. It was nice to be indulged, especially when Ashni didn't put up a fight to let Nakia do the spoiling in return. It didn't happen often enough. Nakia narrowed her gaze on Ashni, making sure she didn't make any sudden moves. "You're not even going to put up a fight?" It would be just like Ashni to pretend she gave up and then literally flip things, putting Nakia on her back.

Ashni's eyes sparkled even more. "You want me to struggle, kitten?"

Nakia laughed. "You know what I mean."

"I know you want this moment to be special. There's nothing more special than your mouth on me. It's a wonder that you're willing to be with me."

Nakia blinked. "There's no one else I'd rather be with."

"I know, but I still can't believe the gods blessed me with you."

Years into their relationship and it still shocked Nakia. Ashni was probably the most powerful person on the planet, second to her mother. And yet she still thought Nakia was a blessing. *How the hell did I get so lucky?*

"I think it's the other way around," Nakia said. After all, her entire life was made possible through her spouse.

Knowing they could get caught in this loop for hours, Nakia kissed Ashni. Sparks jumped between them again. Ashni held Nakia in arms that had conquered nations. She pressed her thigh between Ashni's legs and drew a moan from this force of nature.

Dragging her tongue down Ashni's neck, Nakia tasted salt and subtle honey, like Ashni ate so many sweets it was part of her. She would never tire of the flavor. And the little sounds from Ashni made things so much sweeter. She made her way down, kissing the tops of Ashni's breasts. Her fingers sought taut peaks and Ashni squirmed as she flicked and caressed.

"Tease," Ashni gasped.

"I've barely gotten started." Nakia latched onto a brown gem and loved it with her tongue.

Ashni cried out. "I love that."

"I know." Nakia had learned she liked to spend time with Ashni's breasts just as much as Ashni did. *Never would've thought that.* She sucked and licked.

Ashni threw her head back. "Oh!"

Nakia smiled. Maybe Ashni would remember this and hurry back. She knew she'd count the days until Ashni's return. *Live in the moment.*

To anchor herself, Nakia slid her hand between their bodies and met welcoming warmth. Ashni's legs opened wider and Nakia eased through her wild patch of hair to reacquaint herself with another gem. Ashni's hips bucked.

"You're already so ready for me, beloved," Nakia said.

Ashni dug her fingers into Nakia's shoulders. Nakia loved the pain. Loved that Ashni grounded herself with Nakia's body. A demigod tethered to this world through her.

"Been ready since last night," Ashni said with a couple of pants.

"Oh?" Nakia plucked a lonely nipple with her lips and reveled in the honey on her fingertips as Ashni trembled beneath her. "Last night you wouldn't let me do this. You wouldn't let me have my way with you. Instead, you wanted to see if you could beat your record."

Ashni chuckled and gave her signature lopsided grin. "Six orgasms before you passed out. Worth it."

Nakia gave Ashni's nipple a light bite as a reprimand. Ashni jumped and cooed. The sound made Nakia's heart flutter. Nakia dipped a finger inside of her spouse, and Ashni cried out.

"Look at that. I have the ruler of half the world at my fingertips," Nakia said. "You're at my mercy. How does it feel?"

Ashni's breath hitched. "Sweet."

Nakia kissed the center of Ashni's chest as she pushed her finger home. Ashni groaned, a flush on her chest growing. Her beloved glowed, a beautiful halo around her tawny skin as she worked up sweat. Her shine could put the sun to shame, not that Nakia would ever say that aloud.

"You're beautiful like this," Nakia said as she stroked Ashni. Seeing Ashni like this, there were times when she thought she might float off into the sky and never come back down.

Ashni whined and moved with her. Nakia latched onto Ashni's nipple again. As she pulled the jewel with her teeth, Ashni arched against her and her hips jumped. After a few bucks, Nakia added a second finger and Ashni crooned, throwing her head to the side, showing a thick vein in her neck. The sound floated through Nakia.

"I love when I get to hear you," Nakia murmured, running her tongue along that throbbing vein.

Ashni ground against Nakia, running her fingers through Nakia's hair. "My shy kitten is gone. Sometimes I miss her."

That was a confession to store away for later. She dipped her head and ran her tongue through Ashni's desire. Sweet slippery liquid exploded in her mouth. This was what happiness, security, and love tasted like.

Ashni's back bowed as she cried out, arching into Nakia's questing tongue. Nakia lapped at Ashni like the lazy kitten Ashni liked to pretend she was and worked two fingers in and out of her beloved. Ashni held Nakia's head with both hands, latching onto her eyes with an intense gaze and stroking her hair out of the way. The sensation of Ashni's hands twined in her hair made Nakia feel like she could be carried away on a breeze and it would only bring her more bliss. She rubbed Ashni's clit, and Ashni howled. That reaction earned a nip and a sharp plunge of Nakia's fingers. Finally, Ashni shouted, the sound reverberating through Nakia.

Sweet nectar coated Nakia's face as her beloved quivered against her. Nakia pulled away far enough to see the bliss settle on Ashni's face as a flush came over her ocher body, making her seem almost like a terracotta statue. With a sigh, Ashni seemed to mold with the bed and an ethereal smile flitted across her face.

Nakia cuddled into Ashni, who purred. "Still miss your shy kitten? She couldn't do that," Nakia said.

Ashni kissed the top of her head. "Only my hellcat can do that, but my shy kitten was so cute. I can still hear you asking me if you're doing it right."

Nakia nipped Ashni's shoulder. "Maybe I wanted to learn how to make you feel good."

"And learn you did!"

She placed her hand over Ashni's heart. "Be careful, my love."

Ashni held her close. "I'll come back to you. Nothing would ever stop that from happening. Besides you're always so busy keeping this thing together, you'll barely notice I'm gone."

Nakia nuzzled Ashni, breathing in her scent, holding her close. *If only you knew, my love.* The gnawing in her gut always noticed Ashni was gone. The shadow that everything could fall apart if she made one misstep would notice Ashni's absence and her father's voice would begin to echo in her mind. *Don't think about it. You can handle things.*

"It's so much easier to govern when you're here. I blame you for everything that's wrong and send all the people complaining to you," Nakia said.

Ashni laughed. "Oh, do you? That's why I always have lines of people waiting to get a lightning bolt in the ass? I'll show you!" She grabbed Nakia, grinning like a lion with its prey.

"Don't you dare!" The threat was too late, and Nakia howled with laughter as Ashni proceeded to tickle her.

***

"You're smiling mighty big. We all know how annoying this will be," Adira said as she, Ashni, Layla, and the military traveled north. They had bid all their loved ones farewell minutes ago, and now they were on horseback and on the move. Farmland slowly rolled by. It would soon give way to forests, which would transform back into grassland and farms as they got closer to the Great River Reve.

Ashni grinned wider, sitting taller on Midnight Thunder, his coat shining like glinting obsidian. "I won several battles this morning." She puffed out her chest, still feeling pure ecstasy flowing through her. She was sure it would gush out instead of her blood if she got cut.

Layla groaned. "If this is a sex thing, keep it to yourself."

Ashni scoffed, eyeing her sister. "As if I'd dare gossip about what I do with my spouse. I tickled her for trying to make fun of me. She's no match."

"You're leaving your wife for weeks and you tickle her?" Adira frowned.

"Some couples kiss and cuddle and make love. You tickle torture. How are you in charge again?" Layla arched an eyebrow. Naren, her husband right behind her, had the nerve to twist his mouth up, like he was confused by Ashni's behavior.

Ashni waved them off. "You don't understand our relationship."

They all knew she hadn't left Nakia with their last moments being tickled, but it kept things light. They had pegged the northern tribes a nuisance, not much of a threat. They needed to keep that idea reinforced for their troops.

"I don't think you understand your relationship," Adira said.

"Or a relationship," Layla added.

"My spouse is happy. Clearly, I'm doing something right," Ashni replied, throwing her shoulders back. Midnight Thunder snorted, and Ashni gagged. "What? My own horse is skeptical. You always take Nakia's side."

"Maybe because she isn't constantly taking him into dangerous situations," Adira said.

"He loves it. He's a warrior like me." She stroked Midnight Thunder's muscular neck. "She sneaks him treats. Hell, she sneaks me treats. Maybe that's why I always side with her. Damn, she got us, boy." The horse whinnied, as if chuckling with her.

The journey went on like that, over a week of nonsense. It was a good distraction as the chill of the north made itself known. It wasn't as cold as it could be, but it was enough for Ashni to grit her teeth. She tended to run hot, and the weather now prickled just under her skin, adding to the annoyance of the tribes not staying on their gods-forsaken crap side of the river.

As they came to the Great River Reve, arrows and stones from slings greeted them along with the miserable stench of the North and shouts from the other side. The arrows splashed into the river, and the waters dragged the stones away. The barbarians knew they were coming, lining up behind some brush, waving weapons, shields, and wasting projectiles. Scouts, perhaps, or they simply could have watched them the moment they came into view from the waterway.

"Those idiots," Naren said, putting his hand up to shield his face from the glare of the sun.

"They just want to remind us that we're not friends and they have no desire to be friends," Ashni said. She had tried that route, but the barbarians' response was to wish her a long painful death.

There just was no pleasing some people, at least until they got to see the war machine they wanted to provoke.

Wicus rode up next to Ashni, looking like the seasoned warrior he was. He had on dark, plated armor, not his usual wear, and it was better for the colder north than his lightweight armor. His sword hung at his side and he had his helmet tucked under his arm. There was a confident tilt to his chin, which his steed mimicked. It was good he felt confident enough in Thia to leave her with his city. *Why aren't more Western men like him?*

"What do you want to do? They know we can't reach them from here and they've refused talks," Wicus said.

Ashni laughed, eyeing the wide river. "I'm going to do the impossible."

She had weapons that could reach across the river, but it would've been like blindly swatting a single fly among hundreds. Nothing more than a waste of time and effort.

"Lay waste to them with lightning so we can all go home?" Naren smiled.

Ashni cut her eyes to him. "I can't hit everything with lightning."

"How do you know? You never try," Naren replied.

"Because I know how my talent works. Besides, the river is too wide to make out proper targets."

"You could blow them back with your wind," Naren suggested.

Ashni looked at her sister, face scrunched up. What good would that do? The barbarians would eventually return. Layla had the nerve to look back at her, like Naren wasn't borderline incompetent. Ashni cut her eyes back to Naren and curled her lip.

"Do you work hard to be this stupid?" Ashni asked.

Layla glared at her. "Leave him alone, Ashni. You're just bitter we're up here in the cold."

"Bitter isn't the word I'd use. We have very few options to stop those pests with them being so far away," Ashni replied. "We'll have to build a bridge." The barbarians used boats to cross the river, but it wouldn't work for an army of this size. They'd clog the river and be easy targets if the barbarians had any secret weapons.

Wicus' mouth dropped open. "Across that? It'll take forever."

"Adira?" Ashni turned to her lead general.

Adira scratched her chin. "A week, less if we can figure out how to work at night without accidents like before."

"Layla." Ashni looked at her sister.

Layla nodded. "Night shift. Understood."

"Then let's get started." Ashni clapped her hands, and her people began to move, officers putting soldiers to work.

Wicus' eyes went wide. "You're serious." He sounded way too incredulous for someone who had rode into battle with her before.

"It's not so difficult," Hafiz replied from his spot by Adira's side. He rode above them, on his massive alphyn, Yata. Having grown in years, Yata now dwarfed any horse he stood next to. He had the body and face of a lion, scales on his thick front legs that met dark brown fur at the thigh, and long talons. Hafiz gripped Yata's dark crimson mane instead of reins, which ran the length of his back down his tapered, dragon-like tail and ended with a tuft of fur.

Hafiz seemed made to ride the creature, taller and wider than all of them. His spirit and mind grew with his body as well.

"I trapped your city with a wall of my own," Ashni reminded Wicus. What she was about to do was as much for her allies as it was for her enemies. They needed to remember her army would do the impossible on her order.

Her military set to work. They'd brought materials for the bridge with them, as this had always been the plan. Grunts and groans filled the air as wood was moved. Thuds followed as pieces were nailed together.

"A bridge in only one week. Are you sure?" Wicus asked as he sat at the evening meal with Ashni and her group. They were huddled outside of Ashni's tent while they still had some daylight left and a flurry of activity around them. There was food between them along with maps and scrolls. Naren was more interested in eating, as usual, while everyone else studied some form of parchment.

"Some materials still need to be shaped, but at this point, it's just a matter of putting the pieces together," Adira said as she put down one report only to grab another.

"We've done it before," Layla said.

Wicus nodded. "How?" He picked at some shredded chicken as he read through a report of his own.

Ashni rubbed her hands together, keeping the slight chill away. "You surround yourself with the right people and anything's possible. If you only have one trick, you won't get far. That's from the top." She glanced at Adira and Layla. "To the bottom." She motioned to the foot soldiers hustling to get their labor in.

Wicus nodded, probably storing that away for later. It was always possible he'd use her advice to try to oppose her one day. He and Thia would eventually realize their positions were only through her grace, if they hadn't already.

The barbarians across the river were trying to burn through her grace, though. They put boats in the water as the sun began to set. *I know they don't think I'm just going to let them row to shore like this is any other day for them.* Ashni didn't even need to give orders. She could hear weapons being readied, the snap of thick ropes, and splashes along with wood splintering and shouting. Large projectiles turned the barbarians around quickly; some even had to swim back to their shore.

"That'll keep them wondering what the hell to do for a while," Adira said.

"If they're smart, they'll take those little warning shots and drag their asses back into the interior of the north," Ashni replied.

Adira shook her head. "You know they're going to stick around, trying to figure out what we're up to and make our lives Hell while we get the bridge going. We really should've put some forts on the shore."

"If we knew people lived in that graveyard, yeah, but they should all be dead." And, if they were not being pains in the ass, Ashni would've been happy they were alive. It would've been pleasing to find out that asshole Caligo Mor hadn't murdered all of his subjects, but now they were behaving like vermin, a survival tactic for sure. While she had no plans to wipe them out, she couldn't let them do as they pleased as she tried to reorder the West. In the long run, this might even help them. They might learn to live off of their land, revive their land.

The work done at night had the barbarians baffled. Reports from Ashni's scouts came in on how the tribes marveled over how more bits of the bridge appeared. During the day, the tribes didn't dare put their boats in the water again. Since their arrows and stones couldn't reach Ashni's people yet, the barbarians seemed content to merely watch Ashni's soldiers. When the bridge got close enough, the barbarians tried to set it on fire with flaming arrows. But, Adira's people had thought of that. The bridge was covered in animal hides treated with special alum and other retardants created by the engineers to make setting it ablaze nearly impossible. The barbarians would think it was magic.

"This is remarkable," Wicus said, eyes full of awe as he took in the sight of the completed bridge. The tribes across the water had to feel that even more so. There was a full assault right before them, lined up, ready for war, and the barbarians didn't have the numbers to stop it.

Ashni scoffed. "This was the easy part."

They didn't have a bunch of furious soldiers in their faces as they did this. Construction was easy without constant bombardment.

"Yeah, ask me to do something hard now," Adira said.

Layla held up her hand. "Us. Ask us to do something hard now." She pointed to herself, her husband, and then Adira.

Ashni raised her chin in the air. "Make sure these mangy mutts never trouble one of my cities again."

Hafiz rubbed his large hands together. "We asked for a challenge and you give us that?"

"Then show me," Ashni said.

Ashni led the army across the bridge. They marched slowly, orderly. The barbarians needed to see every disciplined, armored soldier. Every piece of tactile equipment. Every monster that one of her officers claimed was a warhorse, Hafiz especially on Yata and Layla on her demon-horse. This wasn't an army. This was an unstoppable entity. It was a creature built to change the world. What did they have that could match it?

For a long moment, the barbarians seemed stuck. They stood from behind the brush, gawking. Maybe now they understood what the Roshan was.

The bridge groaned. Soon, arrows, rocks, and caltrops came their way, but it wasn't enough to stop them. Shields and armor protected against the projectiles and they brushed aside any caltrops. The closer they came, the more the barbarians disappeared into the brush.

Landing on the other side of the river, the air changed to a mismatch of recovery and decay. Fresh grass mixed with rot, a leftover from the king of the dead, Caligo Mor. He'd always hold a special hatred for Ashni and Adira; Ashni for daring to marry her hellcat and Adira for disrespecting the dead.

The small, dry leaves fluttered on the trees, but the trees were thin, cracked, and spaced far apart. Shrubby and colored flowers dotted the land. And the noise! Birds flew and twittered, and the wind blew a gentle breeze through the sparse trees. To think the Northerners who survived Caligo could be enjoying the new life, but instead wanted Ashni to finish what that rotten bastard started.

"According to reports, one tribe set up an ambush for us," Adira said.

"They still didn't unify after watching us build that bridge?" Ashni asked. What the hell was wrong with people? The smart thing would've been to come together as one while Ashni and her people were getting across the river.

"No, but some were impressed," Adira said.

Ashni rolled her eyes. "But not enough to negotiate?" Which would've also been smart but didn't seem to be on the barbarians "to do" list.

"A show of force should do." Layla smirked. "We need to remind them how we conquered the West in the first place."

It was exactly what Ashni wanted and the easy way to accomplish that was to destroy the ambush. The army split up. Ashni and Wicus led the major force to the ambush while Adira took some light infantry forces to come in from the left. Hafiz took cavalry to come from the right. Layla and Naren had their group and would come from behind.

"You barely discussed this plan before you each moved to your part," Wicus said. His face was mostly hidden under his helm, but she could hear the slight confusion in his tone.

Ashni shrugged. "We've been together long enough to know how this works. Adira's brain is almost identical to mine in terms of warfare, and Layla is me."

This wasn't the most intricate strategy, but it would get the job done. She and the troops came to a narrow passage with a high cliff to one side. As soon as they were on that ledge, the onslaught began.

Midnight Thunder's ear twitched as a couple of arrows zipped past them before a storm of arrows and boulders came from above. Echoes of them thumping against shields hummed low in her ears. Midnight Thunder paused as hot oil rained down on them, but as soon as it was gone, they pressed on. Ashni was more concerned with not being able to see the action up top than anything else.

"Careful as you cross!" Ashni called down her lines. They were bound to lose more people due to mistakes than this lackluster effort.

Swords clashed above them, screams filling the air. Adira made her presence known. That had to be an unpleasant surprise.

Dirt slid down the cliff but less projectiles rained down. Ashni got to join in on the action as she came to the end of the narrow ledge. The barbarian warriors showed their hand too soon and revealed themselves the moment Ashni was on more solid ground. Faces painted with ash and fur-covered bodies rushed her with spears in hand. If they only wanted to dispatch her, perhaps this tactic would work, but if they had hopes of catching more of her troops off guard, they had blown that opportunity. Most of their ambush had been killed already.

Ashni drew her swords. Midnight Thunder pushed forward, itching for a challenge. Several arrows headed for her but Ashni sliced through them all. She leaped into a crowd of foes. They were scrawny compared to her warriors. Hungry in all the wrong ways.

Without armor, her blades sailed through their flesh with an ease she had forgotten existed. A couple of her opponents stared as she sliced someone in half at the waist. Their eyes, hollow until then, flashed with fear.

"If you think that's something, you don't want to see me throw lightning," Ashni said as she turned to take down another one. Did these people not understand she was the Chosen One? She was the carrier of her father's legacy and he was the Son of the Sun. She was divine.

Ashni turned to see how her army fared. They flooded into the area from the cliff side and decimated the enemy's meager forces. Their lines were as thin as they were in a matter of minutes. Barbarians retreating from the top of the cliff came into the space, trying to escape Adira, Hafiz, Layla, and Naren. They ran from one slaughter to the next.

Cutting through another foe, blood splattered onto her face. The droplets ignited more of a fire in her, and she cut her way through more barbarians. As the noise of battle died down, Ashni turned to look for Adira or Layla, checking to see if the fight was really wrapping up. She caught a glimpse of Adira at the top of the cliff. Pointing, Adira seemed to be giving orders. Ashni stalked around for prey but found none.

"Good job," Wicus said from nearby, still atop his horse, with corpses at his feet. His helmet and bloodied sword glinted, as he waited for something else to happen. His face glistened in the sun, sweat dripping from the tip of his nose.

Ashni raised her sword in thanks and opened her mouth to respond. A sharp pain caught her in the back of her shoulder. She gasped. Turning, she saw an archer not too far away. The arrow caught her in the gap between her armor and neck. She broke the shaft, cursing herself for not seeing the man. One of her soldiers cut the archer down.

She didn't think anything of the arrow.

But then, the world tilted.

She stumbled.

Falling to one knee, she leaned forward, trying not to throw up. Blood dripped from somewhere, and she watched the droplets hit the dirt, causing a small crimson pool. Spots floated in her vision.

"Poison," she muttered.

Ashni had been poisoned before, but she had never had this sort of reaction. The world went black. She thought about Nakia. Her face hit the dry earth, and then nothing.

Chapter Three

PEOPLE ASSUMED NAKIA DIDN'T have time to miss Ashni, but there was always a dull ache, hollow in her chest. Haunted by the specter of her beloved, she felt it most when on the throne.

Their throne was wide, meant for two. Nakia patted the cool, empty space of the pillow next to her. She and Saad, one of her engineers, were trying to figure out plans for the canal they needed to construct to keep Thia and Wicus happy. Saad had no good answers with his dark green eyes looking everywhere but her face. *What if you have to come up with something? We both know you can't actually do this on your own.*

"Why is it impossible to get the canal done in this time frame? Once the military returns, we should have the resources to start," Nakia said. They had to keep the soldiers busy to justify paying them anyway.

Saad shook his head, long, wavy, ebony hair fanning around him. "It's not about manpower. It would be impossible to get the materials in that time." He tugged at his flowing emerald sleeve of Roshan-style robes.

Nakia frowned. That didn't sound right. She had seen the military work miracles in the battlefield and most didn't have anything to do with fighting. "And if I get a second opinion?"

Saad twisted his mouth and shrugged. "Highness, no one will tell you otherwise."

She pursed her lips. "Even Saniyah?"

"Highness…" He bowed, probably to buy time to order his thoughts and not insult her mentor. "Saniyah's a great war engineer, but not an expert on earth works."

"No, Saniyah has enough imagination to solve issues on battlefields she's never been on. I once thought you had the same amount of imagination. This is disappointing." Her frown cut deeper, as a nasty voice filled her head. *You're more disappointing.*

He flinched. "Highness, I promise you, I will work this out." Then he scurried away, leather sandals slapping against the stone floor in his haste.

"You were hard on him," Varaza Sur said. She stood off to the side, dressed in unassuming clothing. Her size made her quite noticeable, but from her casual tone, not many people would guess she was the captain of Nakia's personal guard, and she liked it that way. Ashni liked it that way.

Nakia waved the words off. "I know he can do it. If not, I'll have Saniyah figure it out."

Varaza gave her a lopsided grin. "She's a genius."

"He's one, too." He had proven that several times. She needed him to do that once more.

Varaza shrugged. "Not all are equal. There are levels."

"I don't expect him to be on her level, just near it." Nakia eyed the large woman. "We made a promise, and we like to keep it."

Varaza chuckled. "I know. It's how I got this gig, after all."

Nakia fought down a smirk and shook her head. "I think there was a hope it would mature you as well."

"Never! Though it did help me meet my future spouse."

"You better stop chasing that boy around."

Varaza clicked her tongue. "He's cute. Besides, I've noticed being yourself seems to pay off, thanks to you and yours."

Nakia couldn't argue that. Her attitude had caught Ashni's attention. Ashni thought she was bold, brash, and beautiful, even when she was putting up a front. For all of her disquieting thoughts, she maintained her attitude. It had brought her this far. *Put up a facade and hope no one challenges it? You're setting yourself up, just like when you met Ashni.* She ignored the hateful thoughts.

"What do I have to tend to next?" Nakia asked, needing to keep busy. There were servants milling about, but she wasn't addressing any of them.

Varaza didn't answer. It was her way of letting Nakia know it wasn't her job to keep track of appointments, but to keep Nakia safe, Varaza had to be aware of Nakia's schedule. Her next appointment entered, Layla's father.

Badar never failed to make the hair on the back of Nakia's neck stand up. He looked pleasant, friendly, almost soft. Tall and lean, there were times Nakia thought his students could break Badar in half. She knew better.

"Are you ready for your lessons, Highness?" he asked with a bow. He was always polite to her. He never tried to be domineering with Nakia, the opposite of her own father.

"I'm glad you showed up today," Nakia replied.

He taught her self-defense, but there were times he couldn't make the lessons. In his stead, he sent his mother or his wife. They were possibly the toughest teachers Nakia ever had.

Badar smiled, showing all his teeth. His dark eyes sparkled. It wasn't until Nakia met him that she understood how Layla fell for Naren. Seeing that easy, almost carefree expression all of her life, it probably caught her by surprise to see it on someone her age. "I see no reason why our hour should be interrupted," he said.

"You say that until you get word your other pupils are reading the wrong passages in your sacred text and then I'm forgotten," she replied with a smile of her own. He had run out on her a few times to tend to his true students, warrior monks, she guessed. No one ever called them anything after they stopped being students. They learned religion, philosophy, martial arts, mystical arts, magic, and other lifestyles from Badar, though that might just be the education of all Shadow Walkers. She got a small taste of it without having to make her way to their Temple of Darkness or Badar's academy.

"That is why I send my wife or my mother," he said.

She flinched. She still preferred Badar to Samar or Iamar. Part of her wondered if she was trying to make him her father figure. She tried not to think too hard on it, especially since she could hear echoes of her father in the back of her mind.

"I want only the best for you," Badar added.

Nakia snickered. "You don't have to pour it on."

They exited the Grand Hall and made their way to Nakia's personal training room adjacent to an open garden. The room gave off more of an office vibe. There were scrolls lining the walls, all given to her by Shadow Walkers she knew, including Layla and Naren. There were texts Layla felt Nakia needed to know if she was going to learn anything from a Shadow Walker, even if she wasn't learning more than the basics. The gesture was funny but endearing. They were excited about their craft and culture and liked to share if they deemed a person worthy.

Badar always reminded her that she was learning how to defend herself in order to get away, not start a fight. Nakia didn't want to be a brawler, but she didn't want to need rescuing all of the time. Badar was kind and patient with her, even when she stumbled.

They started with stances. How she was expected to use her weight to get people off of her or away from her. Whenever she was angled wrong or her footing was incorrect, he showed her how she should be. If she didn't correct herself, he would ask permission to touch her before shifting her. She had seen this same man lay out his daughter if she left him an opening. Then again, she had also witnessed Layla do the same if her father gave her a chance.

Beyond stances, she learned holds, how to throw simple punches and kicks, weak points on the body, and pressure points. There was practice with using knives and darts, weapons she could conceal in her clothing.

Badar was comfortable with throwing her to help her understand the move, but he still tried not to hurt her. Hitting the floor often hurt, regardless. Demonstrating her comprehension of the lesson was tougher than that.

It was easier now than when she started, as self-defense was different than anything she had ever done. She was fortunate to have the body for it, even if her muscles still ached after each session. Ashni claimed she could feel the difference, but Nakia didn't see any added muscle. Still, training made her feel good all around, physically, emotionally, and even spiritually.

Badar also introduced Nakia to the basics of the way of Darkness. It was more than religion for his people. He called it "more than a way of life." He made it seem like this vast entity that no one would ever understand, but everyone was connected to.

Nakia was able to add it to her own religious beliefs. Darkness was unknown, but it wasn't to be feared. The unknown wasn't to be feared. *So, don't be scared to do your duty on your own. You can do it. Find the strength within you because it's around you.*

Darkness didn't conceal the truth but was part of the truth. To find the truth, sometimes one needed to seek it in the unknown. This helped her navigate her responsibilities as consort, especially when Ashni was away.

"Good. Your movements have tightened and are smoother," Badar said, grinning when their session ended.

Nakia tried to fight down the flutter in her chest from his praise. "Thank you so much for this."

"I'm always here for you, little moon." He ruffled her hair. Maybe, sometimes he looked at her as one of his children. "Until next session." Badar vanished into a shadow.

Sore, Nakia had a bath to relax, looking forward to having lunch with Saffi, Bashira, and Saniyah next. It was the only free time she had during the day to see them until the evening meal. That lack of free time was one of the most annoying things about being in charge. This was why Ashni was often cranky, wanting to do so much, but having to be responsible.

"How goes your day?" Saniyah asked as they made themselves comfortable in the garden. Lunch waited for them, a spread of breads and cheese, fruits and wine. Several candles burned to keep the insects away.

Nakia folded her legs underneath her. "Things are going well, though my lead engineer told me the projected time for the canal was wrong."

"Isn't that what you promised to Thia's husband?" Saffi asked.

"Yes, and Thia won't let it go now that I've given my word," Nakia replied.

Bashira grabbed a hunk of bread. "Not that you'd let it go since you've given you word."

Nakia's word was good, especially since it was the word of her spouse as well. If she said something could be done and it couldn't, it would mean Ashni was a liar.

Saniyah tapped her chin a couple of times. "Why wouldn't he be able to do it on time?"

Nakia shook her head. She surveyed the choices of food to buy herself time, but nothing looked appetizing now. "He doesn't think we have the resources for it. I disagree once the military returns."

"You're right." Saniyah frowned and stared off into the distance for a moment. "Perhaps he's worried they'll be assigned to other projects."

Nakia glanced at Saniyah. "I assign people."

"He knows you're in charge of these things and Ashni will back you." Saniyah rubbed her hands together. "Have him put his worries in writing, including all of the logistics. I'll tell you if his concerns are valid."

Nakia nodded. "Maybe I'm relying on him too much. He might be spread too thin and doesn't want to admit it. He's doing two other projects for me."

Bashira scoffed. "That's not a lot. Especially when compared to how much you do."

Nakia took one look at Saffi, who kept her head down, and decided to stop complaining. Saniyah and Bashira were used to listening to her problems, but Saffi wasn't. She didn't want Saffi to hear her whining about being in charge when Saffi's life had been upended for daring to be heard.

"So, how are you settling in?" Nakia asked Saffi.

Saffi didn't meet her gaze even now, a month into her stay. Nakia imagined how Saffi's life could have been hers. It could have been all over if Ashni had been a little less amused with her. But her present could be Saffi's future. Saffi was born-to-rule to only end up a scared mouse.

"It's odd to be back in my old rooms," Saffi whispered.

"Would you like different ones?" There were probably more bad memories than good in those rooms. Nakia's old rooms had been an escape from an oppressive world, and now they were an oasis from a demanding one. She thought the same could be true for Saffi. *Perhaps not.*

Saffi shook her head. "No, they're fine. I used to sleep on a cold floor, after all."

Nakia held in a flinch. Saffi had been married to a king and forced to sleep on the floor, like a dog. When she first came, it had been hard for her to hold down food, not used to eating her fill.

"How could they treat you that way?" Bashira grumbled, cutting off a slice of cheese and stuffing it into her mouth. "You were a queen."

"I didn't do my duty and give him a child." Saffi clutched her knees, holding onto her robes. Veins popped in her neck, and Nakia leaned over, making sure to do it slowly. If Saffi didn't see it coming, she tended to jump. Nakia caressed her shoulder, and Saffi looked up long enough to give her a watery smile. The expression slammed into Nakia's gut.

That could've been me, and it wasn't, thanks to Ashni. I can't crumble. She thought she could hear her father laughing from his distant island in exile, but it was cut off by Saniyah's voice.

"It baffles me that there are places who believe that's all a woman should do, have babies." Saniyah pulled a sour face. "Thia proves a woman can have children and competency to rule. Our empress proves it can be done without a man at her side. And our queen shows women can lead on the battlefield. Don't they realize they missed out by holding you back?"

Saffi sighed. "You've named anomalies to the system. No one else could've led Tyra, just as no one else could've led Phyllida."

Nakia couldn't believe her ears. "You speak madness. It's clear with right guidance you or Thia could've led." There was no denying that when they were both at home, Saffi was the smarter and bolder of the pair.

"But we have no military experience," Saffi replied.

Saniyah scoffed. "No one is born with experience. You get military experience the same way you get any other experience. Adira didn't have experience until the Great Amir. First when he invaded her village and then when he put a spear in her hand and took her into battle. Greatness has to be fed and nurtured or it'll spoil like anything else."

Saffi shook her head again and scratched at her knees. "Adira's an exception, not the rule."

"Almost half of Ashni's army is female," Nakia said.

What happened to her sister who didn't care about gender? Who argued matters of state with a nobleman only to be punished by their father because she won? Those barbarians had abused Saffi's nature out of her. *Saffi must still be in there somewhere.* Nakia refused to believe anyone had the power to destroy someone's soul.

"Under the circumstances, an odd woman is likely to think more women are odd and inspire them to be odd, but it isn't the way," Saffi replied.

Nakia wasn't sure what else she could say. Thankfully, a servant rushed in with a scroll. He bowed as he handed it to Nakia. She barely glanced at it before her heart cracked and scattered in her chest. Ashni had been wounded, badly. Nakia's throat burned like everything inside of her wanted to escape, but it couldn't. Instead, it charred with a bubbling acid.

"Is everything all right?" Bashira asked, putting her hand on Nakia's leg.

Nakia opened her mouth, on the brink of sharing, but something held her tongue. She shook her head. Everyone didn't need to know this just yet. "I have to tend to this matter. Saniyah, if you'd accompany me."

Nakia and Saniyah bid their companions farewell and then Nakia rushed off to the nearest private room with Saniyah hot on her heels. Nakia made a quick sweep of the room to be sure they were alone.

"What happened? The color has drained from your face," Saniyah said.

Nakia rubbed her cheek. "This is from Adira."

Saniyah paled now. "Is she all right?" Saniyah asked, a tremble in her voice.

"She's fine, but Ashni was shot. An arrow to the neck."

Saniyah gasped, eyes wide and a hand over her mouth. "Dead?" She said it as if it were impossible.

Nakia shook her head. "Close to it. The arrow was poisoned."

The look of relief on Saniyah's face didn't make Nakia feel any better. It felt like she was the one shot by a poisoned arrow. Everything inside her wanted to decay. According to the letter, Ashni was alive, but wasn't doing well. *If she dies, what will you do? You're nothing without her.* Was life even worth it without Ashni? *You would have to carry on her legacy. You would have to face the unknown, alone.*

Saniyah forced out a laugh. "I should've known she's too stubborn to die."

Nakia wanted to laugh with her, but her body refused to make the sound. She decided to tell Saniyah the whole letter. She couldn't think beyond that.

"Adira says they'll send her as soon as it's safe, but she worries negotiations will be impossible. Her authority isn't on par with Ashni, especially with Ashni incapacitated." Nakia tried to swallow, but her throat refused to cooperate. Maybe because her heart was stuck in it. *Calm down. She's alive.* Except that could've changed since the letter was written. How long had it taken for this to reach her?

Beyond that, Adira was right. If the negotiations fell through, things would get worse. The towns the barbarians had been harassing would think the Empire let them down. Ashni's whole dream, along with all of Roshan's dreams and her father's legacy, could collapse.

"This is a mess." Saniyah gnawed her lip. "In the time it would take you to get there, something else could happen."

Nakia read more of the scroll, needing something to hold onto. It was all business after the report on Ashni's condition. "Wait, she informed me of their solution."

Saniyah breathed a sigh of relief. "Good. What will they do?"

"The obvious. Layla's in charge there, leaving me to my duties here." The things they knew best. While Nakia had done peace talks before, she usually had more information to go on and more time to prepare. She also didn't usually have to worry about her spouse dying. "So now I can panic about my beloved."

And just like that, her chest tightened. She couldn't breathe. She wanted nothing more than to be by Ashni's side, to know she was all right. Ashni was poisoned. She had seen Ashni through a lot, but never poisoned. What if she was dying slowly? What if she was in constant pain?

A sob escaped her, rattling her chest, and she couldn't recall the last time she made such a noise. It was like something inside of her had been torn and wailed in agony. *Ashni could die.*

Not being able to gauge Ashni's condition made it worse. All she could see was Ashni withering in her mind. Withering and alone. Ashni shouldn't have to be alone right now. Her family should be with her, comforting her, making sure she pulled through.

Instead, it had to be business as usual.

But this wasn't usual.

Saniyah hugged Nakia, whispering, "It's all right. Ashni will be fine. She's been poisoned before."

That did nothing to push air in her lungs, but she hid her face into Saniyah's shoulder, fabric soft against her cheek. "Before?" Pleased to have missed the other times, she wished this time hadn't happened.

It reminded her of when the captain had pressed a deadly vial into her palm, involved her in Amal's nonsense, and expected her to assassinate Ashni. How often did Ashni have to deal with such things? Then, she thought of her father. To her knowledge, he had dodged several poisonings. How many did he dodge that she didn't know about? It only took once.

Saniyah gave her a tight squeeze. "On more than one occasion. It's one of the reasons she's certain she's the Chosen One. Poison hasn't killed her yet."

Nakia knew that was supposed to make her feel better, but her stomach pinched. It was a miracle she didn't throw up. Maybe past occurrences had merely dosed Ashni wrong. Just because she came out of those unscathed didn't mean she'd do the same now. She wished people would stop taking Ashni's injuries lightly. It influenced Ashni to take injuries lightly as well.

According to the letter, Ashni was in a coma. There was no cure for a coma, and Nakia didn't know how long a body could last in one. She tried not to think about it and the letter offered assurances. Ashni had no choice but to lie there and heal. She couldn't fight the doctors over treatment or snicker with Layla when she skipped medicines. That was good, but it meant nothing if she wasted away and died without regaining consciousness. What medicines were there to wake Ashni? To keep her from wasting away?

"It's okay. It's okay," Saniyah said, but they both knew that wasn't true. "Let it out."

So Nakia did. The wail hurt every part of her, and she doubted it would ever stop hurting, not until Ashni was by her side. *Ashni could die.* Nakia wouldn't breathe easy until Ashni was with her.

Saniyah wrapped her arms around Nakia's shoulders. It felt like the pressure held her together, but she might still shatter in the embrace.

"Come," Saniyah said. "You still have duties to perform, and you have to prepare to receive Ashni. Her carelessness and disregard for her safety and your heart deserve a good scolding."

Nakia laughed, but it sounded as forced as it was. It broke into pieces, just like a fragile cup. With Ashni gone, how could she perform duties? There was no way she could hold things together on her own.

"Nakia, I've got you," Saniyah said. "I've got you."

The words thumped through Nakia. The only reason she was standing was because Saniyah held her. The moment Saniyah let her go, she'd sink like a stone.

After Nakia dried some of her tears and took a couple of deep breaths, Saniyah led Nakia out of the room. She went willingly. It wasn't like she could hide for the rest of her life. She had duties to perform, however badly she might do once Saniyah stopped holding her hand.

Chapter Four

LAYLA RUBBED HER EYES for what felt like the hundredth time. The darkness inside the medical tent bothered her. Occasionally, tears would sneak into her vision, but she banished them before they fell. She couldn't let the healer see her weakness. She didn't think such a thing was possible. *I can't take this.*

It was difficult to see Ashni, wrapped in medicinal linens and animal furs. To see her sister the color of sour milk with strange purple lines crisscrossing her body as if her veins had turned to creeping ivy was almost too much. She smelled like smoldering coals with a hint of spoiled meat. It was weird. Nakia would probably fall apart at the sight.

"She'll be alright," Layla whispered. If she put it out there, it would be true. Or so she hoped. She'd feel better if the doctors knew what Ashni had been poisoned with, but they could only guess at this point.

Ashni had never looked like this before. Was she decaying or something? What foul substance flowed through her that even changed the smell of her body? Why couldn't the healers figure it out?

"No, no, no. Ashni will be alright," Layla said.

Could they continue their march West without Ashni? Who could lead it? Nakia wasn't interested in battle and she wouldn't have the authority to do so anyway.

The military was technically property of the Empire and Ashni was allotted the right to use it only through the Empress' grace. If Ashni couldn't lead the military, then Chandra might recall the soldiers to use them for a different purpose or disband them. *Why the hell didn't Ashni think of this shit?*

But why would Ashni think about not being able to lead the military? If anything knocked Ashni down, she got back up. She always moved forward. It never occurred to any of them she'd be paused to the point where she might actually stay down. What was there to do now? It was a question she'd been asking herself for days.

The tent flap opened and Adira stepped inside. Layla winced as the brief flash of light illuminated dark, indigo bruises under Ashni's eyes and along her cheeks.

"Any news?" Layla asked. Their message should've gotten to Nakia a couple of days ago, so they should have a response soon enough.

"Nakia agreed that you should conduct any and all negotiations. You're just as much Ashni as she is, and we've got to get this done before any of these barbarians realize who some lucky ass archer shot." Adira glanced at Ashni. "There are several leaders willing to meet, and I've set it up. We've got a day to put something together to properly awe them. Hopefully, we can bring these tribes to heel and accompany Ashni back."

Layla would love nothing more than to return her sister to her precious spouse, but they had work to do. "If not us, Naren and Hafiz are to ride with her."

"Agreed."

There was a long stretch of silence between them. They stared at Ashni, listened to her light breathing. It sounded like gurgling, but Layla didn't want it to stop.

"Were you able to find out what poison was used?" Layla asked.

"It's animal based, a frog or toad. They mixed it with some sort of magic powder. Unfortunately, the powder could be any fucking thing," Adira replied.

"Do you have the powder to study?" Layla and Adira had to help Ashni. Ashni would move mountains to save them if she had to. They couldn't let her down. "Five days is more than enough."

Adira nodded. "Indeed. I've got my hands on the powder."

"And?" Layla scratched her biceps, feeling like she was about to come out of her skin. Why was Adira dragging this out?

"We have people studying the powder now, as well as the poison, but there's nothing at ready to counteract it." Adira took a deep breath. "We just have to pray Ashni's body does what it always does and pulls a miracle." Adira's dark eye shifted to the doctor lingering by Ashni's head. "Any changes?"

The doctor shook his head. "Her highness' breathing is shallow, but consistent. The worrisome thing for me and my colleagues is a dark substance she gurgles up every now and then. And her coloring appears to be getting worse."

Layla looked closer. A fresh pastiness had spread through Ashni's already sickened complexion. Her golden tan had been wiped out, not even a trace of it left. The purple lines seemed darker, too. What the hell had those barbarians done to her? Did it hurt?

"And the smell? It's an odd scent for decay," Adira said.

The doctor rubbed the bridge of his nose. "It doesn't appear to be decay. We made a small incision to look and everything looked as expected."

"Is that incision healing properly?" Adira asked. That would be helpful.

The doctor winced. "No. However, it didn't appear to be festering."

"That's something. Okay, at least we know she's not crumbling inside, even if she's not exactly healing," Adira replied.

Layla frowned. "Then what the hell is that smell?"

He glanced at Ashni. "It might be the poison simply interacting with her system. When we cut her to sample her blood, there was a mint smell, which was then accompanied by the aroma of rot."

"Have you ever smelled mint before when someone was poisoned?" Layla asked.

The doctor's round face twisted. "Not in my experience and not according to any notes I've read. Maybe the northerners mixed it with something else."

"Your colleagues are studying the powder," Layla pushed. Surely, they must know something. Anything.

"Yes, I'm sure that'll help. We haven't found anything just yet," the doctor replied.

Layla grimaced, hating being in the dark about her sibling. Poison was meant to kill, and Ashni was a known enemy. They might have made this poison especially for her, designed to take down a demigod. Layla's heart pounded as though it might break through her ribs. For a long moment, it was all she could hear.

"Will she live?" Layla found herself asking. Never did she fear she might lose her older sister. *What would my life be without Ashni?*

The doctor took a deep breath. "I'm not sure, your Highness. It doesn't look good."

Layla lurched forward, like she had been punched in the stomach. She gagged. Bile rushed from her throat. She slapped a hand over her lips and although barely any sour liquid came out of her, it felt like it was everything inside of her.

Adira took Layla around the shoulders. "You know nothing stops Ashni."

In the past, Ashni had moved, spoken even, through the poison in her body. Slurred nonsense, yes, but words. She had moved like a drunk, but she moved...until someone made her sit down anyway. The worst of it took her a couple of weeks to fully recover from. Whatever she messed up, Layla and Adira could easily clean up. How the hell could they clean this up? This land wasn't even part of their desired conquest. It was a joke. A bad joke.

Adira gave Layla's shoulder a squeeze. "There's still work to be done. Ashni will be cranky when she returns to form and finds we didn't finish it when we had the chance."

Layla nodded. "My mother will be able to treat her when we get her back to the city anyway." Her mother worked miracles.

"Of course."

"And my mother has brought many people back from the brink of Darkness to fulfill their purpose before returning to the Void and Oneness." Layla couldn't help but cling to her beliefs. The Darkness couldn't have Ashni yet. They had so much more to accomplish.

Adira chuckled. "Ashni will be fine. No need to get religious."

Layla opened her mouth but found all her words were filled with references to the Darkness. She didn't want her sister to return to the Void. Ashni thought she'd walk with the gods in death and find her place among the stars. Neither sat well with Layla.

"Mind on the mission," Adira said.

"Understood." She had to get her head on straight. She was the one who could end their troubles with the North. "Who agreed to sit down to negotiations?"

"I have the leaders of five tribes so far. I'm working on more. There are about twenty-five different tribes." Adira curled her lip.

Twenty-five? Layla blew out a breath. "That's ten more than your earlier reports."

Adira scowled. "Oh, believe me, people are being chewed out for the misleading information. I had to rework many ideas. The five we have are some of the more influential. Be Ashni, as you are, and bring them in. Others will follow and those who don't will be devoured."

Layla nodded. She was Ashni. She had been Ashni before. In the past, though, it wasn't because Ashni flirted so closely with death and the Void. *Stop thinking about that. You have a job to do.*

Taking a breath, Layla knew she would honor Ashni by bringing these tribes into their fold. She'd show them the reason why being allies with the Roshan was the right thing to do.

"We have a day, right?" Layla asked.

Adira nodded. "A day to work out what we should demand and show them what we have to offer. You ready to set up?"

It was something to do and it would take Layla's mind off of Ashni. She took one last look at her fallen sister before leaving the tent with Adira. Before they even made it a step away, two healers went into the tent. Hopefully, they'd help.

Layla and Adira put soldiers to work and then went over what Layla needed to know. It wasn't hard, but she clutched it like a lifeline to keep her mind off of Ashni.

Soldiers hastily threw together a banquet hall. It was a collection of the best tents in camp, coming together as one large tent. They made sure the fabric was spotless and smelled like a spring day. All of the lanterns made it seem like the place was bathed in sunshine. The colorful pillows and blankets sparkled like they were covered in gold. While Layla wasn't impressed, it had to look magnificent for people who didn't have enough trees to build homes.

"You did a good job," Layla said.

Adira arched an eyebrow at her. "Of course."

Layla swallowed and hoped she didn't say anything else that stupid ever again. *Get your head on straight. You are Ashni.* She turned her attention to the plentiful dishes perched on tables around the room, to feed their guests and guards along with the Roshan soldiers sitting in on the feast. For the meal, they grabbed food and treats from the closest town across the River Reve—a few types of meat, fish, fruits, nuts, and vegetables, along with cakes, pies, and other sweets. More food than their guests had seen in their lifetimes in this accursed land.

The tribal leaders awaited Layla on traditional Roshan pillows at a table loaded with food, drinks, and even sauces. Their tattered robes looked particularly shabby, threadbare with holes. Despite the poor quality of their clothes, everyone, including the servants, had bracelets and necklaces of unpolished stone. The leaders were decked out in them, but it didn't hide their poverty. There were dirt smears on their sunken cheeks and foreheads, like they couldn't be bothered to bathe even for this meeting. She couldn't believe they turned down Ashni's repeated attempts to solve things peacefully.

The leaders did look suitably impressed with everything, gazing around with wide eyes. She was surprised they weren't shoving bread in their pockets. They probably hadn't eaten everything already because the Roshan soldiers hadn't touched their food yet. They didn't know if it was all right to eat yet since none of the Roshan had started. It wouldn't do to start a political incident in the enemy camp. Layla sat on Ashni's pillow, across from the leaders to give them all proper attention. Adira sat down next to her.

"Greetings," Layla said in Kairon. It wasn't the native language of the area, but hopefully they spoke enough.

A man with cobalt and black stripes painted under his sharp blue eyes bowed his head. "Thank you for hosting us," he replied in Kairon.

"It's my pleasure. The Roshan don't enjoy violence." Possibly a lie, but a useful one. "However, once provoked, we have no issue with closing our jaws around an enemy." Definitely not a lie.

The leaders sat a little straighter, and Layla was pleased with herself. Giving them a quick study, she could see the need for order in the North. These leaders were dressed in dusty furs with patches missing from the pelts. Dark circles wrapped around their eyes and their faces were drawn. Their attendants looked worse, their torn linen clothes hanging off of their thin frames. A war wouldn't do them any good.

Introductions were made, and faces twitched as Layla was introduced as herself and as Ashni. Maybe they thought games were afoot.

"Queen Ashni's my sister and we're of one soul. My word is the same as hers," Layla said.

"Did she not think we were worthy of meeting her?" The one called Andoni asked, a frown cutting across his aged features. Green eyes tried to pin Layla, but she'd seen sharper eyes at home.

"Not at all, as you're meeting her through me. Perhaps you're unfamiliar with the Roshan practice, but a soul is able to be in more than one person. The essence that makes Ashni who she is also lives in me, so I'm Ashni as well. A matter has her, but she's left you in my capable hands. Do you doubt her judgment, her faith?" Layla raised an eyebrow, daring this man to try her. She'd literally walk through him and turn his bones to dust.

"Are you the one they say controls people's shadows?" The leader Balera asked, leaning back. A faded tattoo that dotted her strained neck was less noticeable than the freckles on her tanned face.

"I control many things. Shadows are one. I can do the benign." Layla flicked her wrists and her guests' shadows rose from the ground. They gasped. She wiggled her index finger and the shadows danced. Nervous laughter filled the tent. "Or things can get a bit more grotesque." She crooked her index finger and Balera's shadow shoved its hand into Andoni's shadow. Andoni clapped his hand over his throat, making a gagging noise.

"Incredible," Balera said with wide, onyx eyes.

Layla scoffed. "Tedious." Dropping her hand, all shadows returned to their proper places. Andoni gasped, rubbing his neck. "Tricks I mastered as a child. The damage I can do has only been stopped by one and she is me." Of course, she liked to think she beat Ashni more than she lost, but they stopped keeping track.

"Queen Ashni," Balera replied.

"Then it's true she has the gods' lightning?" The small woman named Clara asked, with a tiny quiver to her pockmarked face, obviously intrigued.

Layla nodded. "She does. It's one of the reasons a legion of Shadow Walkers like myself follow her."

"A legion?" A man named Thrasius swallowed, the large protrusion in his avian neck bobbing. He touched his elbows with tethered, fingerless gloves on his hands, like he wanted to hug himself.

"Enough talk about that." Layla waved her hand and they flinched. She bit back a chuckle. "Please, eat your fill and let's come to a peaceful solution to our current circumstances."

Layla watched as their guests immediately reached for items to feast on. She had dough balls as they ate and drank and ignored bread and other portable things disappearing into bags and cloaks.

"Good job with the shadows," Adira whispered while their guests were distracted, lips smacking against their meals.

"If only you knew the restraint it's taking not to crush them all." They were the reason Ashni was near death. Them and their foolish raids.

"Oh, believe me I know. Let's close this matter and tend to your sister," Adira replied.

Layla's attention went back to the guests, ignoring everyone's face glistening with meat grease. "You seem to be enjoying the flat bread," she said to Thrasius.

Thrasius glanced up at her before dipping his third piece of flat bread in his stew. Thick broth dripped from his scruffy beard and he spoke around a mouthful of food. "It doesn't overpower the meat." He sucked his teeth and swallowed.

"So, the goat is to your liking?" Layla asked.

He coughed and put the flat bread down. "You don't save goats for sacrifices to the gods?"

"We usually sacrifice bulls," she replied.

"Bulls?" Thrasius repeated as if in shock. The rest of the leaders stared at her. Clara dropped the mutton in her hands, mouth slightly open. They probably hadn't ever seen a dead bull, let alone a live one.

"Our gods demand great sacrifices for their blessings and our empire has been blessed enough to grow bulls large enough to fell a tree. Our gods like the heart, liver, stomach, and lungs. We may eat the rest." Layla motioned to the beef dishes lining the table.

All eyes went to the beef. Layla glanced at Adira, who gave her a brief nod.

"The Empire delights in sharing goods. We're always in search of new wonders or even fresh spins on known items," Layla said. If the idea of trade appealed to these leaders, they might be able to talk the other tribes into deals and put an end to the raids.

"How do we know you won't simply use your dark magic to enslave us?" Andoni asked, eyes narrowed.

Layla shrugged. "It doesn't appeal to us."

"Besides." Adira leaned forward, pointing at them with a hunk of bread. "Without Ashni, you'd all still be hiding in fear of Caligo Mor."

They gasped. "You dare say that demon's name in our presence!" Balera growled, fire in her dark eyes.

Adira waved that off. "I dare because I was there when Ashni dispatched him and freed you from his death grip. You repay her actions by harassing her people."

"He was just a monster slain by another monster. We're not indebted or beholden to her. She removed a tumor, but remained a cancer," Thrasius said.

Layla arched an eyebrow. *Bold!* "How so? What has she taken from you?"

"Stability," he replied, as if it was obvious.

Layla's mouth almost dropped open. They missed the stability brought on by Caligo? Well, his presence probably ensured one tribe wouldn't attack others. No one wanted to call attention to themselves and die.

"We can reestablish stability and bring wealth to the region, bring life back if that's your wish," Layla said.

"We won't have you rule us," Andoni said, chin in the air.

"We don't want to. It's too cold." Layla wasn't sure how they were expected to bring stability then. Either they wanted someone to be in charge or they didn't.

"But you can't raid our territory and think we'll just accept it," Adira said.

"We have no desire to push north, but we also have no problem destroying the whole area." Layla would prefer that, considering her sister was near death, thanks to these useless bastards.

"We would resist," Andoni said.

Layla couldn't help rolling her eyes. "My people resisted too, and it didn't do much good. And not to brag, but I could kill everyone in this room right now by myself."

Adira cleared her throat, and Layla glanced at her. She was pretty sure if push came to shove, she could kill Adira. She wouldn't walk away unscathed, but she'd walk away.

"We were absorbed, just like others and if you thought my talent was something, imagine hundreds of us. That's right, hundreds. And the Roshan conquered us anyway," Layla said.

"My people were also conquered, and yet we've thrived with the Roshan," Adira added.

"Here's what I'm willing to offer you; food and goods in exchange for food and goods, provided you have something to wow me and my general here." Layla motioned to Adira, who looked unimpressed. "Failure to impress us will result in total annihilation of your people."

"There's no pleasure in this for us. We want to be with our families, just like you, not fighting in a war," Adira said.

The guests shifted their gazes for a long moment. The silence hung in the air. When their gaze came back to Layla, she kept her expression blank. She didn't care what they decided. Ashni's will would be done, no matter what.

"We want homes," Clara said.

"Excuse me?" Layla wasn't sure what she meant.

"We lack the materials to make homes, so we live in caves like animals, like we did when the demon was in charge. You built a bridge in a week. It was as if the gods themselves worked with you," Clara replied.

So, Ashni's plan with the bridge worked. Kind of. "Building materials aren't an issue. What do you have in return?"

"This land's dead. You've seen it. How could we offer you anything?" Balera inquired.

Layla frowned. There had to be something. And then her eyes fell on the dark beads they all wore. Clearly status symbols as they had them in abundance around their necks and wrists. Baubles, but baubles she had never seen before.

"May I see your bracelet?" Layla leaned forward, hand out.

"Yes?" Balera eased one off of her wrist and placed it in Layla's hand.

The weight was more than expected, made up of glass beads and precious stones. The glass beads looked simple, but the stones intrigued her. All dark. There seemed to be words carved into the stones, though she didn't speak the native tongue.

"These stones need to be polished," Layla said. The stones were raw but rare.

"No time or tools," Balera replied.

Layla nodded. "You can pay us, though. We can polish the stones. Do you have a mine?"

"We use what we find," Thrasius answered.

"Then let's start simple. Stones in exchange for building materials. If speed becomes an issue, you pay us to help with construction. After that, I suggest you try mining more stones or produce a good worthy of trade," Layla said.

"Sounds like a threat," Andoni said.

Layla smirked. "This sounds like the makings of a deal. A threat's more, give us the stones and we won't water the healing earth with your blood."

"What goods were you known for before Caligo Mor took over?" Adira asked.

Balera smiled. "We once made the most beautiful blankets, lined with fur. We had giant deer with tender meat. We made decorations with their antlers and a special wine with their blood and wildflowers."

"It seems to me that, in the future, you'll have things our empire might want. We can wait. We know the land has to heal and so do you. So let's start with what you do have." Layla held up the bracelet and then passed it back to Balera.

"You'll sell us materials and labor?" Clara asked.

Layla nodded. "We can come to acceptable terms."

Her guests gave faint nods. It was a small step forward, but it was a step that could send them all home, including Ashni. The other tribes better go for this.

***

Nakia shifted on the throne, leg tingling from sitting too long. She sighed as she finished reading reports from Layla on the northern front. They had settled a deal with the five major tribes and opened talks with more than half of the others. Ashni hadn't changed, but she was on her way home with Hafiz and Naren. According to Layla, her mother and a group of Shadow Walker healers would be waiting to receive Ashni. Layla wanted any input Nakia might have for dealing with the northern front.

"We should build bridges across the Great River Reve, using the excuse of transporting materials. You and Adira probably know the best places. We'll protect them with fortifications that'll be trading posts..." Nakia barely finished writing her response before there was an announcement outside.

"A royal party just entered the city gates!" a servant called out.

Nakia's heart thumped heavy in her chest. *Ashni*. "That was fast." Ashni must be even worse than Layla made her sound if they rushed like that.

"It's King Jay and King Asad."

And just like that Nakia's heart went from hopeful to dread, like ashes ran through her blood. *What do they want?* They weren't friendly with Ashni, and they had no kind of sibling relationship. In fact, Asad's twin had attempted to steal Ashni's kingdom and even murder her. Did they know what happened to Ashni? She knew in the pit of her stomach that those two were going to try something.

"Prepare to greet our guests!" She had to plan. She wouldn't let Jay or Asad finish what the North tried, namely killing Ashni.

Chapter Five

NAKIA COULDN'T FIGURE OUT why Ashni's older brothers were in the Kingdom, but it couldn't be good." They had only seen her family once since Ashni moved her base to the West, and that was because the Empress wanted a look around. To stay on their mother's good side and pretend to support Ashni, her older brothers had flocked to Chandra's side.

Fahim and the younger twins, Kek and Kiran, wrote often. Fahim, especially. Through letters, Nakia got to see the positive influence of the Great Amir. Ashni and her brothers had so many things in common. There was never a word from Jay or Asad. There was no reason for them to be here unless they knew something they shouldn't.

"What's going on?" Saniyah asked as she rushed into the throne room.

"You know?" Anyone close to Saniyah and Ashni probably knew. Why wouldn't someone inform her?

"I was informed. What're they doing here?" Saniyah's expression was as confused as Nakia felt.

"I wish I knew." Nakia shook her head. "Do you have any information?"

"No, but you don't live with someone in charge of intelligence gathering as long as I have and not learn a thing or two. Layla's parents will sit with you when they arrive."

"I already ask too much of them. I have Varaza." Nakia motioned to her guard, who winced. That wasn't a good sign.

Saniyah marched up the dais, staring Nakia down. "That wasn't a request. If they're here to harm you, you need the best. No offense, Captain."

Varaza shook her head. "Can't be offended by the truth. I'm good, but I can't see myself fighting either of them."

"Then it's settled," Saniyah said.

"I don't recall agreeing. I can look after myself," Nakia replied. It wasn't like Jay or Asad could murder her in front of people. She only needed to be careful of them trying to poison her, and she didn't see how Badar or Samar could help with that.

"This isn't up for debate. We need to find out what they're up to, and we need to do it fast. They're subtler and deadlier than Amal could ever be." Saniyah left.

It was hard to believe anyone could be deadlier than Amal. He had tried to poison his own sister once, maybe more. He had no problem with trying to fight Ashni to the death. Jay and Asad came across as haughty jerks, but they didn't seem on Amal's level. Perhaps Amal had learned all he knew from them.

"Make the smart move," Varaza said.

Nakia sighed. They were right, and it wasn't like she had a choice in the matter. Not even ten minutes later, Layla's parents appeared from shadows on the floor, dressed in black robes with black beads on their wrists and necks. Even their eyes were black. They tended to only do that to show their power.

"In your holy attire, too," Nakia whispered, eyeing them. She felt underdressed in her robes. Jay and Asad must be as bad as Saniyah made them sound.

"We want to remind them of our status. They tend to think of us as Layla's parents only," Badar said.

"And they seem to think that means we don't command respect," Samar added, smoothing the beads around her wrist. "Did they inform you they were coming?"

"This is a complete and total surprise. Ashni didn't mention anything, and there's been no letters from them since she left," Nakia replied.

The timing bothered her. Did they have something to do with Ashni's poisoning, or did they put the barbarians up to the raids? Was there a spy in Ashni's ranks who informed the pair Ashni was away, and they were coming to start trouble?

The latter was the most possible, and it meant Jay and Asad saw her as weak. They might be trying to take over before

Chandra could step in. *They think they can run all over you*. Nakia couldn't allow that.

Badar's lip curled as he looked to the front of the throne room. "They know something."

That much was obvious, but Nakia would need to put people on it just to be sure. Not to mention, there would probably be more questions when the brothers settled in.

For now, Nakia needed to prepare to entertain, throw together something grand. If only to play the game. But she also needed to do something about Ashni's arrival. She couldn't allow the brothers to find out Ashni was hurt. Who knew what they might do?

"Can one of you look into them?" Nakia asked.

Badar chuckled. "We're not leaving you. Adira left behind spies. Use them."

Shadow Walkers weren't trained spies, even though their magic, fondness of night, and habit of not making noise should have paired well with spying. Unfortunately, they felt spying was dishonest. Somehow it was all right to torture and kill someone using their shadow. Nakia didn't understand the rules, but now wasn't the time to wonder.

She had never used Adira's spies before. She never had a reason to do so and wasn't sure how to go about it. She cursed herself for rarely paying attention when Ashni and Adira went on about information gathering. It seemed like a tool for warfare. This wasn't war. *Or is it?*

If it was war, she felt woefully unprepared.

Nakia called in trusted servants to prepare for Jay and Asad's arrival. She wouldn't embarrass Ashni. *Wait, Ashni*. If she was still unconscious, Nakia needed to have some place where the brothers couldn't see her.

"Varaza, can you move with stealth?" Nakia asked. It would shock her that Varaza could do anything quietly.

"If you need me to do so," Varaza replied with a bow.

"Ashni trusts you with my life. Now, I want to trust you with hers."

"What do you need me to do?"

"Meet Hafiz and Naren outside the city. They should be on the main road back and will be here soon. Have them bring Ashni in quietly. Make sure no one sees you. I'll prepare a place for her and get word to you where you should bring her."

"I'll go now if you'll be well guarded," Varaza answered.

Badar stepped closer. "We won't leave her side until the brothers have gone."

Varaza nodded and bowed to Nakia before rushing off. Nakia hid a flinch. She hated that she was about to make Badar a liar. It was just Ashni was more important than she was.

Now all Nakia needed was loyal servants to get a room ready for Ashni. Even if Ashni was better, Nakia couldn't risk any leaks about Ashni's conditions.

"When Ashni arrives, you'll need to tend to her," Nakia said to Samar. Her voice hardened. She wouldn't let those plans change just because Jay and Asad were around. Samar would offer Ashni the best care.

"Naren will replace me as guard," Samar said with no argument in her tone either.

Nakia would've preferred Hafiz to Naren. She had seen them both in action and Hafiz seemed to know his business more than Naren. Hafiz's confidence made him a bit of a jerk. However, there had to be something to Naren for Samar to trust him to take over. Something Nakia never got a chance to see...and hoped things would stay that way.

"Do you think Jay and Asad know what happened to Ashni?" Nakia asked.

Badar shook his head. "Layla and Adira would never let something so sensitive leak. Your spies will figure the brothers out."

Nakia's stomach flipped. What if the spies didn't? What if they got swayed by Jay and Asad, true rulers in the Roshan Empire, and not a seat-warmer like her?

"Be bold, little moon. The unknown doesn't need to mean doom. Face it as you have in the past. Be bold," Badar said.

Those close to her liked to say that, reminding her of what they'd seen her through. After all, she had sat down with men who could kill her within seconds and helped broker deals to end wars. She could do this. *Can you, though?* A terrible voice whispered. *All of those are done through the knowledge that Ashni is by your side, and they'd have to deal with her if they touched you. You alone are nothing.*

How long would the voice of her father haunt her? Nakia ignored it as best she could. The voice could talk all it wanted, echo her father, but she couldn't freeze. There was too much to do. Nakia changed clothes, putting on something more spectacular to greet her guests in. Silk robes with actual golden thread and gems sown in a diamond pattern throughout the top.

Multicolored jewels were rushed to her and her best diadem placed on her head. The crown was heavy with precious stones. It wasn't the best she had ever appeared, but it was better than how the brothers would've seen her before the change. Nakia made herself comfortable on the throne. It seemed like forever and no time at all that Jay and Asad were announced at the palace gate and then into the main hall.

"King Jay Akshay and King Asad Akshay."

Horns sounded as they entered. Drums came in after the horns, beating out the rhythm of their steps. The brothers stood before the throne in all of their finery, with their attendants behind them.

A bit much, but not as bad as when Amal arrived. Nakia smiled at them. They grinned back.

Jay had a slight mustache across his fresh face, taking away from his terracotta statue look. He still glowed, like a halo of light surrounded him. Like a bear turned into a man, it was a surprise to find there was enough teal and gold material to make his royal robes. In fact, there were stories that he could become a bear if he wanted. It was more than enough to know he wielded fire, as all of Ashni's brothers did. Nakia hoped he couldn't also transform into a bear.

Asad seemed different. Aged. There was a gray undertone to his once warm, cinnamon complexion. More lines crinkled on his face, as if stress stalked him, burdening him. They might be here for revenge for Amal. Asad was clearly affected by the absence of his twin, even if they didn't spend time together before Amal was put under house arrest.

"Welcome, King Jay. King Asad. It's a pleasure to see you," Nakia said. It was irksome to tell such lies with a straight face, but it was a lesson she learned early on in dealing with people who hated her.

"It is good to see you again." Jay's smile seemed genuine, his amber eyes almost sincere. A better liar for sure. "Forgive our intrusion, but it was brought to our attention that it's been years since we saw our sister's conquest and we should make ourselves familiar with it." He bowed his head a little to drive the apology home.

"After all, this is part of the Empire." Asad smirked, and Nakia knew then and there this was about inheritance. "We should be up to date on it all."

Jay cast Asad a cutting glance. Well, one of them should be up to date and Asad probably wasn't the one. Jay jumped into the conversation. "Yes, like the whereabouts of our sister. Why doesn't she greet us with you?"

"Unfortunately, Ashni isn't here at the moment. She has the heart of a conqueror, much like your father's," Nakia replied. They needed to be reminded Ashni was the one carrying on their father's legacy. She probably had a better shot to the throne than Asad.

"What great lands have stolen her interest now?" Jay asked. His eyes drifted to Badar, as if Badar would react. Badar's jet black eyes stared into Jay's soul. *Is he trying to intimidate Badar?* If he thought he could get something out of Badar, Nakia didn't want to know how powerful Jay thought he was or might actually be. Jay focused on her again.

"The north. It's no secret she won't stop until the world is called Roshan," Nakia replied. Her voice was controlled, even though she felt short of breath.

"There are other ways to honor our father. She leaves you alone too often, Highness," Asad said, as if he were so concerned, but she didn't see either of his spouses.

"I'm far from alone," Nakia replied. She glanced at Badar and he squared his shoulders. Her chest was a little tight. *We need to move this along.* "I put together a feast in honor of your arrival. I set it for later tonight, assuming you'd like to refresh yourselves after such a long journey."

"We had hopes of visiting with our dear sister. Do you have an estimate when your spouse is set to return?" Jay asked. His phrasing wasn't lost on her. Even though Chandra considered her a daughter through marriage, he didn't consider her family. His words set her apart.

"War is tricky," she replied. If anything, once finding out Ashni wasn't there, the polite thing would be to stay for a couple of days to recover from their journey and then return to their homes. That wasn't about to happen.

"Surely she won't be gone for months. Our father taught us the folly of leaving a spouse for so long." Asad smirked.

Nakia's stomach twisted. *That's creepy.* Nakia wasn't sure what he meant, and the hair on the back of her neck stood up. Asad meant her harm. No doubt about that. *Okay, I'm very happy to have Badar and Samar here.* Shadows flickered against the wall but didn't move beyond that.

"Oh, her spouse is quite understanding, much like yours." She grinned, doing her best to look cheerful. She wasn't scared of Asad, just bothered. Her nerves twitched under her skin. *What can I do to get them out of here soon?*

Jay chuckled. "Perhaps we're overtired from the journey and anxious to see our little sister. We should take some time to settle in. We can speak again tonight at the feast."

Nakia nodded. "I look forward to it." *Like I look forward to any form of torture.*

The brothers bowed as servants rushed in to lead them to their quarters. Nakia maintained her regal position for long moments after they were gone, even though she wanted to slouch. Her heart hammered, like it might break her ribs. What the hell was happening?

"They know something," Badar said.

"But what?" Nakia scratched her chin.

"We have to find out," Samar replied.

Nakia wasn't in the mood to deal with intrigue, but she was ready for it. Saniyah would use Adira's spies, and Nakia had a few of her own. Usually, she used them for far more innocent things, such as learning the preferences of visitors to make deals go her way. Now, they'd learn how much the brothers knew about Ashni. Her spies had saved the kingdom before with information. With luck, they could do it again. They were servants, but servants could get people talking. They knew how to win people over and knew how to disappear in a room.

"I'm going to write Chandra. I want to know if she sent them here," Samar said. But why would Chandra send them? To make peace perhaps? That didn't sound like her parenting style.

"That's a good start. I need to make sure the space for Ashni's ready." Nakia climbed to her feet. Ashni would be home soon, and she wanted to receive her beloved without any other issues.

Layla's parents nodded and followed her. The room she had chosen was in the lower levels of the palace, some place she didn't think Ashni's brothers would ever bother to look. The tiny room was supposed to be a shrine area for servants, but Nakia had granted them a larger space closer to their quarters when she moved into the palace. Her generosity paid off now. Servants had prepared the room with a small bed, sitting pillows, a desk, and a few of Ashni's favorite books in case she was awake. Only a couple of trusted servants would be there, just in case.

"What more do you think we need?" Nakia asked, looking around.

Samar pressed a hand to the bed. "Once I assess Ashni's condition, we'll see what we need. I have oils to burn and dark salves to empty the poisoned spaces. I'll probably need a space to mix herbs, compounds, and other medicines to make sure she can fight against the poison."

"All right. May she be awake and clear," Nakia said.

She pressed her hands together in prayer. *Please, to any gods listening, don't let my spouse die.* Her chest burned, on fire with worry. It was as if her insides were about to turn to ash. Ashni had faced, avoided, and cheated death often. Did she have any more great escapes?

***

Everything was black, even when Ashni opened her eyes. Well, she thought she opened her eyes. It was impossible to be sure. *Am I even here?* She looked down but saw only darkness. Even when she tried moving, she wasn't sure if it was happening or not. There was sensation, a prickle under the skin, but not what was expected.

She tried to bring forth her lightning to illuminate the area. No tingle tickled her fingers. No surge of power flowed through her. Nothing to let her know she even still had her talent. *What the hell is going on?*

Still, she tightened her hand, waiting for the inevitable spark. Again, nothing. Her lightning always came when she called. Was this Layla's void? No, Ashni was familiar with that trick and the void didn't feel like this. The void was cold, an endless pressure. This felt like floating.

Maybe some other Shadow Walker had trapped her, but she couldn't see why. She didn't make it a point to spar with many Shadow Walkers. They whined about her talent too much. Had she been helping train the children? Maybe one of them misused a spell or technique. She waited a moment to see if she would be freed...and it didn't happen.

Where am I? She meant to speak them aloud, and though she could hear the words, they seemed to be in her head. She tried again. *Anyone there?*

Her voice carried in the darkness, but there was something about it that let her know it could've been in her head. No response, no echo, no indication there was anything. No sound anywhere.

Am I dead? She remembered a battle. But there was no way she died in a battle. Her father taught her better. She had the best people around her. She couldn't be dead.

Or can I? She needed a sign of something. She listened. There was no sound. Nothing. She inhaled, or so she hoped, trying to catch a smell. Absolutely nothing. Maybe she was dead, and this was the afterlife. No gods, no glory, no joy.

Nothing.

She couldn't accept that. She wouldn't leave Nakia! *Why wouldn't you? Your father left your mother, and he was the Great Amir. Are you anything like him?*

Ashni could never say she was close to the greatness of her father in the sense of his glory. He was the reason the Roshan had an empire, but she was worthy of his legacy. She had practically doubled the size of their empire and treated people fairly. She married the love of her life who could shoulder mighty burdens with her, just as he had. Could she have died like him? Leaving behind so much?

Nakia. Ashni wouldn't be able to forgive herself if she left Nakia to deal with their kingdom alone. *How often do you ride off to battle and leave her to deal with what's going on at home?*

Ashni tried to shake away the thought. Nakia understood her dream. Her mother supported her father through it all, just as Nakia did with her. And what did that get her mother in the end? A dead husband, seven children, and vultures circling to pick her bones clean as they decided who would rule the empire her husband built.

And that's how you left Nakia. The wolves would come for her hellcat. Nakia was strong, and she had Layla, Adira, and others as backup, but Ashni was supposed to be by Nakia's side, loving her, ruling with her, supporting her. Keeping the wolves at bay.

What sort of queen was she? In her drive for her father's dream, had she made the same mistakes he did? Had she basically become him in all the wrong ways?

No. Her father hadn't done anything wrong. She hadn't done anything wrong. And she wasn't dead. She still had so many things to do. So much world to conquer. So much love for Nakia. And she needed to kick Layla's ass one more time. She could already hear how Adira would scold her if she had the nerve to die, and she scolded herself just as much.

S.L. Kassidy

Chapter Six

NAKIA SAT IN THE banquet hall with Samar and Badar during the feast for Jay and Asad. She watched, wanting to see if anyone who shouldn't be with them so much as glanced in their direction. The room was packed with the usual nobles and officials. Some seemed restless, shifting on their sitting pillows, passing up food and wine as it was offered, and glancing at the exits rather than delighting in the party.

Nakia understood. Her robes felt heavy, her mind thick with annoyance for having to even do this. The music was more a whining noise than anything else. She'd like to get off of her teal pillow and walk out, having better things to do than entertain unannounced guests.

No one was happy to greet Jay and Asad. The few people the brothers brought with them seemed to be enjoying the party, following the lead of the kings. Raising their golden goblets, they downed imported wine like it was cheap swill. They stuffed their faces with rich foods, much of it from farther west than they would ever travel. They groped the dancers to their hearts' content.

"Anything look amiss to you two?" Nakia asked. Samar and Badar were better at this than she was, noticing when subtle things were off. As a doctor, Samar was trained to find and solve problems most wouldn't be able to.

"No, they're the same as they tend to be," Badar replied. He leaned forward on his fluffy, black pillow, as if needing a closer look.

"Badar, you could go ruffle their feathers a little." Samar nudged him with her shoulder.

Badar groaned. "I don't want to go reprimand them. You know how that goes."

Nakia arched an eyebrow. "You can reprimand them?" They were kings, children of the Empress. They acted as if they were untouchable, except when their mother was involved.

"We know their parents and technically share daughters. I might be able to rattle them a little for their behavior, since they should've contacted Ashni before coming. They were like naughty teenagers the last time I spoke to them, so we'll see how infuriating they'll be this time," Badar replied.

Nakia could only imagine. Badar stepped away, pushing through the crowd of people and making his way over to Jay and Asad.

Samar leaned closer. "Would you like to hear the conversation?"

Nakia blinked. "You can do that?"

Samar's smile widened. "I can listen through Badar's shadow."

"How the hell can you do all these things through damn shadows?" Nakia squinted as she tried to make sense of that. She couldn't believe it. Their powers didn't make sense.

"All things are possible through the Darkness."

Nakia sighed. "What does that even mean?" Usually, she accepted when they said things like that—Darkness was supposed to be beyond even the gods according to them—but really, how could a shadow act as a conduit to hear a conversation?

Samar put her finger to her lips. Nakia huffed through her nose and folded her arms. Samar then pointed to the brothers and Badar, so Nakia turned her attention to them.

"It comes through like a whisper," Samar said. Nakia nodded, listening to the shadow Samar leaned toward. Their voices did indeed whisper, carrying past the revelry in the hall, clear as if Badar stood right next to her.

"You two usually have better manners," Badar said to the brothers.

Asad scoffed. "What does a beast like you know of manners?"

Nakia flinched at the blatant disrespect. She had never heard anyone speak to Badar in such a manner. She glanced at Samar, who scowled. Maybe the bold behavior was new.

Jay held up a finger. "Just because you knew our father doesn't make you the man."

"And just because you're his son doesn't make you the man," Badar replied. "A pale comparison truly. Your father never showed up as a guest unannounced, nor would he ever treat his hostess as if she didn't exist."

Jay sucked his teeth. "An emperor doesn't have to announce himself in his own lands when all of his subjects are at his beck and call."

Badar tapped his chin. "Has your mother died then?"

Jay's whole body jerked. "You keep my mother out of this, beast."

Badar sighed. "You know how she would feel about this. Hell, you know how your father would feel. Why do you do these things?"

"We don't owe a beast like you any explanations," Asad replied.

Nakia gasped, appalled that he'd have the nerve to say something like that to Badar. The fool.

Badar chuckled. "Funny, since I'm certain if I felt like it, I could crush both of you right now. Only my respect for your parents saves you. You should do well to remember that, along with your manners."

For all their bluster, neither brother spoke after that. Badar stared at them for a long moment before returning to Nakia. Jay and Asad watched him from across the room.

Nakia patted the pillow next to her and Badar sat down, frowning.

"That was useless," Badar said.

Nakia didn't think so.

Samar curled her lip. "Well, thanks to you we know Chandra didn't send them, as Jay got flustered. They're still the immature sterlings they've always been."

"That'll never change. I don't understand how they're Khalid's sons. His eldest. They should be him," Badar said.

Samar chuckled. "Like Layla is you?"

"Layla is like my mother." He waved the comment away. "Does it seem like Asad might actually be in charge of this?"

Nakia turned to him. "Why do you think that?"

"Jay has no reason do something this stupid. The Empire will surely be his upon Chandra's death. Asad's too closely linked to Amal," Badar replied.

Samar frowned. "You're thinking too logically. In their minds, Ashni has always been Chandra's favorite. Jay's here to prove he's better than Ashni and should get the throne. This could be his chance to show Chandra he can handle the now very vast empire."

"Or this could be revenge. Asad wants to hurt Ashni for Amal," Badar said.

Nakia felt those were both good points, but she didn't get a chance to voice her opinion. Jay strolled over, a confident tilt to his chin. Samar's and Badar's eyes flashed and went all black again.

"Highness, is everything to your liking?" Nakia asked, making sure to keep her tone polite.

Jay gave her a strange smile. "For all of the festivities, I noticed Saniyah hasn't joined us. Is everything all right in the Gyan household?"

Her gut churned and it took everything in Nakia to keep a straight face. Saniyah. Did he know she was using Adira's spies to round up information as to why he and his brother might be here?

"Her niece hasn't been feeling well, so she's tending to her. She sends her regards, of course," Nakia answered. Bashira wasn't in the palace on orders from Nakia, Saniyah, and Layla's parents. And Nakia made sure Saffi stayed away for the moment, too.

Jay nodded. "Very well." And then he was gone, back to his seat.

"Oh, dear. He still pines for Saniyah," Badar said.

Nakia's eyes went wide. *He what?*

"Oh, please. He doesn't care for Saniyah. He's upset she picked Adira, a barbarian as far as he's concerned, over his precious sterling blood," Samar said.

Nakia rubbed her forehead. "I feel like I'm learning too much right now, and yet not enough."

Samar shook her head. "Not nearly enough. Jay only wanted Saniyah when she showed an interest in Adira. His hatred of Adira is almost legendary, so he tried to steal Saniyah away. The only thing Saniyah didn't do was knee him in the balls when he made the suggestion that she become his spouse."

Nakia stored that information in the back of her mind. Though it didn't explain why the brothers were there, only adding to trouble they could cause. There were too many moving parts. She hated it.

***

Whispers kept Ashni company in the darkness. She strained her ears, trying to gauge a direction, but it sounded all around her. The voices became clearer, more distinct, and Roshan. They spoke her native tongue. What luck! *They might see me and help. Then I can get back to Nakia.*

"She looks just like that barbarian woman."

Barbarian woman? Nakia? Ashni would make them pay for their insolence.

"None of them look like her."

What?

"She's obviously not his."

Wait a second. The conversation sounded familiar, like it had happened to her a long time ago. *Am I dreaming?* That would make sense.

"Her looks are proof enough of what that hill witch did to our emperor and he doesn't even know it."

Ah. She looked nothing like her father, the Great Amir, so she couldn't possibly be his child.

"He's blinded by her."

"She's bewitched him. How else could you explain him accepting her? She looks nothing like him."

"At least that ghost woman delivered on princes. Those boys are clearly his."

"He might suspect. Shamans and priests have come to him and offered mystical ways to determine that girl's lineage, but he turns them down."

Because I'm his, you jackasses! The emperor is my father! Ashni groaned. She wanted to scream at the top of her lungs, but her voice remained in her own head. This bullshit again. *Why the hell would I bother to dream about this?* She had heard it all from the time she could remember. *This is a waste. I could be coming up with ways to get the hell out of this void.*

Before she could figure out what was going on, the blankness gave way to light. There were blurs at first, shapeless, floating objects that slowly morphed into forms, people, rooms. Four nobles, dressed in Roshan finery, tucked in the corner of the hall of the Grand Palace. Home. *Wait, I remember this.* She looked around the room before staring at a tapestry against the wall by the group, seeing her younger self's tiny feet tucked out of view. Years ago, she'd heard the nobles loud and clear.

"He refuses to see what's clear because she's bewitched him, just as she did to get him to marry her. She's a powerful witch. We all know it."

The nobles weren't wrong about her mother being a witch, but that was the only thing they got right.

"She needs to be stopped."

Ashni remembered how tiny-her wanted to leap out from behind the tapestry and defend her mother, to declare Chandra was more than some hill witch, she was the daughter of a volcano god! Only she could be a match for the Son of the Sun. She couldn't, though. She didn't have the words to say the things she felt in her heart.

So she did the next best thing.

Mini-Ashni, all of five years old, flung back the cloth and launched a surprise attack. The bruising she left on their shins lasted a week. The scolding her father gave her lasted a lifetime.

"You're destined for great things, my princess. Never let people pull you below yourself if it's not necessary. Those nobles can say anything they want about you, but it doesn't change who you are. You're my daughter. You're your mother's daughter. The blood of gods flows through you, fuels you, and one day you're going to light up the world. You'll burn so bright you'll blind them," her father said in a vow she could still feel in her heart.

And then her mother added to it. Words she'd never forget. "You're going to change the world someday."

She liked to think she did that...in spite of her mother, not because of her. After all, her mother probably told her brothers the same thing.

***

With the feast over, the first thing Nakia did was check on Saffi. If Jay and Asad were willing to drag Saniyah into it, Nakia wanted to make sure her sister was safe. They probably didn't know about Saffi, but she needed to be sure.

"Saffi, is everything okay?" Nakia asked as soon as she entered Saffi's room.

The space was furnished with small tables, and thick tapestries and mosaics with calming scenes decorated the walls. Moonlight poured into the room from several windows. Saffi sat propped up on pillows in the corner with a history book, a thin blanket covering her legs pooling around her. Nakia smiled. It was good to see Saffi reading.

Saffi looked up. "Everything's fine, Nakia." Her tone sounded clipped.

Nakia's stomach sank and twisted against itself, sure something was wrong. "You didn't have any unknown visitors?"

Saffi shook her head. "I've been here, not bothering your guests."

Bothering? Nakia rushed to kneel by her sister. "No, Saffi, that's not it. It's not about you bothering them. It's about them bothering you. I want to keep you safe, make things good for you." And it hurt to think she couldn't yet, that the brothers had disturbed this time with her sibling, like a stab to the ribs.

Saffi's lips formed a hard line across her face. "By locking me in my room?"

Just like their father would do. Nakia hadn't thought about it at the time, but that was exactly what this was. *That's because I'm part of you. You're just like me.* Her father's voice rang in her head and made her skin crawl.

"I'm so sorry." Nakia put her hands on Saffi's knees. "I just don't want you to get hurt again."

Saffi closed her book. "At a party?"

"It's who the party was for. They're not good people."

"It's difficult to be good and rule."

Nakia shook her head. "That's untrue. I'm not trying to trap or control you. You can leave your rooms whenever you want."

Saffi nodded, but Nakia didn't feel believed. Her throat burned with worry and tears stung her eyes. She didn't want to lose Saffi's trust in her, not when she just got her sister back, not when they were able to actually have a connection and build a relationship. *You don't know what you're doing without Ashni here. You're drowning, and it hasn't been a full day yet.* She wasn't sure what she'd do next.

***

The world went fuzzy. Hope lifted Ashni's heart. Was she waking up? And then the world only shifted to another part of her past.

Directly in front of her, mini-Ashni was with her father. They sat on a grassy hill and stared at the night sky. Stars seemed to be everywhere, splashes of white on a dark backdrop. Fireflies fluttered around them. Ashni could still smell the wildflowers, even if it wasn't real. Despite everything, calm overcame her. Mini-Ashni stared at her father as if he had hung each star individually just for her.

"Now, Ashni, I know you're my little heavy hitter, but you can't hit everybody," he told her, voice soft and almost boyish. So different than the battle-hardened warrior he portrayed.

"But, Daddy, they said mean things about Mommy."

He scooped her up in a hug. She relaxed against him as he kissed her chubby cheek. "Well, I've learned over the years your mother can handle herself. It's good that you stood up for her, but you don't have to. She can fight her own battles."

She pulled back. "So, I should tell her what they said and let her fight them."

He laughed. "I love your enthusiasm and loyalty, but you don't have to tell her. She already knows. This is nothing new. Sometimes, people will say or do mean things for no reason."

"Like when Amal takes my books."

He sighed. "Yes, like when Amal takes your books. You have to learn what battles are yours to fight."

"I fight Amal all the time."

He chuckled. "I know you do. However, you don't always have to stand up for someone. Sometimes, people need to stand up for themselves. Sometimes, people handle things in ways we wouldn't understand. And sometimes, letting other people fight their own battles helps you grow."

She nodded, even though she didn't really understand. But the lesson had stuck.

Ashni watched as the two grinned at each other. *Why am I dreaming about this? Are there battles I shouldn't be fighting?* She hadn't even stopped fighting her mother's battles after this conversation. She was honor-bound to defend certain people, especially when they weren't around to defend themselves. *You taught me that, Dad...I think.* Looking back, it might have been a lesson she made up on her own.

How does letting someone fight their own fight let me grow? Ashni felt like she should stand up for people. Hell, it was what her mother did, although quieter than her father in a lot of ways. She should stand up for people. *I do.*

***

Nakia sat on the throne and wished she could breathe easy for a little while. Jay and Asad didn't appear for a couple of days after the feast. Their absence made her nervous, but she had people watching them. There were no reports of them doing anything out of the ordinary. There were letters going out, but they only seemed to be discussing how Jay and Asad made it to their destination and checking on their respective kingdoms. It gave her a chance to focus on Ashni's arrival.

She was still a couple of days out, but everything was prepared for when her beloved arrived. The short trip had become a journey due to Ashni's condition. They traveled slowly because she was so delicate. It seemed like any wrong move could be the end.

"What do you think would happen if Jay and Asad knew about Ashni?" Nakia asked Samar and Badar as she took care of some paperwork. They stood on opposite sides of the throne.

"Nothing good," Samar replied.

"They've never been kind to her. We assume that's why she took to Layla the way she did," Badar said.

Nakia's brow wrinkled. "What about Fahim and the little twins?"

Samar shrugged. "Fahim is a completely different person. I do believe Ashni loves him with all her heart, but he's unique. I'm sure if Kek and Kiran didn't have each other, they'd fawn over Ashni."

That made sense. "Ashni's an odd cutting point for the Akshay siblings."

"Khalid and Chandra might have changed their parenting style when the baby girl showed up," Badar said.

Nakia wasn't sure. From what she knew about Khalid and Chandra, they weren't the type to treat Ashni differently.

"Changed how?" Nakia asked.

"They got a little more protective of the children, watchful, and careful who was around them. It might've been too little too late for the older set or it might've just been how Jay, Asad, and Amal were." Samar shook her head.

Nakia couldn't let Jay and Asad just do whatever the hell they wanted, especially since Saffi was wandering about. *I'm not made for this*. She couldn't protect the people she needed to.

Before her thoughts could spiral, Saniyah marched in. Nakia motioned for her to come up to the throne. Saniyah kneeled at Nakia's feet.

"What do you have?" Nakia asked.

Saniyah glanced up. "Nothing much. Adira makes the spying business seem so easy. Jay and Asad don't seem to know what happened to Ashni, but they began making their way here almost as soon as Ashni left for the North."

Nakia scowled. "So, whatever this is has to do with Ashni being gone. A coup?" That couldn't be right, unless they were planning to co-rule. Asad would have to have something damaging on Jay for that to happen, or Jay really had a soft spot for Asad.

"I'm not sure yet. A coup is more than likely, though I can't see them playing nice together. Perhaps Jay will give Asad this end of the Empire for his support. Ashni will be in competition for the throne until she dies," Saniyah said.

She could be dying right now. Nakia's heart skipped a beat and she gasped. Saniyah put a hand on her knee, giving it a squeeze. Samar ran her hand through Nakia's hair.

"Calm down. Her brothers have been trying to get rid of her for years. She's done crazy things to almost get rid of herself for years. She knows now if she dies, you and Adira will scold her for all eternity," Saniyah said.

Nakia laughed in spite of herself, but the remark had the desired effect. She refocused. She had to keep her eye on Jay and Asad and wanted to mend things with her sister. "Have any of you seen Saffi, by any chance?" Nakia asked.

Since the morning after the party, Saffi had been out and about, and Nakia hadn't been able to keep tabs on her.

No one had an answer. If Jay and Asad might kill their own sister, Nakia didn't want to think about what they might do to hers. She needed eyes on Saffi. Now.

***

The memory faded, and Ashni contemplated her father's words about letting others fight their own battles. The words echoed around her in the darkness and hummed through her, making her feel like she did something wrong. *Why shouldn't I stand up for people?* She didn't have the answer, which might explain why the endless black shifted to color again. A new memory.

Mini-Ashni stood in a palace hallway with tiny-Jay. Looking at his thick eight-year-old frame compared to her small five-year-old stature showed why he always seemed like a giant. He dressed in all the finery of the Crown Prince, but he trembled with fury. He balled his hand into a tight fist, and he appeared one move away from tearing the world apart. Mini-Ashni waited for that to happen.

"Why don't you do something? They said bad things about Mommy," mini-Ashni said. She stepped forward. It didn't matter that they were at a royal gathering or that it was a big group of older noble teenagers. They dared to talk about her mother. "I'll do something then."

Jay grabbed her by the hand before she got too far. "Don't bother."

"What?" She glared at him.

Warrior Class Blood Rain

The scowl on his face could've cut diamonds. "They're going to keep doing it. I've seen them, hit them, even told on them, but they never stop."

Squinting, she studied her brother's face for some sign of a lie. "What they said isn't true. We can't just let them get away with it."

"We can't stop what they say without hurting them really bad and that's not good. People wouldn't like us or let Dad and Mom be in charge if they didn't like us."

That didn't sound right to her. Neither Mom nor Dad ever said they got in trouble over her behavior. Who told Jay these things? How could the emperor and empress get in trouble? So many questions, so she went with the most pressing one. "So, we can't do anything?"

"Mom will handle it. It won't stop them, but they'll learn to be quiet about it. Some of them, the smarter ones, will never do it again. Come on." He yanked her to him and threw his arm over her shoulder. He was heavy, bulky. She'd never forget his weight against her.

A ping went through Ashni as she watched the pair. For a long moment, she could almost feel Jay pressed against her, him holding her close, conspiring with her. There was a time when she mattered so much to that big idiot.

Jay snickered. "Let's go have some of those sweet breads while no one's looking."

Ashni watched them go. *Am I smiling? It feels like I'm smiling.* Her eyes burned, too, like she might cry. Why did she have to remember this?

Jay had helped her better understand why she had to pick her battles. *Back when this idiot taught me stuff on purpose.* While Jay hadn't stated he never stood up for her, at the time she thought he did. She couldn't prove otherwise, and he said he stood up for Mom. Why wouldn't her big brother stand up for her?

Beyond that, sweets had been his answer for everything when she was riled up as a child. He always knew where the best candies were and sneaked them for her. Then, one day, it stopped. One day, he was gone and then all that was left was the Light.

Darkness came once more, giving way to something new, focusing on the day she found out about her talent. It had been a hell of a day. Still small, she sat in the grass of a flat plane, thrown from her horse. Her brothers laughed as she wiped blood from her busted lip.

"She can't even ride a horse!" Asad guffawed, pointing at her in case Jay and Amal missed her in the dust.

"I can so ride a horse!" Ashni hopped as she climbed to her feet and stumbled. Her leg hurt, because she had cut it. Blood soaked into the fabric of her robes.

"Then come on." Jay flicked his wrist with one hand.

"I bet what they keep saying is true. You can't be Dad's. You can't possibly be a Roshan and not know how to ride a horse," Asad said.

Amal snickered. "Well, Mom and Dad found her in the snow. That's why she's so light."

It didn't even make sense, but it stung. Since she could comprehend, she had heard similar things, but others whispered them. Her own brothers said them to her face. Her belly twisted and her blood flared as they laughed. Dark clouds gathered over the meadow, blocking a once clear sky.

"She's related to Yetis," Asad said.

"Mommy's way lighter than me!" Ashni couldn't understand why everyone acted like she was the lightest thing to walk the globe. She was only a few shades lighter than her brothers. Mom was the same complexion as a cloud, and no one said anything to her.

"Mommy can also ride a horse," Asad replied.

"Mommy's more Roshan than you and she was born in some backward hill country," Amal said.

"I can ride a horse and I am Roshan!" Ashni stomped her foot. Lightning crackled above them.

Jay scoffed. "You must be from another place. One without horses. There's weird sea people just beyond the Empire. Maybe they lost you."

Coming from Jay, it cut to the bone. "I. Am. Roshan!" Lightning flashed. The wind picked up, howling like a pack of separated wolves. Thundered boomed, like the world was about to come apart. Her brothers looked around.

"It's about to storm," Jay said. "Ashni, ride with me, so we'll make it back before the rain."

"No! I won't ride with you. I can ride my own horse." Lightning struck a nearby tree.

"Stop being foolish! You can't ride and we can't leave you behind. Now, let's go," Asad said.

"I can ride!" Ashni threw her hand without really knowing why. Lightning shot from her fingertips toward her brothers. It smashed against the stone next to them.

Her brothers yelled. The steeds reared up, whinnied, and threw her brothers from their backs. Her brothers gawked at her. She stared at her hands. It felt like her nerves were going to jump out of her body.

After long, quiet moments, the sky cleared, but the atmosphere was different. Everything had changed. Her brothers never quite looked at her the same way again. And maybe she never looked at herself the same. *Why would I be the same? I wielded the power of gods*. No one ever had any answers as to how or why.

***

Nakia was ready to jump out of her seat when she got the news that Ashni had arrived, but she kept her cool. After disappearing for two days about the palace and city, Jay and Asad popped up at random times, as if checking to see if she was working. According to the servants following them, the brothers seemed to be getting familiar with their surroundings. Almost as if they planned to stay awhile.

Yet Nakia just wanted her beloved. She announced loudly she would be taking lunch in her rooms, in case Jay or Asad sought her out. Instead, she rushed to Ashni's side and stopped dead in her tracks when she laid eyes on the fallen queen.

She could hardly believe it was Ashni lying motionless and covered by a thin blanket. While her fingers itched to touch Ashni, she was scared. One false move and Ashni might fall apart. Ashen, practically gray, with bruising around the eyes and mouth. Her cheeks had sunken in on themselves. Deep, dark lines ran like vines over every visible part of her body.

Despite her fear, Nakia placed her hand on Ashni's arm. She expected it to be cold, but it was hot, almost as Ashni was fever-ridden. Then there was the smell. She expected someone in Ashni's condition to have an aroma of death, but that wasn't the case. The faint scent of mint hung over her.

Sniffling, she pressed a little harder. Ashni's body was squishy. That couldn't be good, so she pulled away, afraid she had damaged Ashni.

Nakia trembled at the idea that Ashni's body was decaying just under her skin. She clapped a hand over her lips, holding in a sob. Badar wrapped his arms around her.

"She'll be all right. Samar has her now," Badar said. His quiet voice held so much promise.

Nakia glanced at Samar. Samar examined Ashni. Nakia's stomach churned, burning her throat. Her heart ached. How could Samar fix Ashni? Unable to look at her beloved like this any longer, Nakia turned her attention to Naren and Hafiz.

The pair had certainly seen better days. Dirt and oil covered their faces and hair, which was out of their usual braids. Their plain clothes, worn to help them blend in as they transported Ashni to avoid any unnecessary trouble after finding out Jay and Asad were around, looked just as dirty as their faces. But their shoulders were squared and faces stony, ready for orders.

"What happened to her?" Nakia asked.

Naren handed over a sealed parchment. "Adira wrote everything down that she could find out about what they did to

Ashni, but it's not much. She thinks some Northern death magic might be involved. None of the doctors or healers could figure it out."

Nakia accepted the scroll and read through it. Her eyes seemed to automatically find the part about death magic. Her throat burned to the point it felt like she might vomit. What if the barbarians knew the things Caligo Mor knew? Ashni might never wake up. She might become an undead. There were so many possibilities. She passed the paper to Samar. Hopefully, she could make something of it.

"How was the North?" Nakia asked. She needed at least one problem out of the way.

"Things seemed favorable when we left," Hafiz replied.

"There's an agreement with the biggest tribal leaders, but we still need the other tribes to agree, or they'll keep raiding us," Naren said as he gave her another parchment. "These are the things Layla negotiated and approved."

Nakia nodded, but her body felt like she was crunched up into a tiny ball. It hurt to breathe. She'd look at the negotiations later. "All right. Well, we have a little snag in the plans."

Naren sighed. "Does it have to do with bringing Ashni down here or why Varaza met us halfway out?" Varaza stood in the corner of the room. She looked more rugged than she did when she left, like years had passed. She had done her job well, made sure they got into the city and palace unnoticed, but seeing Ashni in such a state, someone she viewed as a god, was probably difficult.

Nakia nodded. "Her brothers showed up a few days ago."

Hafiz's eyebrow ticked up. "The kings are really here?"

He seemed much too interested for Nakia's taste. He worshipped the ground Adira walked on, but he was one of the few sterling Roshan in their group and still seemed to think sterling meant better.

"They are, and they cannot know about this," Nakia said.

Hafiz nodded. "They'd take advantage of what Queen Ashni has worked for."

Maybe he does get it.

"We have to let Layla and Adira know," Naren said.

"I've sent word. I want them to return, and you two can exchange places with them. They have more experience in dealing with Jay and Asad," Nakia replied.

Hafiz rubbed his forehead. "Then no one will have the on-site authority to negotiate with the barbarians."

"Hold them off, boy. Learn to stall," Badar said, his calm voice settling around Nakia like a hug.

"We might all have to." Samar put a hand on Ashni's discolored forehead. "I've never seen anything like this."

"You can save her, right?" Nakia feared she might die on the spot if she didn't get the perfect answer for this. It felt like there were claws ripping down every inch of her.

"Everything is possible through the Darkness," Samar replied.

The way Nakia's heart squeezed into itself didn't allow her to lie and say she believed that. But, if it saved her spouse, so be it. "Okay, okay, okay. We need to keep it together." *You need to keep it together.* "Samar, you stay here with Ashni. Varaza, you're down here with them. Hafiz, Naren, you'll go back. I'll keep an eye on Jay and Asad."

"And I'll keep an eye on you," Badar said.

"I'll return with you for right now. Varaza, keep an eye on Ashni," Samar said.

Nakia nodded. It made sense for Samar to return with Nakia and Badar to avoid arousing suspicions. The trio returned to the grand hall. Jay and Asad waited for them, standing by the dais, murmuring to themselves.

"Highnesses, is there something I can do for you?" Nakia asked as she made her way to the throne.

"Bow to us when you stand before us," Asad replied. She arched an eyebrow.

Jay waved him off. "Any word on our sister?"

"Still north, negotiating with the tribes. She's not sure how long it'll take," Nakia replied, sitting on the throne. With luck, that response would get rid of them.

"Then perhaps you should entertain us while we're here. We're your guests, after all," Asad said.

"And what would be entertaining for you, Highness?" It took all of her willpower not to bite her tongue with the question. *Why do they think I have the time?*

"You're queen here, are you not? You should know what to do," Asad replied with a sneer.

Nakia smiled. "My guests do tend to do the honorable thing and make themselves known ahead of time, so I can clear my schedule and make plans."

A flicker of a frown painted Jay's face. "We are honored to be your guests."

"We're grateful to have you. I'll do my best to see to your needs now that my schedule has been shifted to accommodate you." That was far from true, but she couldn't allow Jay to out-empty pleasantry her. "We can have dinner together and figure out what you'd like."

The brothers bowed their heads and took their leave. As soon as they were out of sight, Nakia huffed. Jay was being far too nice. She didn't have a chance to think about it because out of nowhere, Saffi pinned herself to Nakia's side.

"I was told you're having dinner in honor of Ashni's brothers," Saffi said, beaming.

Nakia grimaced. "How did you find out about that so quickly? I just made those plans."

"One of my servants told me. You didn't think I was ready for a great feast with them, dear sister, but surely I can take dinner. They must be great men if they are related to Ashni. You must introduce me. Must," Saffi said.

That didn't sound like a good idea. When Nakia glanced at Layla's parents, she could see they shared her doubt. Ashni's brothers didn't need to be aware of anyone close to Nakia or they'd use the person against her.

"Saffi, eat with me first. I've been busy all day." Nakia led her to another room. Servants moved to prepare an early lunch.

"I'll never get used to these pillows," Saffi said as they sat.

Nakia nodded. "It does take a while."

They ate for a while. Nakia introduced Saffi to some nobles, but Saffi only wanted Jay and Asad. It felt like a test, if Nakia denied her, it would prove Saffi had traded one prison for another. So, against her better judgment, Nakia invited Saffi to the dinner. The way Saffi smiled had been enough to light her heart, though it didn't quell the dread that sat heavy in her belly. At dinner later that evening, the moment Asad's eyes landed on Saffi, she knew this was a mistake she couldn't take back.

Chapter Seven

ONE AFTERNOON, NAKIA FOUND herself being dragged along by Saffi to their lunch spot. Usually, Bashira and Saniyah would've been there waiting, but Jay and Asad lounged on the decorative pillows, like they belonged there. Gut churning, Nakia took her usual spot and Saffi went to hers. She wished Bashira and Saniyah were there, if only for the sense of normalcy, but Bashira was forbidden to come to the palace and Saniyah refused to come while the brothers were there.

Jay grinned. "Good afternoon, ladies."

His eyes drifted to Badar, who stood off to the side. Badar was in all black once more, eyes darker than ink. Jay didn't look bothered and didn't focus on Badar for more than a second as though he didn't matter.

"How has the day treated you thus far?" Nakia asked with a small smile of her own. Her face hurt from the falseness of the expression, but Saffi's giggle was disconcerting. *Please, Saffi, no. Don't be taken by them.*

"Fair. The weather here is beautiful," Jay replied, tugging on his top teal robe. It was warm enough for them to sit in the garden, enjoying the clear sky. A large umbrella protected them from the bright sun.

Nakia laughed. "Say that to Ashni in the winter."

"She's become accustomed to her desert, which is how it should be," Asad replied.

Nakia arched an eyebrow. "Why is that?" Were they trying to take Ashni's territory? She wanted to rub her face; except she didn't want to show stress.

Asad made a show of waving a hand. "The Empire is as vast as it needs to be. Anything more is unnecessary."

That argument surprised her, not just because she assumed Asad wanted Ashni's bit of the Empire, but because this was the son of a conqueror. Nakia didn't think any of the Great Amir's children would frown at conquest. "How so?"

Jay glowered. "She's not considering what it takes to maintain an empire every time she adds to it, much like our father. If she bothered to speak with our mother, she'd know she's doing more harm than good."

"And maybe she needs to consider that it's time to surround herself with people who know those things," Asad said, chest puffed out.

"And you're here to educate her?" Nakia couldn't believe their arrogance. Jay sounded like he believed those words. If he did, what were they after? Jay wouldn't get caught up in revenge for Amal.

Knowing the Roshan, Nakia could understand Asad craving some twisted form of justice for Amal. The twin bond was supposedly more than sharing a soul. It was something like being born twice. Without Amal, Asad probably felt like he was missing not just a piece of himself, but all of himself. Jay, though, had no part to be missing.

"We're here to help her understand what's necessary, especially if she's expanding across a river," Asad replied. He stared Nakia down.

Nakia shook her head and popped a date in her mouth, eyes never leaving Asad's gaze. "She has no desire to expand north."

"Yet she's up north right now." Jay leaned over and gathered a few items to eat, as if it was safe to do so now. Was it just a way to make it seem like Nakia gave in because she ate first? Nakia didn't want to overanalyze the lunch.

"You've misunderstood her mission. She's up there because there are barbarian tribes coming into our land and harassing our citizens," Nakia replied.

She glanced at Saffi. Saffi had her feet tucked under her, her hands on her knees, and her gaze downward, like she was trying to stay as quiet as possible to avoid troubling the waters. This was definitely more intense than Saffi banked on and it seemed all her excitement had fled.

Asad rolled his eyes. "You speak of barbarians and say, 'our land and citizens.'" He finally decided to eat something but didn't break eye contact with her. She hoped the fish tasted like ashes in his mouth.

Nakia leaned in a little. "Am I not her?"

Jay held up his hand. "He means no disrespect, just pointing out you've mentioned barbarians, but then you say she doesn't want to conquer the north. What else is to be done with barbarians?"

"She needs to stop the barbarians from attacking our towns." Nakia arched an eyebrow. *Are they not listening to me?* "She wants to continue her conquest of the west."

"Which is still a waste." Asad shook his head.

Nakia rubbed her palms together and looked between the pair. "Are the economic and trade opportunities a waste? There are more markets than ever before. You cannot deny the money going to the Empire from the West as well as the new goods. Let's not forget there have been new inventions introduced to the Empire from the West. Products, food, jewels, medicine, and so much more. Those are only made possible through Ashni's actions."

"How much is it costing to connect all these new trade paradises?" Asad showed all of his teeth. For a moment, he looked almost...demented.

Nakia shrugged. "Money sometimes has to be spent to be made. That's the cost of the Empire." War was never cheap. It was when the war was done that the actions yielded benefits. She had seen this herself, read about it in histories.

Jay let out a loud, clearly forced laugh. "Ashni has prepared you well with her line of thinking. If it were up to her, the Empire would be the world."

Nakia tilted her head and squinted as she studied Jay. "Was that not your father's dream? Ashni's honoring the Great Amir."

Jay sat up taller, towering over the four as he did. Saffi clutched her knees more tightly. Nakia was torn between staring Jay down or comforting Saffi, who seemed overwhelmed. Part of her hoped this might be the thing to keep Saffi away from the brothers. In the end, she reached over and took Saffi's hand.

"There are other ways to honor him. He was more than a conqueror," Jay said.

That's true. Nakia read up on the Great Amir. He seemed like a playful, good-natured person. There were tons of stories about him doing things with his children, honoring his family with his actions, and passing several laws to help the average citizen. She could see those things in Ashni.

There was a law entitling every Roshan citizen to bread, but Ashni included meat with that. Usually rabbits or rodents. It was illegal to murder a slave in the Empire, but in Ashni's territory, slaves could sue over maltreatment. Ashni carried on her father's legacy through those laws, her way to honor him. Why did Jay want to pretend he knew Khalid better than Ashni? *They act as if they're better than she is.*

Asad sniffed. "Besides, conquest sullies the Empire. Dad allowed everyone under the sun to be Roshan, but not everyone deserves it."

"Because Roshan culture is superior to all others?" Nakia raised an eyebrow.

Asad motioned to her with both hands. "You tell us. Have you not forsaken your culture for ours?"

Nakia gave Saffi's hand a squeeze before letting go. Saffi looked up, seemingly a little more confident. Jay and Asad glanced at Saffi, but briefly. They kept their focus on Nakia.

Nakia shook her head. "Not at all. There are things about Roshan culture I like, so I've adapted to my own. There are things from my culture that I like, so Ashni and I mix and match. That's what this whole city is about. Ashni does that because her father did that."

Asad frowned as he chewed on a piece of glazed jerky. "He did so much more."

Were they trying to test her knowledge of the Great Amir? Was she some pretty-faced barbarian that Ashni liked to keep on her lap? For a brief moment, doubt gnawed at her stomach, but she refused to let it bait her. She'd show them.

Nakia put her hands to her mouth for a second, covering a frown as she thought. When she lowered her hand, a smile lingered on her lips. "Did he not want to bring people together? Unite everyone? Ashni has the same desires. She doesn't look down on people because of where they were born or their social status. I think that the Roshan allowing for upward mobility is wonderful, and Ashni's taken it one step further and used it to great effect."

Ashni used the flexible class system of the Roshan to gain loyalty. Well, Nakia hoped they were loyal. Thanks to spending time with Hafiz, she understood how some of the pureblood Roshan looked down on the assimilated citizens. If push came to shove, would the sterlings abandon Ashni for bringing in so many barbarians? Would the barbarians abandon Ashni for want of autonomy? *The brothers might stir things up and start a revolt.*

Jay cleared his throat. "Maybe now isn't the time for such a discussion. We can talk to Ashni. Has she gotten word to you of when she'll be back?" He sampled some of the flat bread and diced goat.

"From what I've been told, they're talking to the top five tribes, but there are dozens scurrying around up there," Nakia replied.

Asad sucked his teeth. "Ashni hasn't won them over with her charming personality and might of the Empire already? Can she even still call herself a conqueror?"

Nakia kept her calm, even though she desired nothing more than to snap at him. "She's not always a conqueror. Sometimes, she's a liberator. In this case, she's a defender." She was tired of Asad trying to tear Ashni down. What had he accomplished to outshine his sister? Nothing she knew of, beyond being the older twin to a psychopath.

"Ashni rescued me," Saffi said, voice low, eyes on the floor. The lunch was definitely more political than she bet on. The brothers scowled at her, seemingly offended that not only had she spoken out of turn, but she contradicted them.

Nakia placed a hand on Saffi's knee again, which got her to look up. Saffi smiled and Nakia couldn't help smiling back.

"As a gift to her beloved spouse, undoubtedly," Asad said.

"Deep down, Ashni wants to protect people," Nakia replied, knowing he probably couldn't understand.

"We can't protect everyone and trying to take on too much will simply lead to everyone's demise. If it were up to Ashni, she'd pull every drowning slob into our boat until we all sink," Jay said.

Nakia knew the logistics of working things out in an empire this size. Whenever they had to wait for a response from the capital, it showed. Even when Ashni tried to keep up to date with Khenshu, it was maddening sometimes. But it didn't mean they should give up. Not when this was Ashni's dream, her father's dream, her people's dream. Besides, Ashni's march West helped many people, not only the Roshan. Ashni would never stop, unless that poison in her system took her out.

***

Ashni couldn't be sure how long she was lost in darkness. She felt like she was nowhere and everywhere as she watched the tiny version of herself. *Why do I need to see this? I already lived it.*

Tiny-Ashni dipped and dodged as her martial arts master, Mahir Qabil, came after her. She thought she was fast and then she was on the floor and her little butt hurt. Mahir was never gentle with her, even though she was small. He glared at her with hard dark eyes and posed to strike with thick muscles and powerful hands. It would definitely hurt if he hit her, even if she managed to put her guard up, which was unlikely. He was about to teach her a painful lesson. One she learned many times. One she didn't want to learn again.

Mahir's hand twitched. Her heart leaped into her throat, and it felt like she was about to come out of her skin with fear. The air grew heavy, and sparks jumped from Ashni's hand. Right before

98

he was on her, lightning crackled from her fingers. Gasping, he leaped back. For a long moment, he stared with wide eyes. She almost apologized, but instead scrambled to her feet, in case he was being coy.

"The rumors are true," he said.

Ashni clutched her hands into fists as small bolts of lightning popped around her. Spasms shot under her skin. Taking a breath, she flexed her fingers until the lightning faded.

Mahir took one step closer. "You can control it?"

She shook her head. "I've only done it twice. I just calmed down, and it went away."

He nodded. "I suspected your talent would come soon. Your brothers' Fire didn't come until they were seven. You're barely six. And lightning? Lightning is meant for the gods!" His face broke into a grin that eased her heart out of her throat and back into her chest.

"So, will I get my Fire then?" She was tired of Amal acting like he was so great because he could beat her in a match, but she'd take him apart with fire. Maybe Asad and Jay, too. Okay, maybe not Jay.

He rubbed the back of his neck. "I'm not sure, Highness. Talent like yours is quite rare."

"But I'll get it, right?" Her brothers had Fire. Her father had Fire. She had to have Fire. She couldn't be different again.

He kneeled down to her level. "You might've been blessed with something different."

Ashni scowled. She didn't care what lightning was about. She was supposed to have Fire, just like she was supposed to have a richer skin tone. She didn't fit the Akshay family, and this only further proved that. She didn't need that.

"I want Fire," Ashni said.

"It's not up to me."

"I want Fire!" Thunder boomed outside and the wind howled loud enough for them to hear it. Ashni could feel that it was her. It was like the storm pulsed through her and fled her to the outside world. "I don't want this. I don't want it."

Tiny-Ashni took off and the scene dissolved into the throne room.

"Mommy!" Tiny-Ashni leaped onto the high throne, landing on her mother's leg.

Her mother grunted. "Careful. You'll break my leg."

"Is Dad back yet? He has to tell the gods I don't want it." He was the son of a god. They had to listen to him, right?

Her mother stroked her head. "He'll be back in a few days. Why do you need him to talk to the gods?"

"Because he's the Son of the Sun. Khurshid will listen to Dad and give me the right talent!"

Her mother laughed. "And what's the right talent?"

She glared at her mother for being so dense. "Fire! Lightning doesn't fit. All the boys do Fire. You're even the daughter of a volcano god. I'm sure Khurshid will want to fix his mistake."

Her mother's pink lips pursed. "Are you saying the king of the gods made a mistake?"

"How else do you explain lightning?" Tiny-Ashni stared her mother down.

Chandra smiled at her, eyes shining in a way Ashni had learned to hate, but now missed. Her mother looked at her with such love. Her mother looked at all of them with nothing but love.

Chandra ran her hand through Tiny-Ashni's braids. "The same way I explain how a conquering prince showed up to my tiny village to take over and ended up marrying me. Sometimes, life doesn't make sense to us until far down the line. Questioning the gods rarely helps."

Tiny-Ashni scratched her forehead. "So, this is for a reason, but we don't know what it is?" *It was a damn good reason. Forgive my young insolence, Khurshid.*

Her mother nodded. "Gods have different goals than we do. They sometimes have different plans for us, and we don't discover those things until later. Don't fight this blessing. Embrace it and see where it takes you."

Tiny-Ashni nodded and the scenery faded again. Ashni stared at the darkness around her now. *I took that to heart.* As a child, she used to hold her mother's words in high regard, but her lightning changed how she viewed the world. The world opened up to her, for better and for worse.

＊＊＊

Nakia sat down to yet another meal with Jay and Asad. She didn't want to make a habit of this or the fact that Saffi invited herself again. Lunch should've scared Saffi off or at least bored her. Nakia wasn't sure if her sister was simply exercising her freedom and wanted to spend sister time together or if Saffi was infatuated with the brothers. *Please, be the former.*

Badar sat with Nakia. He didn't eat. He watched, probably expecting poison. And honestly, he wasn't the only one. Nakia eyed the fruit dripping with honey.

"Any word from our dear sister yet?" Jay asked.

She wanted news about Ashni as badly as Jay pretended to want to hear from her. Samar was busy reading up on medical texts now after her initial tries failed to clear the poison from Ashni. Thinking about it made Nakia's stomach turn, and that was only the top of her worry list.

It was still a mystery as to why the brothers were here. Saniyah continued to investigate, but nothing was conclusive. Servants reported the brothers never spoke about it. It was like they were on vacation, enjoying palace life, eating at all hours, drinking whenever they wanted, and playing with any free persons who would let them.

Nakia sipped her wine and surveyed dinner, needing comfort food. She grabbed some bread and spread jam on it. "She's planning to stay in the North."

Jay arched an eyebrow. "Oh?" He bit into a roasted chicken leg.

"Yes. She means no disrespect to you, of course, but the tribes up North are a danger to many of her citizens." Nakia glanced over at Saffi. She looked better than the last time, nibbling on a skewered squid.

"She couldn't even spare us a direct communication after we traveled all this way for her?" Asad inquired much too innocently.

"She wouldn't need to, as I am her." Nakia ate her bread. The jam was delicious, and the sweet taste helped settle her.

The brothers bristled. They understood Ashni considered them one and the same. They were of the same soul, mind, body, heart. The fact that Jay and Asad pretended otherwise was an affront to her, Ashni, and their marriage.

"How long will it be before she returns then?" Asad asked through gritted teeth.

Nakia picked up a bowl of rice, mixing it with some shredded chicken. "She's not sure. She plans to oversee the building of fortresses and bridges as we get more northern tribes to agree to work with us. Lives are on the line." She wanted to emphasize that, so they couldn't claim Ashni had dodged them.

"So, we should just go home?" Jay asked with a tilt of his head, his long braids shifting to the side of his head.

Nakia shrugged as she scooped up the meal with some flat bread. "You could ride to the frontier. I'm sure Ashni would enjoy the company."

"There's nothing but misery in the North," Saffi muttered.

Nakia looked at her sister, pride burning inside her. There was a flash of the old Saffi. She had never been to the North, but she had educated herself. She read up on it and had an opinion. With any luck, this Saffi would show up more often rather than the one who seemed intrigued by Jay and Asad.

Covering her joy, Nakia scoffed. "Believe me, I know. I've seen it."

Saffi nodded. "It was once scouted by the Tyra, hoping to find a new home. It was considered inhospitable, even by them."

It said something that the Tyra used to live in a dark swamp and even they thought the North was terrible.

"One of the many reasons Ashni doesn't want the area," Nakia said, pleased with Saffi's help. She wasn't sure if it was on purpose or not, but she'd take it.

"Ashni should've burned it to the ground then," Jay said, carelessly waving the chicken leg in his hand. Skin fell from the food and then he tore the rest of the meat from the bone with one big bite.

Asad chuckled. "Only she can't." He grabbed a handful of diced venison. He actually put his hand in the dish, as if he was the only one who would eat it. *Was that some weird display of dominance?*

"Ashni isn't in the habit of utterly destroying things. Even though she conquers, she respects. Something she learned from your father," Nakia replied.

"Yes, *our* father," Asad said.

More of the "Ashni isn't Khalid's daughter" nonsense. Nakia wanted to roll her eyes. *Great.*

Jay leaned forward, motioning to himself and his brother with one large hand. "You sit in judgment as if you know our father or our beliefs or us."

Nakia had played this game long enough to know that was a trap. He was angling to get her to admit she didn't know all she thought she did. He could be trying to trap her into inviting them to stay longer, and she wouldn't fall for that mess. Taking a breath, she ate a little more and maintained eye contact with Jay.

"I cast no judgment. I'm sure you learned many lessons from your father as Ashni did. Different personalities pick up on different things," Nakia said. She and her sisters learned plenty of things from their father. Nothing he intended to teach them, but they each picked up their own lessons for their own survival.

"And one of the lessons Ashni missed is family togetherness," Asad replied before eating more of the venison in his hand.

This from a guy who wants to impress upon me that Ashni's not his father's child. Nakia sipped her wine, letting the sweet liquid quell her anger.

Asad grabbed a piece of bread, tearing it in two. "She should leave the frontier to her fisherwoman for a few days."

Nakia blinked. "Fisherwoman?" Then it dawned on her. "Do you mean General Adira Gyan?" *The disrespect!*

Asad shrugged. "The fisherwoman."

Nakia bristled. "I hear that fisherwoman destroyed a whole unit of Roshan warriors with a spear and someone saw such potential in her that they gifted her with a war spear, horses, a sword, and a command." She wouldn't let them besmirch the name of the woman who personally carried her from Caligo Mor's citadel.

Jay waved the whole matter off. "Through the grace of the Amir. Without him, she's a fisherwoman and, really, he pitied her more than anything else."

"So, once he died, her status reverted?" Nakia asked.

"She no longer leads a Roshan army, only a branch of it," Asad replied.

"Then she's not a fisherwoman," Nakia said.

Asad glared at her from across the table, but he didn't have a rebuttal.

Jay interjected. "The Great Amir used her for what he could, but she's nothing much."

"Nothing much? She rose from a fisherwoman to a general," Nakia said.

Jay scowled. "There were much greater sterlings. My father seemed to think the outsiders were special, though, because of our mother. Something else Ashni picked up from the Great Amir."

An announcement from a nearby guard interrupted their conversation. Layla and Adira were back.

Jay arched his eyebrow again. "Layla, but no Ashni?" he asked as if it wasn't possible.

"Layla's back to make sure home base can support the building of the forts on the Northern front," Nakia replied.

The way Asad's face twitched meant Nakia had to come up with something better. She sent for Layla and Adira then focused on the skeptical Asad.

"Ashni sent Layla back because Layla can move between both sites the fastest," Nakia said, when Layla and Adira came over to them.

Layla nodded, sitting down. Adira maintained eye contact with Asad, as if challenging him, but he didn't take the bait. Jay glared at Adira, though Nakia couldn't even begin to understand what that glare was about.

***

Tiny-Ashni wanted to ask her father why the gods would give her lightning for a talent and make her so different again. But when he came home, he spent time with Jay. She would've joined them, except the moment she came upon them, Jay glowered at her. It was more than enough to freeze her and stop her heart.

"Hey, Ashni, I hear your talent came in," her father said with a grin. She barely heard the words, too focused on how Jay treated her like some kind of enemy.

"It's lightning," Jay said before Ashni could mutter a word. She felt a stab in her chest as he said it with such disdain and as if he were tattling on her.

Her father continued to smile as he nodded. "Nice. I don't think anyone's ever had lightning as a talent. The gods really shone on you, huh?"

Jay growled. "No one in our family has that."

"No, you're right. But, like I said, I don't think anyone's had it before. Lightning is special. It comes only from the sky."

"Fire's better. Fire is from Khurshid himself," Jay said.

Her father nodded. "This is true, but Dima wields lightning, and she can even block Khurshid himself."

Jay scowled. "Yes, and Dima's children wield lightning, too. And they like to walk among mortals sometimes."

Ashni wasn't sure what her brother meant at the time, but it clicked when she was older. When her lightning came in, he believed she was the daughter of the storm god. She was proof their mother strayed from their father. Beyond that, she was not their father's child, so she had no claim to anything, not even him.

***

Nakia sat by Ashni's bedside holding Ashni's hand in both of hers. Ashni's hand was squishy, as her body was, like everything inside of her was made of wet mush. Still, she was warm, and she was breathing. There was hope.

Layla sat across from Nakia, with her eyes pinned on Ashni. Nakia wasn't even sure Layla blinked. Layla refused to touch Ashni, which was worrisome. Was there a problem with touching Ashni? Nakia couldn't help herself and Samar hadn't stopped her, so she clutched Ashni whenever she could. Adira paced behind Layla, looking like a caged animal.

"They can't know Ashni's incapacitated," Adira said, scratching her forehead.

"They know something's up. I don't think they're going to leave," Nakia replied. *What should I do?* She held off on asking. She was in charge, after all, so she needed to figure it out.

Layla shook her head. "Well, that doesn't do us any good."

Adira rubbed her chin. "They have to know something happened to Ashni. They wouldn't be flaunting their presence otherwise. The question is, how do they know that."

"A mole." Layla growled.

"I would think so. We'll have to check that out. What I don't understand is why the hell they're here, even if they know something happened to Ashni. I can't imagine Jay wants this territory," Adira said.

"This has to be revenge for Asad, even though he didn't act like a twin to Amal. He likes to pretend he's Jay's sidekick," Layla replied.

Nakia's face contorted. "But Jay wouldn't want revenge."

"I disagree. Jay probably wouldn't think of it as revenge, but he's hardly a fan of... well, any of us really." Adira motioned around the room. "Saniyah has been avoiding him, yes?"

Nakia nodded. "She's hardly been around and kept Bashira away."

"You might want to get Saffi to avoid them. I've already heard talk that she's intrigued by them. Discourage that." Adira wagged a finger at her.

With a shake of her head, Nakia sighed. "I tried. It only enticed her more." She was certain Saffi wanted to be around the brothers because Nakia tried to keep her away that first night. She wasn't sure what she could do about her sister. She probably already messed that up. *Like you mess everything up, like you'll mess up running the kingdom without Ashni, and like you'll mess up handling her brothers.*

"Watch out for her." Adira leaned forward. "Jay might seem sensible, but he's the one who taught Asad to bite. Those nobles did a number on them, but Jay truly thinks he's a god."

Nakia saw glimpses of Jay's ego. He spoke as if whatever he said was the only truth.

"Do any of us have the authority to tell them to leave?" Nakia asked. As far as she knew, even Ashni couldn't do that, but they might know something she didn't.

Layla snorted. "No, and even if we did, they wouldn't listen. Jay thinks being the oldest makes him the highest authority outside of the empress, so he'll pretend that's true. At the moment, it actually is. We can't force him out. It's his decision."

Nakia sighed. "So, we've got nothing."

"Nothing I can think of, unless there's trouble in their provinces and we can't start trouble there without tempting the empress into acting. Jay came along thinking we'd focus on Asad, but I know he's the true demon here," Adira replied.

Nakia wasn't sure if that was true or if Adira was speaking out of Jay's open interest in her spouse. It didn't matter either way. The brothers were bad news, but with no information to act on, they were frozen.

"Samar, do you have news?" Nakia asked, and all eyes went across the room.

Samar, who had a small laboratory at the other end of the room, didn't respond. Not a good sign. She had spent about an hour muttering to herself before this. Now, she was bent over a small pot, dripping a dark liquid into it. All of her liquids, powders, and balms gave the room a strange, muddled scent of earth and smoke. Candles heated up several concoctions, adding melted wax and humidity to the room. It was enough to give anyone a headache if they were there too long, but Varaza never left, nor did Samar. Samar might have forsaken sleep at that point.

"Ashni's a fighter," Layla said.

Adira nodded. "No way she dies from one arrow by some archer who got lucky. She's the Chosen One."

Those words weren't just for Nakia. Layla and Adira needed to believe it, too. This was so much. *And it will break you.* Nakia hated that fucking voice.

*　　*　　*

Tiny-Ashni moved her chess piece, checkmating Amal for the third time that day. It wasn't a surprise when Amal slapped the board away, setting it on fire. Asad had to duck the flaming wreckage without bothering to look up from his book. Amal roared, flames shooting from his nose.

"So, no fourth game?" Ashni asked with a smirk. He was the one who asked her to play. It was raining outside, and their mother encouraged them all to spend time inside together. Jay abandoned them almost immediately, going off with people Ashni didn't know. At first, Amal asked Asad to play, but Asad brushed him off as being no competition. Asad wasn't wrong.

"You're a cheater!" Fire jumped from his finger as he pointed at her.

"No, I'm just better than you," she replied.

"You're not! I'm the son of Emperor Khalid Akshay!" He threw out his chest.

"And I'm his daughter. Your point?"

"No, you're not! You throw stupid lightning."

The aforementioned lightning popped from her fingers. "Watch your mouth."

"I don't have to listen to you! You're nobody and everybody knows."

"Take it back," she said in a low growl.

"Never."

Lightning jumped from her hand and blasted Amal across the room. He hissed and struggled to his feet, throwing a fireball at her. She shot more lightning and it went through the fire, stopping it. Amal stared at her with wide eyes. She smirked. He released a frustrated wail and ran out of the room. He was going to tell their mother. She turned to Asad.

"You want to play?" Ashni asked.

Asad scoffed. "I have better things to do." He went back to reading.

Ashni did not think anything of it. Later, she realized Asad never engaged her the way Amal did, but that didn't mean Asad saw her any differently. His eyes said the same things. Asad never engaged her in general, though. Her lightning was the reason for both.

***

Nakia woke up to news that the brothers had an announcement, and they had the nerve to be doing it in the throne room. Their gall didn't surprise Nakia. She threw on her nearest robes, barely having them tied, and rushed off to the throne room, met by Adira. Layla and Badar appeared out of a shadow, falling into step with Nakia and Adira as they marched deeper into the room.

"What's going on?" Adira asked.

"Something terrible," Nakia replied.

"Of course," Layla said.

"Thank you all for coming," Jay said, standing by the throne with Asad at his side. They wore finery a god might descend to the mortal realm in.

"Maybe they're leaving," Layla whispered.

"Yes, please," Nakia said, even though she knew that couldn't be the case.

"We've been here for almost two weeks, but we didn't make it clear as to why we are here," Jay said.

"We were investigating if this kingdom was following Empire protocol. Every kingdom is to be headed by one of Empress Chandra's children. This kingdom is not," Asad said.

"Excuse me!" Nakia marched up to them. "Ashni is one of Empress Chandra's children." *What are these bastards playing at?* After all the fuss about being Khalid's child, this was a new argument and one she wasn't prepared for.

Asad looked her dead in the eye. "We know Ashni's dead."

"Now we're in charge," Jay followed up.

"Ashni isn't dead!" Layla stormed over, Adira hot on her heels.

"Then why has no one seen her on the Northern front?" Jay asked.

Nakia's eyes widened. She didn't have an answer for that. It wasn't like they could produce Ashni. It was better for them to assume Ashni was dead than to know she was too out of it to defend herself. If they didn't think she was dead, they might devote their time to make Ashni dead and Nakia refused to risk that. At least they just confirmed someone was feeding them information. She needed to find out who the mole was, and she certainly couldn't cede control without a fight.

Chapter Eight

"THIS IS A COUP!" A man from the Court cried.

Several members of the Court advanced on Jay and Asad. Adira's hand went to her weapon, as one of the few people allowed the privilege in the throne room. Layla put herself in front of Nakia and raised her hands. Badar stepped to Layla's side.

Jay merely smiled, calm as could be. "It isn't a coup. These are the rules. Every kingdom in the Empire is to be ruled by a child of the Empress."

"Queen Nakia is a child of choice by the Empress," Layla said.

"That doesn't hold up any more than her claim that you are Ashni," Asad replied with a smirk. Cruel delight danced in his pale green eyes, an odd contrast to Chandra's eyes of similar color. Whenever Nakia saw Chandra her eyes were always filled with love and kindness.

"We are Ashni!" Layla pointed to herself and Nakia. "And my sister is not dead." Her stern voice didn't seem to make a dent in the brothers' facade. Nakia held in a wince. She didn't want them looking for Ashni.

"Prove it," Jay replied, chin tilted in the air.

"We aren't under obligation to prove anything to you," Nakia replied. She couldn't believe the insolence of these brothers.

"You are, because unless Ashni's alive and well, we're in charge for now." Asad folded his arms, fabric stretching across his muscles.

Nakia scowled. They had to argue Nakia was acting as regent. Technically, Ashni could appoint anyone she desired in that position. "Ashni appointed me as regent."

"Which is void if Ashni's dead. Until the Empress decides who would take over, we're in charge by virtue of being here," Jay replied.

Layla scowled. "And your territories just happen to have regents in place with you gone."

"Of course," Asad replied. "The only issue here is that Ashni died."

"And you seem so broken up about it." Nakia curled her top lip. They probably suspected Ashni was dead as soon as they got here and not once did, they show any signs of mourning. In fact, they had Nakia throw a feast as though they celebrated the death of their sister. *Disgusting.*

Asad stared her down. "Just as broken up as you seem about it."

"Ashni's not dead," Nakia said.

"Then prove it."

Nakia scoffed. "Prove to me my beloved is dead."

"We sent people to that hellhole of the north and no one saw her."

Nakia shook her head. "I'm expected to believe your spies over my own people?"

Adira frowned. "You can't prove your claim any more than we can prove ours."

They were at a stalemate. It would boil down to who people would follow. Glancing around, Nakia wasn't sure the brothers even had the support of the nobles in the throne room. Everyone seemed tense, but it could be the situation in general rather than the coup. This was about to be a big mess, but Nakia wouldn't back down. This was her kingdom. She was Ashni. *But are you?*

***

The scene around Ashni dissolved into another memory. Tiny-Ashni chased after her older brothers. They were on their way to the circus, getting a chance to watch the matches.

"Wait for me!" Tiny-Ashni managed to catch up to them. She panted but kept her stride. Her brothers didn't bother looking back.

"You're too young. You can't come," Amal said, his voice a hiss.

Jay tossed a glance over his shoulder. "It's just for the sons of the Great Amir anyway."

Tiny-Ashni scoffed. "Fahim isn't with you."

"Fahim's too young. Go away," Jay said.

The words wouldn't have hurt as much coming from Asad or Amal. Coming from Jay, it was like being punched in the chest. Until that moment, Jay had avoided her, but hadn't spoken his dislike.

"Jay." Ashni had to hold in a whimper. "Why can't I come? Asad and Amal aren't old enough either." They were short a year.

"They are sons of the Great Amir," Jay replied, and he sneered, as if disgusted. She didn't understand.

"You know, my lightning's a gift from the gods," Ashni said. "Everyone says so."

Jay sucked his teeth. "Yeah, and everyone also says you're not a son of the Great Amir. So, go away!"

"You're beneath us." Asad turned and shoved her.

Ashni walked right into the push, giving it more force than Asad intended. It hurt her chest and she fell off balance, dropping to the marble floor. It was cold and hard against her butt and palms. She picked herself up as her brothers backed her into a wall.

"You can't come," Jay said as if his word was law, and it practically was. He was the oldest and would probably inherit the throne. He didn't care about her gift from the gods.

The harsh tone in his voice froze tiny-Ashni long enough for them to get away. There was a burn in her eyes as she watched them disappear down the hall. Growling, she punched the wall behind her. Pain throbbed in her hand. If only the wall were her brothers. With a stomp of her foot, tiny-Ashni turned on her heel and marched off, not sure where she was going. She wandered by a room where her mother happened to be, sitting with the sleeping baby twins.

"Mommy?" Tiny-Ashni stepped inside.

Her mother put a finger to her lip. "Quietly, my little gift from the gods."

Tiny-Ashni grinned. Her mother thought she was a gift from the gods and since her mother was half-god, it had to be true. She puttered into the room as quietly as her shoes allowed. She was about to crawl into her mother's lap but stopped. A little kid would cuddle into her mother. She wasn't a little kid, even if her brothers thought she was.

"You like sitting with Kek and Kiran, even though they don't do anything?" tiny-Ashni asked as she flopped down on a pillow. The babies were asleep on a mat next to their mother.

"Their presence gives me joy," her mother replied.

Tiny-Ashni scratched her head. "But they're not doing anything."

"I don't need any of you to do anything. I just need you to exist and it makes me happy." Her mother ran her hand through her hair.

Ashni opened her mouth and then closed it. She wanted to ask something but was scared of the answer. Would her father love her, even if she wasn't his?

"You love Kek and Kiran, right?" Ashni asked.

Her mother smiled. "Of course I do."

Tiny-Ashni could feel her face scrunch up as she tried to think how she wanted to go about her questions. "If they had a different talent, like not Fire, would you still love them?"

Her mother laughed even more. "Of course. Your talent doesn't mean anything. Although, I'm still waiting for one of my darling children to come for spell crafting lessons."

Tiny-Ashni held in a scoff. Spells were boring. Picking flowers, measuring and stirring, and tasting nasty things. Who would want to learn that? "You still like us even though we don't want to know spells, right?"

"Of course I do. You're entitled to like what you like."

"And to not like stuff, too?" Then her brothers had a right to not like her. It didn't seem fair. Jay used to like her. They used to do stuff together. He shouldn't be allowed to just turn that off.

"Of course."

"And you'd still love me even if I didn't like the same things, right? You can't just stop loving me, right?"

Her mother leaned down, embracing her. "My precious flower, I could never stop loving you. When you truly love someone, it's always with all of your heart. I love you and your brothers like that."

"Dad loves us like that, too, right?"

"Your father loves you with everything inside of him and he always will. You love us like that, right?"

Ashni nodded. "I do."

"When you love people, you accept they're different from you." Her mother blew out a breath. "I could spend the rest of my life telling you how different I am to your father and how much we love each other."

Ashni twisted her mouth up. "Are you mean to each other?"

"You know sometimes we are, but we don't love each other any less." An attitude she probably hoped her children carried.

Tiny-Ashni took those words to heart for a long time. "Right. You love people in your family, even if they're not your family." Her mother and father weren't born related to each other. They learned to love each other.

Her mother blinked. "One of the things I actually love about Roshan culture is that family is always so much more than something you're born into. You'll meet people you bond with so deeply and you know they can only be your family."

"And what about this family?" Tiny-Ashni made a circle with her finger.

"And we'll accept your new family as our family. That's one thing I love about my culture. You always have your family."

Oh, Mommy. That's why you're this way. I forgot. Maybe her mother was right. You always have your family, but your family isn't always the same. If Jay could cut her off so easily, he never was her family.

Tiny-Ashni squirmed. "What makes you family, Mommy?"

"Love, of course." Her mother shrugged. "You know your family by the way you love them and the way they love you."

It made sense, though her heart sank at the thought of Jay. And it was worse with Asad and Amal. Those were her brothers, but she felt nothing for them. Asad pretended she didn't exist, and Amal constantly lashed out at her. They didn't love her. They treated her as if she was nothing, less than nothing.

Had Jay loved her and then it faded somehow? Because of her lightning...it seemed odd. She couldn't figure out how to ask her mother beyond a general question.

"Can you stop loving someone?" tiny-Ashni asked.

Her mother frowned. "You can, but it takes a lot of work. That person has to mess up very bad."

"I haven't messed up." Tiny-Ashni didn't mean to say that aloud, but she couldn't have messed up. It wasn't her choice to have lightning. The gods made that decision, and the gods didn't make mistakes.

Her mother kissed the top of her head. "No, you haven't."

Tiny-Ashni grinned, but then slapped at the air to get her mother to back up. She was too old for kissy faces. Though this was good. She didn't mess up. Jay was just confused. He didn't understand the gods made a choice, not her. When he figured that out, everything would be fine.

***

"The nerve!" Nakia fumed. She was surprised smoke didn't come off of her as she paced the room hiding Ashni from the world.

"You need to gather noble allies immediately. The more support you have, the harder it'll be for them to make a claim. Then we'll wait on word from the Empress. She'll side with you," Adira said, making a fist.

Her confidence was hardly misplaced. It was no secret the Empress loved Nakia as her own, but if Nakia lost control before the official word came in, nothing would matter. Her people wouldn't follow her regardless of any decree.

"This would be easier if Ashni woke up," Layla said with a glance over at Ashni. She was pale, dark marked, and barely breathing.

Samar shook her head, her voice grim. "The poison damaged much of her body. Sleeping helps the healing process, but I haven't been able to put together any medicine that'll help the process go faster. Don't rely on Ashni simply waking up."

"She's healing, yes?" Nakia's heart jumped into her throat. She couldn't lose Ashni and Ashni's kingdom at the same time.

A frown marred Samar's features. "The information provided by our now allied tribes helped, but it was only the ingredients of the poison. They're certain it's fatal and listed potential potions that haven't done a damn thing. Not to say my own work has done any better."

"So, we're just considering it a victory she's not dead?" Adira sighed and rubbed her forehead.

Samar blew out a breath. "Yes. Ashni has to keep fighting. Right now, it looks like her body is fighting the medicines, but that might not be a bad thing. This isn't the first time she's been close to death."

Nakia's chest hurt. "How is her body fighting the medicine not a bad thing?"

Samar waved the question off. "It means she's fighting to keep herself alive. Ashni's body is strange because she's part god. So, things designed to kill someone don't work on her, but sometimes things designed to help keep people alive don't work on her. Sometimes she doesn't need the help. Her body's trying to repair itself."

"Let's hope that remains true," Nakia said.

With a scoff, Adira waved her words away. "She's lived through much worse. We have to secure the throne for you. You obviously have the Shadow Walkers and their clans, which is good because no one wants to fight them."

"And we will fight them if necessary," Layla said. Her mother made a noise of agreement. Badar, tucked in the corner near Samar, nodded.

Nakia nodded. "I'll go see the nobles of the city and remind them of the good things Ashni and I have done."

"Saniyah will remind the wealthy nobles around us," Adira said.

"Merchants should be easy to secure. We offer more trade routes than anyone else," Nakia said.

Adira scratched her chin. "There might be more than enough existing trade to keep the merchants happy and expanded routes tend to be less secure in the beginning. They might not want to chance it."

"True," Nakia said, thinking fast. "I should be able to count on the military."

"Of course, but most of the military is up north building forts. You don't want to take them off of that detail or the barbarians will see it as a sign of weakness," Adira said.

Nakia shook her head. "I had no plans to call all of them back. If necessary, I'd recall a third and fill some numbers with new recruits." There was never a shortage of people willing to join the military for adventure and status.

"Good." Adira nodded.

"Should we get Wicus and Thia?" Layla asked.

Nakia bit her lip. "Not yet. Wicus and Thia might look at this as a chance to regain their autonomy. They could back Jay and Asad, especially if Jay is serious about this being too much land for the Empire. I love Thia and I believe she loves me, but she has people to worry about as well. She'd do what she feels is best for her people. I can't fault her on that."

Adira nodded. "We'll secure your position and then contact her if necessary, but we have to make sure surrounding cities stay with us. We need to watch for any sterlings that might betray us and worst of all, we have to find the fucking scum feeding information to those two bastards."

Layla pointed to the door. "We should move on it then."

"Can't move without a plan of attack," Adira replied.

They came up with a list of groups Nakia needed the support of to remain in control and moved out to make it happen. Nakia met with people in the halls on her way out of the palace. People flocked to her, wanting to pledge their allegiance. As she looked at the throng of people, Nakia smiled. So many people wanted to talk to her that she never even made it out of the palace. Maybe things would be all right. Though she hoped Adira and Layla made it further than she did.

"Nakia, what's happening?" Saffi rushed to her and looped her arm around Nakia's. She steered Nakia away from the crowd, who respectfully didn't follow.

"What do you mean?" Nakia asked.

"Are the kings in charge now?" Saffi sounded a little frantic and her eyes darted around the corridor as they walked.

Nakia frowned. "No, I'm in charge. This is my kingdom." Well, her spouse's kingdom, but she'd keep it while Ashni fought for her life.

Saffi tilted her head. "They said it was Ashni's?"

"I'm Ashni's spouse. Hell, I am Ashni. We share a soul. They can't take that from me any more than they can take my kingdom." She didn't expect Saffi to understand, but she wanted to reassure her sister as best she could.

Saffi's pale forehead wrinkled. "The rules say otherwise, right?"

"No. They're bending the rules to suit them." And they won't get away with it. *Won't they? You're not equipped to fight them.* She growled at the voice in her head, trying and failing to ignore it.

"How so?"

"Why?" Nakia didn't see the reason for Saffi to need that information.

Saffi shrugged. "I want to know what's going on."

"Why?" Her sister hadn't been this curious before.

"Perhaps I can help."

"Unfortunately, you can't." There was a gnawing in Nakia's gut. She suspected Saffi and hated that. Nakia had gained such an appreciation for family over the past few years. She wanted to be able to go to family with anything, but she couldn't trust Saffi right now, not with how intrigued her sister seemed Jay and Asad.

Even if Nakia trusted Saffi, she wouldn't share everything with her right now. Saffi had been through so many traumas. She wanted to make Saffi's life easier, comfortable.

"This is my kingdom. Not only was I left in charge by Ashni when she left, I'm Consort," Nakia said.

Saffi pursed her lips. "Does being Consort count since she's a woman?"

"Of course it counts!" Nakia held in a growl. "Excuse me, but I have things to do."

Nakia didn't wait around for Saffi to respond, rushing off to seek more support. She had forgotten how many people could be in the palace on any given day. Most people seemed firmly on her side and respected her claim. Eventually, she was able to relax a little.

And it was in that moment Asad eased by her side.

"We should dine together and discuss the transition of power from you to me," he said with a smile, daring to wrap his arm around her waist.

Nakia didn't know she could move so fast until she was a safe distance from Asad. "You seem to think you hold power over me. I'm in charge here." She placed her palm against her chest.

He chuckled, and it sounded so dark she wouldn't have been surprised if tar-colored smoke came out of his mouth. "If you have to say you're in charge, then you're not in charge."

She gave him a sickly smile. "Then, by your logic, you and your brother aren't in charge. You had to announce it in the throne room, after all."

Asad glared at her with more malevolence than she could've imagined, like a demon, trying to destroy her soul with his eyes. "You're nothing if I say you are. You only exist by my goodwill, which will no longer extend to you if you don't learn how to behave."

Nakia sneered. "Good luck making me not exist then. It might prove harder than you think."

No one seemed to be in the brothers' corner yet. Besides, she had stood in front of more powerful people and didn't blink. He wouldn't be the one to change that.

***

The scene melted to another one, Ashni just a helpless passenger as all her memories swam before her, all her lessons learned in youth. Tiny-Ashni was on the outside looking in, quite literally. She stood in the doorway, watching her father spend time with her baby brother, Fahim. Fahim liked to read stories and tiny-Ashni understood even at this young age how smart her little brother was. He was barely four and read better than any of his older siblings, Ashni included. She liked that about him.

"Can I listen, too?" Tiny-Ashni stepped inside the room.

Her father looked up and smiled. "You're listening anyway. A front row seat is the best."

Tiny-Ashni nodded and zipped over to the pair, flopping down on a pillow. Fahim grinned in a way that reminded her of their father and continued reading. His voice was squeaky, but he read at a good pace and it was fun to watch his eyes light up when he got a hard word correct.

Her older brothers didn't know how to exist in a space like this. Maybe they couldn't exist in a space like this—quiet, small, almost out of the way.

"I'm going to get another book." Fahim got up and went to his stack of books.

"Fahim tells good stories," tiny-Ashni said.

Her father nodded. "He does. I miss them when I'm out on campaign."

"You should take the books with you."

He laughed. "But they're Fahim's favorites. What would he do?"

She glanced at her brother. "He'd get new favorites. He reads a lot. Or you could take him with you."

Fahim slammed his book down. "I don't wanna be away from all of the books. We might leave one I want to read."

Their father laughed and scooped Fahim up, hugging the toddler to his chest. "Well, one day you're going to have to be away from your precious books and ride with me because I love it and I love you!"

"No!" Fahim laughed and squirmed as their father tickled him.

"I'll ride with you." Tiny-Ashni hopped to her feet.

"Well, you have to save your brother first." He swung Fahim around like he weighed nothing at all.

Tiny-Ashni wasted no time attacking her father. If she jumped, she could reach his neck. He moved out of the way. She spun into a kick as soon as she landed, hitting him in the knee. He hissed and jumped away.

"Fahim, your sister must love you very much. She's trying to hurt me!" Their father moved Fahim in front of him, like a shield.

"Put him down!" Tiny-Ashni pointed at her father and lightning shot from her finger. She yelped, as did her father.

Her father ducked in time to miss a face full of lightning. Chuckling, he glanced behind him as he put Fahim down.

Tiny-Ashni twitched as shame slammed through her. "I'm so sorry, Daddy!"

Her father flashed a carefree grin. "It's okay. I love when you do the lightning!" He yanked her off of her feet. "It's so amazing. I don't think I've ever seen anything like it in all my travels."

Fahim tugged on their father's sleeve. "Can I get lightning?"

Her father gasped. "You don't want my talent? What's wrong with my talent?"

Fahim scoffed and waved it away. "Everybody has it, but only Ashni has lightning. Mommy said Ashni was chosen and I wanna be chosen with her, so we could be together and get strong."

Her father beamed. "She could use the practice. I mean, that poor wall." They all looked at the charred hole in the wall.

Tiny-Ashni stared at Fahim. "You like my lightning?"

He nodded. "It's different. I want it so we can match."

"Well, you can't have it. It's mine," tiny-Ashni said, but she beamed on the inside. Her younger brother flattered her.

Fahim pouted. "Oh." His distress ate at her with a speed she never thought possible. She didn't mean to hurt his feelings.

"Hey!" She held up both hands. "I was only playing. We can both have lightning! Just like we can both join the same guild when we get older."

Fahim's face brightened. It felt good to make him feel good. She didn't want to hurt Fahim any more than she wanted her older brothers to hurt her. It wasn't fun when it happened, so she didn't want to spread that.

"So, what guild are you two joining then?" her father asked, finally putting tiny-Ashni down.

Tiny-Ashni poked her chest out. "The Lion Guild!"

Fahim made a tight fist as he held his hand up. "Of course!"

"My warrior guild. A fine choice." Her father mussed her hair, literally ruffling her feathers that were braided into her light ocher hair. "However, you're not old enough to be in a guild, not yet."

Tiny-Ashni was aware of the rules. "We could get me a lion cub now. I'll take the best care of him until I turn thirteen."

"I'll talk to your mom. We only just got Jay his bear brother. Both of them are growing like weeds."

Tiny-Ashni nodded, even though she didn't care about the rules. She wanted things to happen now, especially since her father liked her lightning. And she had Fahim to back her up. Her father had enough faith in her to want her to join his warrior guild. She wouldn't let him down.

The scene melted and Ashni sighed into the darkness. She had been so thrilled about joining the Lion Guild in her youth. *The poor kid didn't know the tragedy waiting for her, but at least Fahim let her know she was a good sibling.*

***

Nakia sat down for dinner with Layla and Adira. Badar stayed behind with Samar to make sure she didn't work herself to exhaustion. Layla and Adira would keep her safe. They compared notes. It seemed most of the nobles backed Nakia's claim to the throne. Many religious leaders would rather wait for word from Ashni or Chandra, but almost no one backed the brothers.

"Nobody likes them," Layla said.

"Nobody likes who?" Asad stalked over and sat down next to Nakia.

Layla stared at him. "You."

Asad smiled. "Being liked is overrated. Not everyone likes my mother, and she's still Empress." He inched closer to Nakia, invading her space. "Hell, there are times I don't like my mother, but she's still Empress. That's just the way things are."

"Are you admitting treason?" Adira asked.

"Of course not." Asad chuckled, snatching some berries off the shared plate. "I'll follow the Empress' decisions, although that doesn't mean I always like them. Don't you feel that way about what she's done to Amal?" He moved to put his arm around Nakia, and she caught his wrist.

"Don't touch me," Nakia said.

A low wheeze filled the room, and both Layla's and Adira's blades were at his throat before anyone could blink. He continued to smirk. His eyes darkly evil.

His gaze flicked to Layla. "Are you sure you want to point your sword at me, Shadow Beast? Need I remind you whose territory Tariq and Tiq sit in? One word from me and those places will not only be burned to the ground, but everyone will be raped, the children slaughtered, and the rest will be sold into slavery." The way his voice remained low and steady drove home that promise. He tapped his chin. "Or maybe I already left that standing order. You know, should something happen to me while I'm here."

Layla didn't waver but cut Nakia a glance. Nakia was flattered by Layla's loyalty. Still, she couldn't trade so many lives and anguish for her. She gave a small nod and Layla's jaw tensed as she put her weapon down.

Asad chuckled. "Good dog." He turned to Adira. "I don't think anyone noticed, but Jay went to go see Bashira dance. He hoped to get a private show."

Adira snarled. "You are a fucking monster!" She sheathed her blade.

Asad laughed, and the sound cut through Nakia like a serrated blade. He was worse than Amal, and Adira said Jay was worse than him. At least Amal brought the fight to Ashni, one on one. Amal never made it personal in that sense whereas now innocent people Ashni cared about were in danger.

"Have a seat, ladies. Let's celebrate this peaceful exchange of power." He put his arm around Nakia's shoulders and yanked her to him. She cringed as his strange cinder scent surrounded her. His demonic laugh filled the room and drained all feeling from Nakia. The brothers had entire towns as their hostage and Jay also had Bashira. *What's my next move?*

Chapter Nine

FOR ALL OF HER life, Ashni wanted to be a member of the Lion Guild, like her father. They were the top warriors as far as she was concerned, a perfect mixture of intelligence and strength. They always had each other's backs. Her father practically bounced when she received her cub, Tau.

"Look at the size of his paws!" He held up the paw of the five-month-old cub. The sleek yet tiny golden cub yowled.

"I'm going to make him fierce!" Ashni held his leash tight, and her father put Tau on the ground. They had a journey back home, walking from the arena. Crowds parted for them, mostly due to recognizing the Great Amir.

He laughed. "I'm sure you will. It's about time one of my kids joined my guild. I mean, Jay and the damn bears. The betrayal!" He put his hand to his heart. "And the twins with the wolves. The wolves! They're a bunch of sneaks!"

Ashni threw her shoulders back, giddy. She'd grow Tau up strong and fierce to make her father even prouder. Tau was already big for his age, which was one of the reasons she picked him. He would be huge when he matured.

"Treat Tau like your brother, Ashni. He's going to protect you for the rest of your life, like Hamza did for me." Her father's fingers went to the lion teeth around his neck. He had a number of lion tattoos along with eagle tattoos, honoring his guild and his godfather. She wanted the same.

"I'll give him the best life," she said.

Her father gave her a sort of sad smile, his eyes wet. She didn't understand his tears at the time.

Tau was her brother in every sense of the word, cuddling her whenever Amal bothered her, whenever Jay and Asad ignored her, and listening to Fahim read. He stole bits of her dinner and trained with her for hours. She wasn't sure they spent any time apart in three years and in less than a minute they'd be separated until they met again in the circus.

When she turned thirteen, the day was upon her to finally join the Lion Guild, and she wanted to run. *No, I don't want to see this again.* Ashni sat in the dusty, shadowy corridor in the circus. She could hear people cheering the match outside, but it was like a dull hum.

Her focus was on Tau, her lion brother. He was three now, mature for a lion. He was as big as she'd hoped he'd be, solid muscle, big teeth, and an even bigger heart.

Ashni hugged Tau, his short, dark mane tickled her cheek. People liked to tease her and say they had the same hair, same coloring, though she liked to hear it. "I'll never forget you, brother. You've been with me through tough times."

He blew his hot breath in her face, and she laughed. He nuzzled her, and she cried in his mane. She wanted this so badly, but she didn't want it this way. *You don't think about it when you first pick your brother. You don't think about it when you're bonding over the years. You're too young to figure it out and then it hits you when you're sitting in the damn dirt at the fucking circus, and you can only go through with it.*

"I'm so sorry." And she apologized up until men came for Tau and took him away. She was given a spear, helmet, and chest plate, and she walked onto the circus floor.

It happened like a blur. She recalled the smell of incense, as this was a holy rite of passage. The audience sounded like a buzz to her ears. She didn't understand why. Tau lay dead at her feet, her spear in his chest. How dare they applaud that? She had killed her brother. Was the Guild worth it? She wanted to say yes, but it wasn't until it connected her to her new family, to warriors who would always be there for her, with her.

Ashni wasn't sure how long she stood there, covered in the blood and the scratches of her lion, and then an arm around her shoulder pulled her away. Her father pulled her close.

"I know," he said.

Her father knew because he had to kill his lion in the circus. Every warrior in every guild had to. She wasn't alone. They all knew how she felt, but it still didn't fill that void. Wearing Tau's teeth around her neck, so that he was still always with her, protecting her, didn't fill the void either. It was the second time in her short life she learned not to ask for something, because you just might get it. First her talent, now her brother. Life wasn't fair.

***

Nakia sat with Ashni, holding her clammy hand. It still felt like her skin covered damp cloth rather than muscle and bone. She had hoped it was a step up from it feeling like thick cereal was under her flesh. Each breath rattled in Ashni's chest. Nakia said silent prayers for her beloved over and over. She wished she could leave offerings at a temple, but Jay or Asad might have questions or take it as proof that Ashni was dead.

Asad had followed her around after dinner and she allowed it, to give them a false sense of power. To get down to see Ashni without him knowing, she had Badar transport her in a shadow.

"I don't understand your brothers, Ashni. I don't understand how they're your mother's children," Nakia said, her thoughts spinning with the brothers' betrayal.

"They were actually raised differently. The brothers had more parents than she did," Samar said from the corner of the room, reading. She and Layla were there while Adira had gone to check on Bashira and Saniyah, taking Badar as backup. *They'd better be alright.*

"More parents? Did the nobles really have that much influence? Why didn't Khalid or Chandra stop them?" Nakia shook her head. Why hadn't they done *something*?

Samar sighed. "Well, I don't have any insight in that, but I've met some of the nobles who shaped them. Helli's filled with snakes. Their venom reaches far and wide."

Nakia sighed, but that made sense. She knew that from growing up in the palace of Phyllida. The nobles tried to influence

129

her life, knowing at the very least that whomever she married could end up with a great deal of power.

What sort of nobles got to the brothers and let them think taking towns hostage was all right? What had those nobles done so the brothers didn't mourn the death of their sister? What had those nobles said so that Amal had been fine with trying to murder Ashni on so many occasions?

"Royalty almost always breeds intrigue, even in the best of families," Layla said.

Nakia nodded, though she wished she didn't have to think about it. How would this affect her own family? She only just got her sisters back, and her nieces and nephews from Thia. One day, would there be intrigue between them? How would Thia react to this attempted coup, and what was going on with Saffi?

"We're going to come out on top off this," Layla said with a confident nod.

"How can you be so sure?" Nakia asked. *How can Layla have such faith?*

Layla motioned to Ashni. "Because she's not dead and my mother will find a way to get the poison out of her system."

So many lives are in your hands now. Nakia's throat went dry. It was hard to breathe. She was one step away from losing not just Ashni and Ashni's kingdom, but Layla's people, Adira's family, and possibly her own sisters. *This will break you.* And this time, the thought stuck.

*** *** ***

Ashni scowled as she stared at a closed stable door, warning signs all over it. Warning signs she had ignored when she was thirteen. *Why the hell is my life flashing before my eyes?* It was annoying.

Even in her glory, Ashni wasn't interested in herself. She jeered at plays when there were characters based on her. After murdering Tau, she went straight to Midnight Thunder. He had been in the royal stables, a prize for anyone who would dare try to tame him. He kicked down doors, jumped fences, and even killed one unfortunate soul with a swift smack to the jaw. There was talk he was a demon in horse form.

Ashni had been hurt enough, curious enough, and maybe even depressed enough to check out this demon horse. She'd need a horse soon. She was a member of a guild now, a warrior. She could join the military. Her father would definitely take her on campaign within the next year or so.

The first time she met Midnight Thunder, he bit her. Lightning in his face kept him from coming back for another piece. He didn't try to bite her again, though he still fought her for months. Her life became training and fighting Midnight Thunder. It helped her work through the pain of losing Tau.

"I don't care how difficult you are. I'm not giving up on you," Ashni said as Midnight Thunder refused to let her on his back.

"Give it up, princess. He'll make good barbecue!" one of the stable hands told her.

"No! He's a great horse." Other people couldn't see it, but she knew he just needed someone to be there, to understand him. She leaned closer to the horse. "Do you hear that? You keep being an asshole and they're going to eat you."

Midnight Thunder didn't care. He was a jerk of a horse. He beat her up so often that her brothers would come watch.

"You think you're going to war? You can't even break a horse!" Amal said from a safe distance. Asad and Jay snickered.

Ashni ignored them, hating to think they had a point. Warfare was more than the ability to kill someone. Warfare was about decision-making and look at her stupid decisions. She was fighting a horse that hated her. She wanted to be in a warrior guild so much she had looked her best friend in the eye as she ran him through with a spear.

It didn't matter if others had done it. It didn't matter that those were the requirements. Tau deserved better. She wasn't worthy of any of that. She wasn't worthy. So, she gave up.

Not too long after that the stable worker who told her to give up let her know Midnight Thunder was going to be put down, so

Ashni had a chance to bid him farewell. At first, she wasn't going to, but she thought of Tau. Midnight Thunder deserved a goodbye, deserved to know at least one person thought he mattered. When she got to the stables, Midnight Thunder actually whinnied as if he was pleased to see her. He nuzzled her, like he missed her.

"I guess I don't have to ask if you've been being good," Ashni said, stroking his muzzle. "If you were being good, you wouldn't be in this mess. You could've made a great war horse, you know? We could've gone into battle together and you could've kicked, bit, and head butted all the enemies you wanted, but you want to be a jerk."

He snorted and she laughed. It was like he knew he was a jerk.

She kissed the side of his head. "Bye. Maybe the gods will see fit to reincarnate you as something who can just run free."

She turned to leave, but he followed her and nudged her with his head. Workers rushed to wrangle Midnight Thunder. She didn't look back as the horse cried out, fighting. A yank on her robes stopped her.

"Hey!" She spun and Midnight Thunder pushed her with his head again. "Look, it's over. I tried. You and I want different things. I can't save you." He had the nerve to blow his hot breath in her face.

"If you can't save him, who can?" her father asked, appearing through smoke.

Ashni practically jumped out of her skin. "Dad!"

"I was coming to make sure you were okay. I didn't think the demon horse would still be here." Her father motioned to Midnight Thunder.

"I wanted to say goodbye to him." She caressed the side of the horse's head.

Her father frowned. "Doesn't seem like he's ready to say goodbye."

"It's too late."

"How so? He's here. You're here. You like him. He seems to like you."

Ashni was about to object. Then Midnight Thunder rested his head on her narrow shoulders. Okay, so maybe he liked her.

"Then why are you such a jerk?" she asked, like the horse could answer. He snorted in reply.

"Sometimes, it might seem like someone doesn't like you or you might be an acquired taste, though it seems like you've grown on him. It happens. I grew on your mother, like a fungus she likes to say."

Ashni snickered. "She calls you mold sometimes."

"Yeah, I'm her mold." He threw his shoulders back, proud. "Maybe you're the demon horse's mold. More than that, never say it's too late to save somebody. It's never too late. It's a matter of wanting to or not."

Ashni swallowed. He was right. She wanted to save Midnight Thunder, except she wanted him to want her as well. "Okay, you jerk horse. I'll save you. But after I save you, you're either going to start treating me like a friend or I'm not coming back here, okay?" she asked, and the damn horse actually nodded.

Her father laughed. "That's right. Try to do the right thing for someone, and also for yourself. You're coming along nicely, kid." She beamed back.

Midnight Thunder treated Ashni like he knew she saved his life. He trained with her, and it was then she became known as the Chosen One. The gods had to have picked Ashni for something, not because she wielded lightning, but because she tamed the demon horse no one else could.

***

Being outmaneuvered using promises of mass murder was horrible and having to endure Asad touching her the next morning at breakfast was almost enough to make Nakia call his bluff. Except with the way Layla practically laid down for him, Nakia was all too aware Asad's words were no bluff. They had fought the wrong war and lost. It was time to regroup.

The moment Nakia could get away from Asad, she called Layla and Adira down to Ashni's resting room. Adira brought Saniyah with her, but Bashira hadn't been home yesterday. *We have to get her back from Jay.*

"What's your plan?" Layla asked, sitting in the corner with a scowl. "I've thought of five hundred ways to kill him, and none of them save Tariq."

Adira shook her head. "He most certainly has standing orders to put Tariq and surrounding areas to slaughter should something happen to him."

Layla punched the floor. "And I'm just going to let a void eat Jay if he hurts Bashira. She doesn't have shit to do with this!"

"I will destroy Jay just for disrespecting Bashira." Adira's voice was dangerous, promising. "She's a fucking Roshan noble."

Saniyah held up her hand. "Please, let's think of something rational and that has a chance of working. We owe that to Bashira."

Nakia sighed. "We could contact Thia. It was one thing when this was just about kingdoms, but I don't think she'd leave me to be harmed."

"Put out feelers. Don't play the hand too quickly, though," Adira said.

Nakia nodded. She didn't want to risk Thia jumping in before they had all the facts. Wicus would never forgive Nakia if she set up a losing battle for him.

"What can we do about Bashira? I won't stand for her being used against us." Saniyah visibly shook. Adira wrapped her arms around Saniyah, who tore away from her for one second and then buried herself in Adira in the next. Adira held her close.

Nakia's eyes drifted to Ashni and her stomach twisted. *Will I get to embrace her again?* Samar's voice brought her back to the topic at hand.

"Jay can easily die in his sleep," Samar said casually, as if just passing on a fact. It wasn't surprising. There were many tales of Samar putting enemies to sleep.

"No, we don't know how the Empress might react if we assassinate her child. I mean, yes, she likes all of us well enough, but we know how she feels about her children," Adira said.

Layla's lip curled. "And she'd know it was us. I doubt there'd be any hesitation."

"No, there wouldn't." Badar frowned at Samar. Samar ignored him.

"Well, I can't just leave her hostage to a brute," Saniyah said, tears building in the corner of her eyes before she could wipe them away.

"None of us can." Layla motioned around the room. Even Varaza nodded. She'd been on her job of guarding Ashni, sometimes even forgetting to eat.

Bashira was too well loved for them to let this go by. Nakia didn't want to imagine what horrors Jay might be capable of. Her skin crawled.

"We'll get her back." Nakia took Ashni's hand. It was firmer than usual and warm to the touch, which made her start. *Is this a good thing?* "Should Ashni's hand be this warm?"

Samar waved her off. "Her body temperature has been rising and falling for a few hours now. I'm not sure why. That's not in any of the notes the barbarians gave and nothing I'm reading about explains it."

Of course it means nothing. Nakia's shoulders dropped. "We planned wrong. Adira, what can you tell me about Jay and Asad? Maybe we can come up with something."

Adira shook her head. "I don't know them as well as I know Amal. Amal was always being a pest, but Asad mostly keeps to himself. If he was with anyone, it's Jay, and they stay in their kingdoms. I can't think of a time when they plotted against Ashni."

"Once the Amir died and land was split, they went their own ways," Saniyah said.

Adira scratched her cheek as she thought. "Asad spent more time with Jay than his own twin when I first met them."

"You said Jay was the real demon between them. Why?" Nakia asked.

Adira, a hardened general who lost her eye in a war, actually trembled. "Jay's the type of person who could kill you but would rather kill your child in front of you and then follow you around the rest of your life taunting you about it. Jay's more poisoned than Ashni is right now. He's just walking around spreading it to others."

Badar nodded. "It was undoubtedly Jay's idea to threaten our hometown, even though it's in Asad's territory."

"Why would Asad be with him?" Nakia asked.

"I think Asad realizes being close to Jay is more advantageous to him as far as advancing and possibly gaining the throne. By Roshan standards, when Amal was out and about, it was strange for Asad to prefer Jay to his twin, even if Jay is the older brother. It's also a little odd for Jay to drag a brother away from his twin."

Nakia frowned. "What would you say about Asad?"

"He probably would have no problem killing Ashni, like Amal, though he seemed to be the type who would burn the palace down and everyone in it to get to Ashni. And apparently, he got that from Jay."

"Asad's unusual, but Jay's a different creature altogether. The Amir could be vicious in battle, except it turned off when not in battle. Ashni has the same. From what I can tell, her brothers could be the same, though since they view us as enemies, it's not turning off."

Layla scoffed. "The Amir and Ashni wouldn't ever go as far as these two. Asad would kill everyone in Tariq and salt the ruins."

"And he'd view it as an act of war. For them, this is war," Adira replied.

"Is there a line they won't cross?" Nakia wanted to know how much danger they were all in.

"I remember when the Amir died. There was talk of putting Jay on the throne, but he wouldn't go against his mother, and there was talk of Asad as well. No one was worried about him bowing to the Empress," Adira said.

That answer made Nakia's stomach tighten. "So, he's more like Amal in that instance." Nakia glanced at Ashni—poisoned, grey—and couldn't help thinking of years ago. "What if he's more like Amal now?"

"You think he had something to do with Ashni?" Layla asked.

"The timing is suspicious, and the barbarians who claimed they would help haven't been much help," Nakia replied.

Samar chewed on her lip. "I don't think he has that much pull. Everything Adira got from the barbarians added up with Ashni's symptoms. It's just they expected the poison to kill her, like it would've done if she wasn't a demi-god. Focus on the battle in front of you, not the poison."

Good advice. Nakia wanted to approach Asad and Jay as vicious animals now. The only problem was these vicious animals happened to be the Empress' offspring, so they couldn't be down like mad dogs.

"Can we create a reason for them to go back home?" Nakia asked.

"Most of the things I can think of or know people can do might be brushed aside if they trust their own regents," Adira said.

"Come up with a list. I'm thinking one of you should stand guard here," Nakia said.

"With all due respect, I'm standing right here," Samar said, arching an eyebrow.

"You're here as a doctor. You worry about keeping Ashni healthy. Someone else should worry about defending her with Varaza. I wish it could be me," Nakia replied.

Adira shook her head. "You have to keep an eye on Jay and Asad while maintaining control, even if they're in command."

Nakia nodded. They broke after Layla demanded first watch over Ashni. Nakia went to her room. Badar left her alone, not wanting to invade her privacy. Nakia liked to think she was safe in her room but found out otherwise as she found Asad waiting just inside of her door. *Keep him at an arm's length.*

"What can I do for you?" Nakia asked with a forced smile that hurt her face.

Asad smirked. "Well, I was hoping we'd be able to discuss your transferring power to me and my brother."

"That's a matter to discuss in the light of day in the Grand Hall." Not that it was ever going to happen. She intended to keep stalling him.

His eyes danced with mischief. "I was hoping to discuss it now, although if you'd rather wait until morning, I could fill my time with seeing your sister. She seemed to like me."

"You stay the hell away from my sister," Nakia said. She might not trust Saffi, but she'd die for her. Saffi deserved peace, and Nakia would do anything to give her that.

Asad chuckled. "Maybe I'll go tell her that."

"Leave my sister alone." Nakia glared at him, trying to set him on fire. She didn't care what type of monster he was. She'd slay him before she allowed him to touch a hair on Saffi's head.

"Then perhaps you should invite me into your chambers." He put his hand on her elbow.

"You're already in here and it's improper." She yanked her elbow away. Servants scurried around in the background, heads down.

He shrugged. "I'll have my servants bring your sister to me, then. They deserve some fun after so much travel time."

Nakia's chest tightened, and her jaw tensed. She took a deep breath. "Please, come in."

He looked outright crocodilian. She had lost again. Now, he knew how much she valued her sister.

They entered her main room, and the servants paused to stare. She waved them off, sitting on her favorite pillow and gesturing to her most uncomfortable seat for Asad. The pillow was flat, but he didn't seem bothered by it. He had a servant bring them red wine, and then spent the next half hour sipping wine and staring at her. Nakia spent that time refraining from throwing her wine in his face.

"This was fun." He rubbed her knee. She desperately wanted to slap the grin right off his face but couldn't risk her sister getting hurt. "Let's do it again sometime."

And then he was gone.

Unable to contain her anger any longer, Nakia yelled and flung the cup. It shattered against the wall and dripped red onto the floor.

***

Fourteen-year-old Ashni was a sight to behold. Lanky, mostly made of elbows and knees, and wearing a helm that barely fit her head. Standing next to her brothers as they prepared for battle, she looked like a wooden slide toy.

Jay looked like a full-grown warrior. With his height, he towered over their father. Jay looked like he could wrestle a bear, which he had almost done when he joined the Bear warrior Guild. He had lost his spear for a moment in the match but managed to collect it again and down went his bear brother. He never seemed too broken up about it.

Jay's armor was clearly custom made while Ashni had pretty much the same armor as any member of the rank and file. Jay could afford the armor from money built up from over two years of riding with their father. Ashni would have to earn the same.

Asad and Amal weren't as convincing as Jay was, though they still had her beat. Glistening, polished armor. Helmets that fit their heads and swords rather than spears. Proper weapons for royalty.

"Ashni," her father said, clapping her on the shoulder. The force pushed her forward a bit and she had to adjust her helmet. "I want you to meet someone. You could learn a lot from her."

Ashni nodded. They stepped inside his tent, and she stood face to face with a woman decked out in the best armor with her helmet tucked under her arm. Her hair was short but pulled into a tight braided ponytail at the nape of the neck. She stared down at Ashni with one dark, intense eye. A scar closed the other.

"Adira, I want you to meet Ashni." Her father pushed Ashni forward.

Adira groaned and curled her lip a little. "Another one of your spawn."

Ashni frowned. "How do you know?"

"You have his eyes." Adira stepped forward.

Ashni wasn't sure what to think of Adira. The seriousness of her gaze spoke of her being a seasoned warrior. It probably helped that Adira thought she looked like Khalid. No one else ever thought that.

Adira glared at her father, no fear at all. "I'm not babysitting."

"I'm not asking you to. I've got Ashni, and I want her to know she should watch you. And you should be aware of her. This kid has potential." Her father patted Ashni's shoulder.

"You say that about all your kids."

He shrugged. "I believe it. That's why I tell them all to watch you. You'll show them the next level."

Adira snorted. "Try not to kill the kid. I have to move my unit into position." She marched out of the tent.

"Come on, Ashni. Let's go get you some battle experience." Her father clapped and moved out.

At first, Ashni feared her first battle would involve just sitting on Midnight Thunder and observing the chaos. Her father hadn't placed her anywhere, beyond the back row of cavalry. As it turned out, Midnight Thunder had his own plans and made a break for the fray.

"Ashni!" She heard the muffled voice of her father.

For a moment, Ashni considered pulling his reins, but why? She had trained for this and killed Tau for this. Dirt, grass, mud, and smoke were everywhere. Her eyes watered. Her lungs burned. But she was alert enough to cut down any enemy who dared to wander too close.

At first anyway.

Midnight Thunder took a spear to the side and reared back, throwing her. She yelped as she spilled to the ground. Her ears rang, but she was aware enough to block a sword coming down on her. Her spear was almost cut in half. A soldier loomed over her. Throwing out a hand, she pushed lightning free and dropped that soldier plus several others behind him.

Ashni climbed to her feet and backed people up with her lightning until she had good footing. Soaked in sweat, her hair stuck to her face. She had no idea where her helmet was. She had no idea where her horse was.

"Ashni! There you are." Her father ran over to her. "Do you have any idea what your mother would do to me if you died in battle?"

She refused to admit this was an accident, although he was sort of right. Her mother would probably skin her father alive if something happened to any one of the children. "I wanted to be in the battle, not babysat by you."

He laughed, but his lip wobbled a bit. "Obviously I should've waited before introducing you to Adira." He put his arm around her shoulder. "Come. We'll get cleaned and checked on before celebrating our victory."

Ashni nodded and followed her father. Her blood pumped from the fight, and she was surprised to discover she was covered in scratches. She didn't remember being touched, but she had to get stitches in several different places. Her father laughed as he stood by her, but it sounded like sobbing. Once she was bandaged, he left her alone to confer with his generals. She went to get cleaned up.

"Looks like you lost the horse and much of your blood on the battlefield. You should be more careful with your things," Asad said as they were eating victory dinner later that night. A few battles later, he actually tried to steal Midnight Thunder and when he couldn't get away with that, he tried to poison her horse. She hadn't told anyone about it, and when she confronted him, Jay came to his defense, promising her if she bothered Asad about "nonsense" again, she'd end up eating that horse.

Jay shook his head. "You're clearly not ready for war. The gods have cursed you and will curse us because you're here."

"Based on a few scratches?" Adira asked as she flopped down on the closest pillow. "At least she didn't get stabbed her first time out." Her gaze drifted to Asad.

The way her brothers glared at Adira made Ashni more intrigued with her. Jay's face flushed to the point where it seemed like a blood vessel burst in his face. "How dare you sit with us, fishmonger."

"Sterlings never mix with barbarians," Asad said. Ashni wrinkled her nose at the term sterling. She didn't see why her brothers used it. They weren't original Roshan either. Their mother was once a barbarian. Her old trainer was once a barbarian as well. Once absorbed into the Empire, though, they were as Roshan as anyone.

"Your father invited me to sit here." Adira ate a date with a smug smile.

At that moment, their father came up and clapped Adira on the back. Adira gagged and choked. Adira coughed and sputtered until the date flew out of her mouth. She glared at him, and he grinned.

"You better not die. I need you to figure out more great moves with your unit," he said.

"Maybe don't kill me then," Adira replied.

He scoffed. "Hell, I'm not sure I can kill you. I mean, if I could, it would've been long before now. Tried it when you had that damn fishing spear, and you took out way too many trained warriors. How the hell were you not a soldier then?"

"Being a soldier didn't exist in my little village when you showed up and took over." Adira curled her lip again.

He smiled like she complimented him. "Nobody told your little village to be sitting in the middle of my supply lanes. Besides, they didn't like you anyway. Not like I do!"

"Why is she sitting with us?" Jay asked.

"I like her." The Amir raised his wine goblet. "I enjoy Adira and her grumpiness, especially when she leads her unit in a surprise flanking move that helps turn things in our favor. In fact, let's raise our cups to Adira." Other goblets and cups went up. There were cheers and drinking, but the Amir wasn't done. "And let's not forget my little one. Did you guys see the work she put in?" He grabbed Ashni by the wrist and shoved her hand in the air. Cheers echoed through their banquet tent as other goblets shot into the air.

"We saw that lightning!"

"It was like she cut the sky!"

"And it saved our asses!"

Ashni had no idea. She threw her lightning around to stay alive. She fought down a smile, even though she hadn't meant to do any of it.

Jay scoffed. "First the fishmonger, now this. She panicked and sprayed her talent all over the place. It's probably only through the grace of the gods she didn't hit any of us. Why do we celebrate mediocrity so often?"

"Nothing about what either of them did is mediocre. They have the gods' touch as much as you do," their father replied.

Jay shook his head. "Dad, we are descendants from gods. It's blasphemous to put this fishmonger on the same level as us." He scowled at Adira.

"Adira fought bravely, taking down their lead warrior with her spear. It's those acts that make us great." The Amir took a deep drink from his goblet. "That make us all great!"

The cheers came louder than before. It was like her father said great acts make people great. Adira did something great, so she was great.

Adira shook her head and focused on the food in front of her. She seemed sullen the whole time, even though she had the Amir's full attention. Other soldiers would've killed for such an honor. But that was just Adira, Ashni learned. Glory was always a double-edged sword with her. It brought her great standing and wealth; except she knew what it meant to be conquered and here she was doing the same. Ashni wanted to know more of her.

Ashni could be great, too, as long as she did something great. Greatness was in her future. *Have I been great, though?* This wasn't greatness to Adira. *What is greatness?*

Chapter Ten

MEETING ADIRA HAD POSSIBLY been the best thing to happen to Ashni. Adira turned her from a warrior to a soldier. Yes, she was a bitch about it, but she still did it. A soldier's discipline had saved Ashni's life many times on the battlefield.

"Recklessness is in your blood," Adira had said to her as she stitched up a gash in Ashni's arm. They were just outside Adira's tent after another battle. They had known each other a couple of years now and she never failed to get on Adira's nerves with her actions, no matter what she did. The sun was warm and felt like a blessing washed over them.

Jay wandered over to their section of the camp. "I wonder how. Not like the Amir is reckless."

Adira laughed, more mocking than amused. "I'm almost certain that's his family name."

Flames danced on Jay's fingertips. "You watch your mouth about my father, fisher-wench."

Thunder boomed through the sky. "You watch what you call one of the best officers in the damn army. She says worse things to the Amir's face, so I doubt he'll mind this," Ashni said.

"What's going on over here?" Their father charged over. Ashni would have to learn to stop broadcasting her emotions, but it was hard to do with Jay around.

"Nothing. Just checking on Ashni," Jay replied.

Her father turned to her and smiled. "You need more patience. You're worse than I was at your age."

"We kept the element of surprise," Ashni replied. She had gone off before she was supposed to in the battle, except she had seen an opening. Adira taught her to take advantage any time she noticed one. Now, it seemed to be a problem when she put it into action.

Her father chuckled. "True enough, but you're worth more than a victory, Ashni. Never think otherwise."

Ashni grinned at him. "Hey, I'll be all right. They don't call me the Chosen One for nothing."

"The Empress is going to kill you when she realizes you turned her only daughter into you," Adira said.

He guffawed. "Maybe that was my plan all along." He puffed out his chest. "And yes, she's definitely going to kill me."

"Ah, I'm sure the Sky Cutter would have your back." Adira rolled her eyes, calling Ashni by the nickname in a sort of sarcastic way.

He chuckled even more and patted Adira on her arm. "When you're done with my impulsive offspring, I need to talk to you. We've got some new war toys to help as we get closer to Shadow Walker territory. I don't need to tell you we'll need every weapon we have to take on their talents."

Jay scoffed. "Those Shadow Beasts won't know what hit them when we show them our Fire. Shadows can't exist in the light."

Their father shook his head. "The Shadow Walkers have lived in Darkness for centuries. They know how to snuff out light."

Jay frowned and crossed his arms, looking down on their father. Jay might have been taller than the Amir, but he was still the son and had to be reprimanded. Their father didn't pay him any mind. Jay's nostrils flared.

"The Shadow Walkers won't be an easy conquest," Adira said.

"Nothing worth it ever is. They have the knowledge and talent to make the Empire excel. Beyond that, there are massive quantities of water in their area. I had hoped for a trade." He shrugged.

"They said no," Adira said, her voice dry.

He grinned. "Well, their response was much more unfriendly than that. So, now we have to be unfriendly as well. Saniyah, a brilliant engineer if you haven't met her, has a few ideas."

"I have not met her."

"Well, she's brilliant. She was trained by Nayyir Gyan and he's been singing her praises since he brought her along. Of course, she's his niece, so it might come across as biased or something, but he's right." It was so clear he was excited, practically bouncing in front of them.

Adira shook her head. "Well, I know how much trust and faith you put in him. I'll be by as soon as I'm done working on Captain Reckless."

"Hey!" Ashni didn't find it fair she got so much crap over something that worked.

"Should I come as well, Dad?" Jay asked.

Their father nodded. "You may come. Bring the twins. Adira, bring Ashni."

Adira nodded. "Let me finish this so we can make your meeting."

That was enough to get rid of her father, and Jay followed him.

Ashni turned her attention back to Adira, awed by her. Maybe it was the level of respect her father had for Adira. It was obvious he trusted Adira with the world...and her.

Adira took a breath as she finished the stitches. "Okay, you're all done. Try not to get wounded in this meeting. I don't think either of us want to hear or see Jay again." That was the truth.

The meeting had several top officers in it who interrupted an eighteen-year-old Saniyah Gyan almost constantly. Her mentor stood, letting it happen. She needed to learn to assert herself.

Adira stood by Saniyah as she presented and explained her work. Ashni noticed their fingertips brush a couple of times but didn't think anything of it. She thought more and more about her father's trust in Adira. She was obviously special, beyond being an officer. *I admired her. I still do. What is greatness to Adira?*

***

Nakia entered the throne room with Asad at her side, his hand on her elbow. Jay stepped behind them, Bashira pressed to his side. Bashira had a bruise at the corner of her mouth and her eyes were red.

At the side of the room, Badar watched from the shadows, hard to spot, though Nakia had become familiar enough with him to know he was there. Not too far from Badar, Layla paced, hand on her sword. Nakia caressed the hilt of a dagger hidden in her sleeve, the temptation to stab Jay in the throat greater than the desire to murder Asad. She sat down on the throne, head high, though Asad and Jay stood on either side of her. Their message was loud and clear.

Saniyah rushed the dais. "Let my niece go." Her voice echoed through the large hall.

Jay held up Bashira's wrist. She whimpered and tried to pull away. He only pulled her closer and her face screwed up in pain.

"She was given to me by the Queen," Jay said, like his words were the stone-cold truth. He winked at Nakia. "Such a fine hostess."

"Lies!" Saniyah pointed at him. "I know Nakia well enough to know that isn't true, so let's put the proper players in place." That sounded like a challenge and Nakia didn't like that. They weren't in the right place to challenge anyone.

Jay inclined his head. "Meaning what?"

"Let Bashira go. She's got nothing to do with royal matters. I am chief war engineer and married to Ashni's top general. I know the Court.

I could educate you." There was a strange, determined glint in Saniyah's eye, like a dare.

Jay practically jumped at it. "Your council would be valuable." He flung Bashira away. "Go away, dancer. Be thankful for your aunt."

"Aunt Saniyah!" Bashira seemed to fly to her aunt's arms, sobbing as soon as she was secure against Saniyah.

Nakia flicked her gaze to Jay. *What the hell had that monster done to her?*

Saniyah held her and stepped back, putting distance between them and Jay. "It's okay now," she said, patting Bashira's head.

"Don't do this, please." Bashira's voice cracked.

"I have to protect you, even at the cost of myself. It'll be fine. This is an old dance," Saniyah said, eyeing Jay.

Nakia could only imagine the history between the brothers and Saniyah. What she couldn't imagine was why Jay would want to treat Saniyah or Bashira harshly. They were the sweetest people she had ever met.

Saniyah gave Layla a nod and Layla vanished into smoke only to reappear by Bashira's side. Dark smoke billowed once more, and both Bashira and Layla disappeared. Saniyah marched to Jay as if she could walk through flames, stopping by his side with a scowl.

Jay smirked. "You know who I'm sure would love to join us?"

Asad tapped his chin. "Saffi?"

"Leave my sister out of this," Nakia said through gritted teeth. She had no idea what had happened to Bashira, but she'd be damned if she let them do anything to Saffi.

"Oh, she's already involved herself. Your sister wants to follow the rules," Asad said.

Nakia's stomach dropped. She didn't want to, though she could believe it. When Saffi walked in, smiling and heading straight for the throne, she knew. She couldn't even be angry. Those damn Tyrans broke Saffi a long time ago. This probably made the most sense to her.

"All I had to do was offer her a chance to be my third spouse." Asad shrugged.

Nakia's lip curled. "Bastard." She couldn't see Saffi wanting to be anyone's spouse ever again, especially if there were multiple spouses already.

Asad smirked. "No, that would be your spouse. Checkmate."

"We haven't even begun to play," Nakia replied. *Oh, really? Because from here, it looks like you lost.*

"The game is over."

Nakia straightened her shoulders. "If this is all for Amal, imagine what I will do for Saffi." She'd tear these bastards apart with her bare hands to keep them from hurting Saffi. Her sister had been through enough.

Asad chuckled. "Saffi isn't your twin."

Nakia leveled a glare at him, needing him to see the promise in her eyes. "You will regret this." Maybe not today and maybe not tomorrow, but soon there would be a reckoning.

***

Ashni knew what the darkness would give way to once it lifted. Why? To remind her of how amazing her little sister was? To remind her of what she and the Roshan took from her little sister? To let her know greatness wasn't what she imagined it to be at first? Before she could determine the reason, the darkness lifted. She watched and wondered.

The battlefield was quiet for a moment, a lull in the fighting. Her father pulled his troops back, not a full retreat, just enough to rethink the plan. Ashni hung in close to Adira as the officers gathered around the Amir. Adira offered suggestion after suggestion, none of which the Amir commented on. Ashni wasn't sure what was wrong with any of them, but kept her mouth closed. Too bad other officers couldn't manage to do the same.

"Fisherwoman, stop bombarding the Amir!"

"Yeah! Learn to keep your mouth shut."

"Why are you even here? This is a meeting for top officers." Jay pushed his way over to her.

Ashni stepped between them. "She's a top officer." Why the hell did her brothers act like they didn't know that? Especially Jay. He always jumped down Adira's throat the second she said something.

Adira put her hand on Ashni's shoulder. "You know you don't have to stand up for me. I'm not scared of him, or any of these other sterlings."

"You should be." Jay blew a small fireball in her face.

Adira didn't even blink as the fire blackened her nose. "I've faced more formidable Fire and come out quite fine. And that was as a fisherwoman."

"That's it!" The Amir came and took Adira by the shoulders. He shook her a little. "You said we should rain down sacred oil on them, right?"

"One of several suggestions, yes," Adira replied.

"We'll mix that oil with the battle oil. The fumes will slow the Shadow Walkers down enough for us to take control of this situation."

"It sounds crazy coming from you," Adira said. His demented smile probably didn't help.

"Well, it's to be done. Prepare!" He clapped his hands together.

"Are you sure?" Jay asked.

Their father punched his fist into his palm. "It's perfect. It's just crazy enough to work."

"You're just plain crazy, but okay," Adira said, which was funny since it was half her idea.

The troops were hastily put back into their lines and battle weapons were put on display. Their enemy moved to put themselves back into their formations. Demons of onyx mist paced in front of them, eyes glowing, ready for battle. They shrieked and the ground shook. A piercing sharp noise rang throughout the space. Ashni resisted the urge to stick her finger in her ear as pain erupted through her brain.

"Set it up!" Khalid ordered.

Everyone scrambled to get the oils mixed and loaded. The Shadow Walkers didn't move when the oil was launched. They expected the oil to ignite and spread fire on the field. The Roshan had done that earlier. The Shadow Walkers had easily countered, engulfing the fires in their shadows or letting their demons put them out. Now, it would be different.

When the new oil ignited, the smoke choked the Shadow Walkers. Any demon caught by the smoke disappeared into mist. The Shadow Walkers broke their ranks, trying to get someplace safe as they burned, flesh peeling when hit by the oil. Their screams rippled through air, but Ashni didn't think anything of it. Wailing was a common sound to her.

Next came the charge, Ashni's cue. Midnight Thunder ran heavy into battle. Her swords in hand, special blades her parents gifted her to make sure they could withstand her talent, cutting whoever she went by, but they hadn't turned things around yet. Roshan charged, going down into a dark pit and didn't come out. Was this a Shadow Walker trick or a void?

As she got closer, she got a better idea. Warriors were being turned to dust by a black cloud that had tiny hands. Ashni let a small blast of lightning go, thinking it would take care of the cloud. Instead, her lightning vanished into the ether and the darkness faded enough to reveal the truth.

Ashni gasped. "A kid? A kid is taking out the Roshan elite?"

The kid looked at her and smirked. A void ripped open in front of Ashni. Midnight Thunder reared back, almost throwing Ashni, narrowly missing being devoured by the black hole. Ashni leaped off of Midnight Thunder. No one was going to kill her horse...even if he was still a jerk sometimes.

Bolting forward, she made a tight fist as she went into the pit. The child waved her hand at her and Ashni moved just in time to avoid another void. Then the kid glanced at another soldier coming with a sword for her. The sword began to turn to dust just as Ashni's knuckles connected with the little girl's cheek. The kid yelped and tumbled into the blackened dirt. She fell in a heap, and Ashni grimaced.

The girl didn't look much older than her youngest brothers and they were barely nine. She couldn't imagine them being in battle, couldn't imagine punching them in the face either. The idea made her stomach clench. She approached the child as the other Roshan went to rejoin the battle.

"Hey, kid, you dead?" Ashni asked with a lump in her throat.

The kid leaped to her feet and put her hands up. Her eyes were completely black, as dark as her armor. Shadow Walkers eyes did that when they were tapping into their true power. A kid shouldn't have been able to do it, shouldn't have that much power.

"Darkness prevails!" she yelled.

Ashni tensed, ready to fight, and then the kid fell right on her face, unconscious. Ashni stayed with her. A kid shouldn't be on the battlefield, except this kid seemed like a different creature altogether.

Ashni could hear the sounds of battle above them and itched to join the fray, but she stayed until the kid woke up some long minutes later. *I stayed.* The kid jumped to her feet, stumbling a little. Ashni raised her hands, ready to defend herself, but the kid didn't do anything. She looked around.

"We were defeated. The Darkness has forsaken us," she said.

"The Roshan war machine is pretty hard to stop once it gets going," Ashni said.

The kid looked at her with such seriousness and it was like the depths of the ocean were in those onyx eyes. "The Darkness will eventually prevail."

Ashni shrugged. "I don't see Darkness beating the Sun or the Son of the Sun, so you guys might as well just give up the water."

The Shadow Walkers did, eventually. The kid didn't give up, though. She hounded Ashni about a rematch and then another rematch. At some point in time, the kid was just with her. She stayed. *I stayed.*

***

Nakia sat at lunch with Asad, Jay, Saniyah, and Saffi. Asad had his arm around Nakia's waist and caressed her hip. Every few moments, she swallowed down acid as he reveled in touching her. She needed to do something before he disgraced her.

Saniyah sat across from her, staring at the table as if trying to calculate the best weapon against Jay. Jay was draped over her shoulders like a cloak, surrounding her.

Only Saffi seemed to be carrying on as if this was normal, chatting and smiling while stuffing her face with figs and offering the brothers food. Nakia hated to think this might be normal for Saffi. She might only know how to operate as a servant. She might think dysfunction and abuse were normal.

"You should feed me some grapes," Asad said to Nakia.

"You should choke and die," she replied with a smile.

"Like Ashni did?" He grinned, too.

"You covet her power just like your twin," Nakia said. What else could be his motive beyond revenge? He could've easily killed her if that's all he wanted. This had to be about proving himself better than Ashni.

Asad scoffed. "Everything Ashni chases and holds is through the grace of our mother. Once our mother dies, she'll lose all of this."

"Unless your mother gives her the whole thing," Nakia replied.

Jay laughed. "That's not happening."

"Why is that?" Nakia asked. Chandra liked Ashni and thought highly of her. *It must be because whoever Chandra wants doesn't actually matter.* Jay and Asad would probably fight each other for control of the Empire anyway. She didn't want to imagine what they might do with Ashni.

Asad ran a finger down her cheek. "It doesn't matter since she's dead."

"You seem so sure of yourself, even though you don't even know how she died," Nakia replied.

"If she isn't dead, where is she? We know Ashni," Asad said.

Nakia cocked an eyebrow. "Do you?"

"Ashni's dead. If she isn't, where's the thunder and her tears from the sky? Where's her tantrum?" Jay asked, looking around.

"Her tantrum almost killed Amal," Nakia said and earned the back of Asad's hand.

Nakia's lip split, and before she could react, Asad grabbed her by the chin. Saniyah moved forward, but a hand up from Nakia stilled her. Jay yanked Saniyah back while Asad forced Nakia to look at him.

"Amal liked to take it easy on our dear sister and it cost him, just like saying his name will cost you." Asad flung Nakia to the side and patted his lap. "Saffi, come sit with me."

Saffi gasped, glancing at Nakia with eyes full of fear as it hit her that this wasn't normal. Nakia glowered at Asad, hand in her sleeve, ready to end him with one flick of her wrist. Remembering Layla's people were at his mercy stayed her hand. Instead, she beat Saffi to his lap.

"Have you ever even been with a man?" Asad's breath burned her ear. "Being with Ashni is neglectful to someone like you. I'll teach you." He ran his tongue over the shell of her ear. It was like having slime on her flesh. Disgust rippled through her and she yanked away, purposefully slamming her elbow into Asad as she did. He grunted.

"Oops," she said, innocently, tucking her elbow in again.

He put a hand on her knee, tightening her hold. Nakia allowed it. Small victories.

The moment Nakia could escape Asad, she did. She retreated to the room where Ashni rested. Adira sharpened a knife, staring at it but her mind clearly elsewhere.

"You heard?" Nakia asked.

"Saniyah discussed it with me. She has to protect Bashira, so I understand the move, but I have to protect her," Adira replied. Her voice was hard. She probably had everything mapped out.

"What's your plan?"

Adira looked at her, eyes flashing. "I'm going to kill Jay for disrespecting her and attempting to defile her." As if it was so simple.

"Attempting?" Nakia felt the disrespect press against her during lunch. Last night was a taunt where Asad forced her to drink with him. He could do whatever he wanted with her.

Adira shook her head. "She'll never be defiled in my eyes. He's defiling his character and embarrassing himself."

"Things won't come to that. I'm going to write Thia and Wicus for help. Jay and Asad are trying to torture us, and I have to do everything in my power to stop that."

And Thia would at least save Saffi.

Samar looked up from a plant she pulled apart. "Even if it means our people?"

Nakia took a breath. "Of course not. Can't we move the army into position?"

"We can't use the Roshan army to attack the Roshan army," Adira said.

"Even if it's to defend the Roshan?" Asad planned to slaughter Roshan using Roshan. He was going to commit mass murder in an empire where killing one person—even a damn slave—was a punishable offense. They had to be able to do something about that.

"They're not sterlings, not the original Roshan" Adira said.

"Neither is the Empress." It was like everything she learned about the Empire meant nothing.

Adira shook her head. "Never come between the Empress and her children. She'll pick them every time." That was a hard truth.

Nakia slapped her hands together. "Well, I'm not going to sit here with my thumb up my ass and wait for Ashni's brothers to rape and ruin us."

"You wouldn't be ruined." Samar shot over to her and grabbed her by the biceps, looking down at Nakia with eyes that seemed to know everything. "You listen to me. You are strong. You're not at fault when someone tries to hurt you, when someone tries to take something from you. They haven't won."

"I can't do anything to protect my people, my mentor, my sister, myself." Her eyes drifted to Ashni. "Haven't they won?"

"They've only won once you submit." Samar frowned. "So, never submit."

"Then what can I do? They can kill your people if we blink the wrong way."

"Sometimes, the battle is won through patience. Play a long game with them," Adira said.

Nakia could do that. "How long?"

"However long you need to win. They don't know what they signed up for when they showed up and you were in charge," Adira said. The glint in her eye was filled with such confidence. She actually believed Nakia would carry them through this.

Nakia nodded and felt Adira's faith in the pit of her stomach. Her words rang true. She had been chasing them and trying to outmaneuver them in a proper fashion. Well, there was more than one proper way to do things.

You'll still lose. The damn voice in her head echoed, but she locked eyes with Samar. The voice quieted. Adira came over and clapped her on the shoulder.

"When you're done with them, you'll have ruined them forever," Adira said. If this hardened war general could believe in her, this person who defeated her father, then the voice in her head that was her father had to be wrong. She'd stop Jay and Asad. She had to.

***

When the darkness lifted, Ashni wasn't sure what to expect, but it didn't take long to realize she didn't want to see it. Her heart was shredded all over again.

The day had seemed so normal. The nobles and leadership met to discuss budgets. Ashni wasn't privy to the meeting, but Jay was invited, allowed to accompany an "uncle" of theirs. Instead, Ashni took Midnight Thunder out for exercise as they were supposed to be going on campaign soon. It would be Fahim's first ride.

She couldn't wait to teach Fahim everything she knew, imagining his wide-eyed stare. He'd probably be annoyed by Layla, but also fascinated with her and her religious beliefs. Adira would definitely be captivated with Fahim. He was too intelligent for Adira to ignore or pretend to be irked with his presence.

Wailing messengers arrived at her little meadow. At the time she couldn't fathom what could be so sorrowful. The day was glorious and soon they'd be out, adding to the Empire. And then, they told her the news that stopped the world. "The Emperor, our great Amir, the Son of the Sun is dead!"

Ashni flinched like she had been struck by a bolt of lightning and rushed off, not realizing she rode Midnight Thunder harder than she ever had in her life. *Lies!* He couldn't die. Wouldn't die. Not with more worlds to conquer, more sights to see, more people to meet. They were supposed to go West. The denials died in her mind when she saw her mother crying. Her body turned to dust. He was dead.

There was a moment when she wanted to join him. *Did you?* He can't die. Blackness washed over everything, smothering the memory.

"No, you're the one who can't die!"

Ashni twisted and turned. *Who the hell just spoke to her?*

"You're the Chosen One."

Dad? She could see only darkness, yet his voice was unmistakable. She carried it with her always, his soothing tones when times got rough.

"Your mother charged you with changing the world. I charge you with leading the world. More than that, you can't leave your family the way I left. You cannot die!"

***

Ashni gasped and shot up into a sitting position. Bright, white light blinded her, burning her skin. Her head throbbed. *Am I dead?*

Chapter Eleven

NAKIA ROLLED OVER EACH facet of their next move while staring into the dark of her bedroom. She'd let the brothers think they won. She talked it over with everyone already, ideas and details coming together over the course of almost a week. It would take time, and it would cost her. It would cost Saniyah pain and suffering. And, in the end, it would be checkmate in their favor. She set it up as quickly as she could, as Asad would want her attention soon.

She contacted Naren first, sending the message with Badar. She needed Naren to, little by little, shift the army from the north, sending them to Khenshu and then along to Tariq, Tiq, and surrounding territories under the guise of needing new training. She sent Badar to them with the story that he had to meet other teachers to discuss techniques for dealing with the Northern barbarians. They would claim they were training in case the barbarians went back on their word.

On their way to Tariq, they would have various cover stories, ranging from visiting family to pretending to be merchants with new goods. Clothes and props would be waiting for them in Khenshu. From there, they'd travel in small groups and smuggle people out using the same ruse as they got in. *We'll see who's in charge.*

The voice in her head scoffed. *The brothers will tear your plan apart.* The voice sounded smaller than usual, though. Adira had put her stamp of approval on this, as did Layla, and they had defeated her father, so his voice could kiss Nakia's ass. She'd beat these brothers. It would just take a different sort of battle. Plus, she already had numbers on Asad's forces. They were a fraction of the army Ashni and Nakia wielded.

She had written to Thia a few days ago, after everyone determined this was the best course of action, and Thia's response came swiftly. She was with Nakia. Thia promised to never let her sisters be hurt again, just like Nakia promised. Neither of them would actually be able to keep those promises, which they both knew, but it was the principle of the matter.

Wicus' forces would return to the north to fill in any gaps made by departing Roshan forces. That way when Asad or Jay noticed the troop movement, she'd be able to explain it. With no hostages, Jay and Asad wouldn't be able to ignore the nobles' and the military's support for her. Then, they could get Chandra involved and let her settle the matter with facts in front of her. *Game on, bastards.*

It was just after that confident thought that Asad knocked on her door. Without waiting for a reply, he entered her personal room. Again. Disgust ripped through her. Terrible manners, yet that didn't seem to matter to him. Servants scurried around, putting up an illusion of busyness and hiding anything she needed out of the way. There wasn't much since she burned any correspondence after reading them.

"Why are you here?" Nakia asked, eyes narrowed on Asad.

Asad smirked. "I figured we could have dinner in a more intimate setting."

"You know how poorly this looks," Nakia replied.

He grinned wider, much like a demon, and motioned to several pillows, ordering her to sit. She sneered but didn't want to do anything more to upset him.

Nakia sat, nodding to the servants but knowing Asad spent too much time in her space for her to keep anything important for long.

"You're quiet tonight." Asad placed a hand on her thigh. His new habit, developed over the past few days.

"What's there to say?" Nakia replied.

"Maybe the company will loosen you up."

And, as if it was timed, Jay arrived with Saniyah. Saniyah sat across from Nakia, holding her head high, even though there was purple bruising around her mouth. Jay draped himself over her again. With their torment focused on Saniyah and Nakia, the brothers had forgotten Saffi, and Nakia had Layla smuggle Saffi out of the palace. One less person to worry about. Eventually, Saffi would be sent to Thia, but for now she was hiding with Layla's clan.

Asad tried to start the conversation again. "You could tell me how you prefer me to Ashni."

Nakia arched her eyebrow. "I don't make it a habit to lie."

Asad wasted no time back handing her across the face. Pain blossomed on her cheek and the slap reverberated through the space. The taste of metal danced on her tongue. Asad probably thought he was hurting her, yet it wasn't much of anything. It physically hurt, but her father had hit her with a bowl that had hot oil in it. She still had the scar. That was pain. This was posturing, intended to frighten her into compliance.

Over the past few days, she learned violence was his go-to reaction when it came to her, much like his twin. It seemed like a way to punish not just her, but Ashni, even though Ashni wasn't there.

"You all need so much encouragement that you're better than someone you've already deemed inferior. It's odd," she said.

Asad raised his hand again.

"Leave her be!" Saniyah lunged forward only to be snatched back by Jay. She turned; hand raised to strike him. Jay caught her hand and squeezed her wrist until she screamed.

"Hey!" Nakia tried to move, but Asad pinned her arms to her side. He head-butted her. A crunch echoed and her skull throbbed. Agony raced around her head.

When he pulled back, she could see her blood on his forehead, and she felt blood drip from her nose. The blood leaked down to her lip.

"Hurting me doesn't suddenly make you better than Ashni," Nakia said.

He grabbed her chin. "I'll always be better than the bastard child."

She smirked. "That's why you all chase her shadow?"

Asad grabbed her by the throat and she gagged, trying to scream. For a second, she thought he might strangle her to death. Saniyah roared, maybe there were words, but Nakia couldn't be sure. Fear clutched her heart. She didn't think he'd run out of patience so quickly and skip right to murdering her.

"Asad," Jay warned.

Asad loosened his grip, yet it didn't un-strike that nerve.

Asad snarled at her and kept his hand on her throat, holding her up as if she weighed nothing at all. She dug her nails into his fingers, trying to rip his hand off her neck. It didn't work. He dragged her into the adjoining room and threw her on the bed, towering over her.

Nakia fought. She kicked and scratched and went so far as pulling a dagger on him. She caught him by surprise enough to cut his arm, but it wasn't enough for him to let her go. Her three years of training proved nothing against his lifetime of fighting. He blew fire in her face, not enough to hurt her, although she didn't know that at first. He disarmed her as she shook away the heat. But that wasn't the only trick up her sleeve.

There was another dagger, and she almost had him right in the armpit until he closed his arm on the blade just in time. He yanked that knife away, and Nakia slashed with a third dagger. He winced as she cut into his robes. She wasn't sure she made it to his ribs when he grabbed her hand.

He snarled in her face, huffing smoke at her. "How many fucking daggers do you have?"

"Enough!" She went to stab him again with yet another dagger. He blocked it with his forearm, knocking it out of her hand. He was wounded, though.

"Yes, enough," Jay said.

Nakia turned to see him holding Saniyah. She had a knife to his throat, but he could set her on fire long before she killed him, and they all knew that. No one moved.

"I'm tired of this. Be a good girl and lie down for him or I will roast all the flesh from Saniyah's face," Jay said.

"You can't!" Nakia replied.

Flames came from Jay's nose. "Do you want to test that?"

Nakia looked Saniyah in the eye. They had discussed this, being ready to sacrifice their bodies if necessary. It was easier said than done.

"You don't have to. He might kill me, but I promise you, Adira will kill him in return," Saniyah said.

Jay growled. "That damned fisherwoman is going back to the muck where she belongs as soon as I get a chance to send her there."

Nakia took a breath. *We made a plan. I made a plan. I have to stick to it.* Lives were at stake, and she was the leader. Sacrifices had to be made to win. Jay dragged Saniyah back into the dining area as Nakia steeled herself for what was about to happen. Nakia had been dreading this moment since Asad had forced his way into her room and made her drink wine with him. Ever since then he had been taunting her with his presence in her space and taking liberties touching her, taunting her, letting her know this was coming. She braced for it as best she could, but the knowledge that Saniyah was a room away, heard her struggle, and tried to help made things that much worse.

"I didn't need the help," Asad muttered.

Nakia would prove him wrong, even as she resigned herself to this fate. He disarmed her and stripped her in under a minute. The violation seemed to last forever. Still, she bit and clawed, causing as much damage as she could. She sank her teeth into his shoulder enough to draw blood. He stopped moving long enough to punch her in the chest. She collapsed on the bed; all the wind knocked out of her. She tried to curl into herself from the pain but couldn't even do that. He was too heavy and all around her, blood from his wounds dripping onto her. She sobbed in spite of herself, agony after agony rippling through her.

It seemed like it took him forever to get off of her. By then, her sobs were silent and her body sore. It was like he skinned her, could see everything inside of her. It was so much worse than she imagined it would be. Nothing she could've done would have prepared her for this. *No, don't think about that. This was a price for your victory*. He stared at her, grinning.

"If your precious Ashni is so great, why couldn't she save you from that? Because she's dead," Asad said.

"You wouldn't dare if she were alive," Nakia replied, trying her damnedest to keep the quaver from her voice. She glared at him, even though she was unable to move.

"I do as I damn well please." He spat on her, gathered his belongings, and walked out.

Nakia shivered. She was wet. Sticky. Gross. Yes, this was her price for a later victory, yet she still cried to herself. Whispers came soon after, and servants entered the room. No one touched her or talked for a long moment.

"Highness, we should bathe you," someone said. She couldn't focus enough to figure out who it was.

"And there's an elixir you must drink," another said.

Nakia didn't fight them, numb to the sensation of them moving her. She could feel was Asad. He was everywhere. The idea made her want to vomit. *Is this what victory looks like?* The voice in her head had the nerve to laugh. *No.*

This was a sacrifice, like Saniyah made to save Bashira. In the end, she would show him. *I will win.*

***

Bile rose in Ashni's throat. There was no way death could be so bad. Cool water pressed to her dry lips turned her away from the sickness. She drank until the water was gone. It gave her eyes a chance to focus and see who blessed her with a drink.

"Samar," Ashni said, voice low, scratchy, as if it clawed its way out of its grave. Her mouth tasted like something had died in it.

Samar gave her a soft smile. "For a long moment there, I considered maybe they got you."

Ashni blinked. "They who? The north?"

Samar laughed. "No, your brothers."

Ashni squinted, mind swimming, thoughts swirling. Her brothers? The ones nobles were trying to put on the throne now that her father was dead? The ones laughing at her for adopting Layla? The ones calling her a fool for learning tactics from a fisherwoman? Or the one who read to her while she tried to train the other two in basic self-defense? What year was it?

"What's the last thing you remember?" Samar pursed her lips.

Ashni stared at the wall. Battle sounds filled her head. Metal scrapped metal. Screaming. She could smell fire, burning, smoke. But what battle was it? Where was she?

"I don't know." Ashni felt like that answered all questions.

Samar frowned. "Let's try something else. Stand."

Ashni nodded and went to move her arms to push herself up. Her arms refused to move as did her legs. Panic pulsed through her. "What happened? Why can't I move?"

Samar rubbed her palms together. "You were poisoned."

Ashni's mouth gaped, words lost on her for a long moment. "Poison did this?" *The hell?* She had been poisoned more times than she could count at this point.

"This poison has left you in a coma for almost a month."

Ashni couldn't believe her eyes didn't fall out of her head from how wide they opened. Poison put her down for a month. She didn't think it was possible. Once, she was poisoned and able to host a party the same day! The look on Samar's face said it all, though. She was lucky to be alive.

She took a moment to take stock of herself. Okay, she couldn't move her limbs, but she hadn't used those muscles for almost a month. It felt like everything under her skin had turned to sand. It was almost itchy, burning like claws scratched down every inch of her.

Before she could open her mouth, Layla sprang up from a shadow, squealing when she saw Ashni. She wrapped Ashni in a hug so tight it could break bones. So weak, it was a struggle for Ashni not to fall limp against Layla, like an empty banana peel.

"You're awake!" Layla tightened the embrace.

"Shh!" Samar put her finger to her lip.

Layla gasped. "Oh, right. Sorry. I'm just so glad she's up."

Ashni scoffed, trying to ignore the pain pulsing through her body from her sister's embrace. Somehow, even her teeth throbbed. "You act like I died."

Still, from the pain of a simple hug, she understood how weak she was. Maybe this time luck saved her. *Or was it Dad?* She remembered hearing her father telling her she couldn't die, couldn't leave her family. *Hellcat.* Her heart thumped at the thought of her spouse.

Layla actually sniffled. "We thought you did, or you were going to."

Ashni groaned. "Obviously, I still have things to do and the gods left me here." Or a god left her there. She had a world to change.

"Then let's get you fit for what you have to do," Samar said and turned to Layla. "Layla, fetch Nakia now."

Layla frowned and held Ashni tighter. "Must I?" Ashni looked at her sister. This wasn't her usual pretense of disliking Nakia. *It's as if she's scared to release me.*

Ashni's already tense stomach clenched at Layla's fear. *How close was I to dying? Am I still close to dying, even though I'm awake?* She'd ask Samar about it when Layla was gone.

"Yes, she deserves to know her spouse is alive, so go fetch Nakia," Samar said.

Layla sighed. There was something strange about the way she looked, almost disturbed. Ashni wasn't sure what to make of that.

"Is Ashni ready for the stress?" Layla asked, finally letting Ashni go.

Ashni's chest tightened. *How could Nakia stress me out?*

Samar scratched her chin in thought. "Ready or not, Nakia deserves the same relief you just felt."

"What stress do you mean?" Ashni asked.

There was a deep sigh as Layla shook her head. "You'll have to see. Nakia will tell you." And then she was gone, vanished into the shadow in the corner of the room.

Ashni's body trembled. "Samar, tell me, why would I be stressed by my beloved?"

Samar began mixing a potion on the short table next to Ashni's bed. "Let's work on getting your strength back for when you find out."

Ashni wanted to argue, but a strange sort of excitement spiked in her. She felt lightheaded. She fell back against her bed and closed her eyes. The bed was uncomfortable, so unlike her bed sheets and down pillows. *Why am I not in my own damn bed to get better?*

"Can you drink?" Samar put a second cup to her lips. She was thirsty, but the flavor was too much. Her throat seized and she coughed, sending warm tart liquid everywhere. Samar frowned, dabbing at the droplets on her face with Ashni's blanket. "We'll keep with your steam treatments then."

Ashni choked a little more as Samar moved away. "Steam treatments?" *I can't even drink medicine. I have to breathe it in.* She stared down at her hands, too weak to move them.

"It's how I've been delivering most treatments to you. Steam and balms. It's been trial and error, but you're strong," Samar replied, heading to the other side of the room.

Ashni didn't feel strong. A breeze could probably break her in half. Samar hummed as she worked, and finally Layla returned with Nakia by her side. Ashni's heart leapt at the sight, her body aching as Nakia launched herself onto Ashni.

"Ashni!" Nakia sobbed.

"My love," Ashni said, hating that she couldn't raise her arms to return the embrace.

Nakia pulled away and studied her with wide, wet eyes. "I'm sorry. Are you hurt? You sound like you're in pain."

Ashni tried to smile, but she could only manage a wince. Then she took in Nakia's appearance. Her bruised face, one eye swollen completely shut. Stitches closed her eyebrow and a cut on her cheek. Her bottom lip was split down the center.

"What happened?" Ashni asked.

Nakia shook her head. "Don't concern yourself. Focus on getting healthy."

"I have to concern myself. I'm meant to protect you." *Who dared to touch my hellcat?* She would punish them for all eternity.

"Sometimes, I'm meant to protect you." Nakia kissed her cheek.

Ashni couldn't even make a fist to express her anger. Whoever hurt Nakia would probably kill Ashni with their bare hands in her current state. That realization sat like hot iron in her stomach.

"So, whatever happened, you did it to protect me?" Ashni asked.

"It happened because people are terrible, but we'll teach them otherwise. For that to happen, you have to regain your strength," Nakia replied.

Ashni wished she could argue, but she was already exhausted, and she had hardly been awake for ten minutes. Nakia held her hand, gave it a gentle squeeze, and that was enough to put her to sleep. At least her life didn't flash before her eyes this time.

***

Nakia kissed Ashni's forehead as she drifted off to sleep. She turned her attention to Samar and Layla. Samar wasted no time rubbing an herbal emollient on her bruises. It stung her damaged flesh, and the slight scent of rosemary burned her eyes. Layla scowled as she watched her mother work.

"You should see the other guy," Nakia said. *That's what Layla and Ashni would do, right? Make light of the situation.* "You'll both be proud to know I fought him. I hurt him."

Layla took a deep breath and scrubbed her face with both hands. "Even though you warned us, I didn't think he'd be dumb enough do this."

"She's going to kill him," Samar said.

166

"If I don't," Layla said, eyes alight with hatred. She raised a hand and shadows rose with it. Her hand was so tense the color drained from her dark honey fingers.

Samar shook her head. "It's not your right." Layla curled her lip and let the shadows fall away. "This is for Ashni."

"She can't kill him. Their mother would never forgive her," Nakia said.

"Ashni won't care. Chandra will simply have to deal with it," Samar replied.

Nakia could see that happening. *You know the lengths she'll go to for* you. However, as long as her plan continued along, there would be no need for Ashni to murder her brother and possibly face her mother's wrath. Nakia had to handle it.

"I should get back so Asad doesn't get suspicious," Nakia said. He kept her by his side almost all the time now, like he knew she used her free time to put her plan in motion. It was too late for him, though. *You really think you'll defeat these battle-hardened, war-tried princes who were groomed to rule? You're—*

Layla took Nakia's free hand, drawing her away from the thoughts swirling in her mind. "Thank you for all you've done," Layla said.

And just like that, the voice in Nakia's mind went silent.

Nakia gave a half-smile. "Don't thank me until it works." Anything with so many moving parts could fail. "I'm also glad your spouse is more reliable than he pretends to be."

Layla beamed. "There's a reason I married him beside the fact that he's cute."

Nakia laughed, then looked at Samar. "Thank you for everything you've done for Ashni. Take care of my girl." Samar nodded before she faded from view as a shadow consumed Nakia and Layla.

They reappeared in Nakia's room and Nakia fell onto the nearest pillow, exhausted. Layla followed her lead.

"Did Saffi make it to Thia?" Nakia asked.

Layla nodded. "She's been there for a couple of days. Tariq?"

"The first warriors are on their way there. So far so good."

There was a long moment of silence. Layla stared at a wall then scratched the side of her head. "Will this work?"

"Provided Adira doesn't murder Jay beforehand...I don't know." They saw less and less of Adira. Nakia couldn't imagine what it was like to watch her spouse being used as Jay's toy, knowing it was nothing more than a taunt against her.

Layla frowned. "I'm sorry you and Saniyah are going through this."

"Not as sorry as they'll be when this is all over." Nakia didn't want to think about what happened to her. She focused on her plans, and how the brothers' dishonor would eventually blow up in their faces. The future was pleasant enough to distance the present.

"Should we watch Adira?" Layla asked. "I'm not sure how long she'll hold off."

"Saniyah knows how to keep her at bay. We just have to get Asad's hostages away from him. We don't even have to worry about military and noble support. Now that Ashni's awake, we can use that to win favor with Chandra rather than hoping she doesn't decide the brothers should get control of this land. We just need to buy some time for Ashni to get stronger, so her brothers can't kill her on sight." She took a deep breath. This had to work.

Layla put her hand on her shoulder. "Never forget, you're strong and we're with you," Layla said.

Nakia scrubbed her face with both hands. *Am I really strong?* Maybe she wasn't, but they were together.

"You're so strong," Layla said, once more, like she needed Nakia to understand her words were the truth.

Layla stood and moved to Nakia's pillow, embracing her. Nakia broke down into sobs, overwhelmed by the support, by Ashni being awake, and by what she had endured, even if it was to save people. Layla held her tighter. It fortified her. She'd remain strong for Layla and her people. *They believe in me. I can do this. For them.*

Asad burst into the room. Layla leaped to her feet, tense and ready for war. Her eyes immediately went black. Nakia wasn't sure she had ever seen Layla do that before. Thick, black smoke swirled around Layla, popping with energy. The room got cold.

He smirked, but Layla arched an eyebrow. Nakia stood by Layla's side. Asad stepped closer.

"Shadow beast, do you want in on the sessions with the little princess?" he asked.

"You're going to regret this," Layla said.

He laughed, even as his hand went to his ribs, nursing an injury from her knife. "And who's going to make that happen?"

Layla smirked. "Her." She jabbed her thumb at Nakia, who winked at him.

His thick shoulders shook with amusement, but then he winced. He still felt the sting of her fight. He growled to cover up his pain. "How is she going to do that?"

Layla's jaw worked like she wanted to spit at him. "What would your mother say if she knew you were doing this?"

His smile vanished and his eyes combusted right before them. The mere mention of Chandra infuriated him, like he understood how disappointed she'd be. "My mother's none of your concern."

"Don't you think she's some wild woman from the hills?" Nakia asked innocently, remembering Amal's words from so long ago.

"Wild woman?" Asad pointed a threatening finger at her, flames dancing off his fingertip. Smoke shot out of his nose. "Watch your fucking mouth, you barbarian wench."

Nakia tilted her head. Interesting. Though Asad wanted revenge for his twin, his ideals didn't align with his twin's. "Your brother called your mother that. Did you ever tell him to watch his fucking mouth?"

Asad moved, but Layla was fast. She had a short, plain knife to his neck before he was a step closer. His eyes trailed down to the weapon.

"You care so little for your hometown? You'd throw them all away for some barbarian bitch?" Asad asked, showing his pearly white teeth in a smile that was more a grimace.

"That's my fucking sister." Layla put away her weapon. She glanced at Nakia and Nakia understood. Layla trusted her to save her people.

"You pretend to be close to Amal, yet your thinking's clearly different," Nakia said. There might be something there to get him to back off.

"Amal allowed people to poison his mind, but he's still my twin, and to be punished as he was for Ashni isn't fair. Ashni betrayed him."

Nakia couldn't believe what she was hearing. "He tried to kill her!"

Asad scoffed. "That was their relationship. He wasn't serious, and she took it too far."

Nakia's mouth dropped open. *He's crazy.* She looked at Layla, whose face was beyond incredulous. Nakia didn't know Layla's sepia eyes could open so wide.

"So, it's her fault?" Nakia finally said.

"They danced this dance a long time and she knew there was no reason to bother Amal for claiming her kingdom. He couldn't keep her kingdom."

"Then he shouldn't have taken it. He hurt a lot of people who were under her protection. Was she supposed to just let him get away with it?"

He threw up his arms. "She was supposed to play the game!"

Nakia shook her head. *What the hell is he talking about?* "So, this is a game to you?"

Asad glared at her. "No, I don't play their childish games. You don't seem to understand the bond between Amal and myself. You wouldn't get it because you're not Roshan."

Nakia arched an eyebrow. "So, the Roshan are the only ones who bond with people?"

"We understand the bonds better than you barbarians. You don't know what it means to rely on each other the way the Roshan do."

"Your own sister can't rely on you." Nakia pointed at him.

He grabbed her wrist and yanked her forward, then slapped her. She fell to her knees, grabbing her cheek. Asad grabbed her hair. She yelped as he yanked her head up. Layla growled, but Nakia shook her head. This pain was tiny compared to what she'd been through already.

"Ashni has never been reliable because she's not one of us. She surrounds herself with barbarians because she doesn't accept us," Asad said.

Nakia grabbed hold of her own locks and pulled, ripping her hair from his fingers. Some hair tore from her scalp, but she was free. The move shocked Asad.

"Because you never accepted her," Nakia shouted. "You don't even think she's your father's daughter."

"There was nothing to accept. She knew what she was. Mom might've been fooled, yet we all knew once the lightning came in and she suddenly thought it set her apart." He stepped forward as if to grab her again, but Nakia slipped from his grasp.

She scowled at him. "What the hell are you talking about? You three shunned her."

"You don't know what happened."

"You're all jealous of her and her relationship with your parents. You hate how people love her. You don't understand why anyone could accept her when you thought it was all right to throw her away. I think you hate that the gods—and your father—chose her."

Asad straightened, fire burning in his eyes, then stormed out, slamming the door behind him. The glasses on the table tinkled together from the impact. Nakia slumped to the floor.

Layla dropped down to Nakia. "We're rubbing off on you in the worst way."

Nakia managed to laugh. "He seems mad."

"You got under his skin." Layla gathered Nakia into her arms and helped her to her feet. "You should be careful, though."

"If he's upset, he's not thinking clearly. He's likely to miss what's going on around him." She would do anything to keep him from discovering what was happening behind his back. "So, sister, huh?"

"Sister." Layla chuckled and hugged her. "And you know what I'd do for a sister."

Nakia smiled and leaned into Layla. Layla would have her back no matter what. That knowledge filled her with confidence.

Chapter Twelve

ASHNI HAD TROUBLE SITTING up in the uncomfortable bed to take her vapor treatment. Aches throbbed through every part of her, and it itched like there was sand under her skin. The thick, black steam of the treatment, heated in a bowl, stung her eyes and scratched the roof of her mouth. Her lungs burned as she breathed in the medicine, which she couldn't even smell or taste. The poison had dulled those senses, as well as her sense of touch. She pushed herself through it.

"Breathe in," Samar stood by her bedside and coached her, breathed with her. It was partly to make sure she didn't go too fast. She needed to hold the vapor in, take her time, even though she wanted to rush through everything. Samar made sure that didn't happen. "Out."

Ashni followed the rhythm. She needed to move, needed her body to stop feeling like she was made of dust. Samar promised the medicinal fumes would help with that, and it was the only way her body would accept treatment right now.

Even though it had been days, she couldn't hold down liquids or food. Well, she thought it had been days. It was hard to tell, being locked in a room with no windows. Surely, she needed sunlight. Looking at her arms, she was pale, close to the same color as her mother. *And Roshan nobles thought I was light before*.

The poison left faded dark lines down her body. Ashni had never heard of a poison making a body look like vines lurked under the skin, so Samar filled her in. The poison, known as dilitro, had confounded Samar more often than not, even with the instructions left by the Northern barbarians.

Ashni couldn't turn her gaze away from her body. Her muscles had decayed, and her skin hung off her bones. She hated it. *Be grateful you're alive.*

"How long until I can move properly?" Ashni asked.

"I'm not sure. For now, focus on breathing in and out to make sure you get the full effect of the medicine," Samar replied.

Ashni nodded. She could feel the medicine down to her toes, tingling as it slowly rebuilt her broken body. Samar stepped over with another remedy as soon as she was done with the vapors.

"More balm?" Ashni asked, even though it was clear by the jar in Samar's hand. The thick goo inside was bright green.

Samar shrugged. "Your body responds to this better than any others I've used. You absorb the medicine through your skin."

Ashni nodded. She was more used to salves for bruising and soreness. Her injuries had never been so severe to be medicated like this. She wasn't sure other doctors would've thought to treat her in this way. *What would I have done without Samar?*

"What did you see when you were unconscious?" Samar asked as she rubbed Ashni down with the balm, starting with her bony arms. It made her skin tingle, like being pricked with needles.

Ashni's brow furrowed. "Why does it matter?"

It was just her life. She lived it once. That should've been good enough.

"Perhaps your mind needs treatment as well if it came up with ways to keep you occupied. Or maybe even your soul, if it went on a journey while your body was down."

"My mind and soul are fine." But...had her soul gone on a journey? She didn't think so, but she was certain her father spoke to her at the end. And reliving her life...it felt like more than a dream. It felt deeper, like being there.

Samar stared her down with dark eyes. "What did you experience?" she asked gently.

Ashni inhaled and got a lungful of medicine from the balm with a hint of a strange citrus scent. *My sense of smell is trying to come back.* She trusted Samar with everything. "My life."

Samar arched an eyebrow and continued to spread the liniment, now to Ashni's thin legs. "What about your life?"

Ashni squinted as she searched her mind. "Relationships? I'm not sure." That seemed to be the breakdown of each vision. Every one of them seemed to be her connection to someone else. *Tau.* She wanted to reach for the teeth around her neck—her brother's—but she couldn't lift her hands.

Samar nodded, massaging the balm into Ashni's feet. How many times had Samar done this for her? Samar was beyond a well-respected member of society and there she was rubbing Ashni's feet.

"Relationships with whom?" Samar asked.

Ashni thought back to each dream. "Family."

Samar moved to her back, slipping her hands under the shirt Ashni wore. "Family in what way?"

Ashni took another deep breath. She wasn't quite sure she could boil it down. "My mother helping me understand how stupid it was to listen to nobles who said I wasn't Dad's."

"That's it?"

"No. There were my brothers and things with them, good and bad. Joining my guild. The heartache of what I did to Tau and how I almost let Midnight Thunder die. Meeting Adira. I could practically feel how jealous Jay was of her."

Samar made a noise, massaging salve on Ashni's spine and neck. "So, relationships that shaped you?"

Ashni wished she could scratch her chin. "I don't think I'd say that."

"Then what? We're going to be here a while."

Ashni did her best to explain her dreams, how she was on the outside looking in. How it seemed like more than a dream, and less like she was actually there. Samar listened and worked, but she didn't say anything in the end. Ashni glared at her the best she could.

Samar arched an eyebrow as she stepped away. "Why that expression?"

"Aren't you going to say anything about my experience?"

Samar gave her a soft smile and tilted her head. "Do you need me to?"

Ashni snorted. "No, but that's never stopped you before."

If Samar and her own mother were anything to go by, mothers were always loaded with advice no one asked for. Unfortunately, they also had good timing and offered advice no one asked for at the right time.

She chuckled as she massaged the liniment into Ashni's neck, just under her chin. "I feel it's pretty obvious."

Is this really all mothers? So annoying and smug. "Oh, really? I think it's pretty hazy, just flashes of my life."

"Very particular flashes of your life. Not to mention, your father's voice at the end."

Ashni shrugged. It took her a moment to realize she moved her shoulders and giddiness fluttered in her belly. *Slowly, but surely*. "Maybe my mind really did break. You have medicine for that?"

"Of course I do. Maybe you needed to see them to sort yourself out. See your past roads to figure out your future path. See who you were on each step of the way to determine who you will become."

That seemed too simple. She felt changed by what she saw, almost like she wasn't who she thought she was. "And Dad's voice at the end?"

Samar laughed. "Are you or are you not the Chosen One?"

Ashni blew out a breath. She should've expected that sort of answer from Samar. Now, she'd end up with more questions than answers. Who was she now that she was bedridden? Where was she going? To conquer the West of course. Her dream. Her father's dream. None of those visions were about conquering the world, which she always thought was the only goal she should have. *Wasn't that what I was chosen for?*

Then, her dad's voice rang in her head, a memory from long ago. *Ashni, you're different, but in a good way. You've been marked. You are chosen.*

Chosen for what? *Damn it.* She needed to figure that out.

"Why do you think I'm here?" Ashni asked.

Samar gave her a deadpan look. "I can't tell you the lesson or you don't learn it."

"That's not how learning works." Teachers told students the lessons all the time.

"That's exactly how learning works when it comes to life."

Ashni rolled her eyes. Samar was a night nymph, so she probably knew everything there ever was to know, and she'd never outright share.

Sighing, Ashni tried to answer her questions. She wanted to conquer the world and make it Roshan...why? Yes, it was her father's dream, but he had a chance to push her to take over the world and he didn't. He told her to "lead the world" instead. *What does that mean?*

Before she could come up with an answer, Adira stormed in. She threw her sword into a corner. The sword clattered onto the floor. Then, Adira threw herself onto a pillow. She scowled at the floor, obviously trying to burn a hole in it. Every time Adira came in, she seemed more and more upset, and the fact that she threw her sword meant that something was very wrong.

"What are you pouting about?" Ashni asked.

Adira snarled. "Shut the fuck up."

Ashni flinched. Her friend's anger seemed genuine. Ashni couldn't remember a time Adira was truly angry with her, and now Adira looked at her like she was the enemy.

"Hey, don't bring that negative energy here. She's healing," Samar said with a frown.

"Then tell her to shut the fuck up. Damn idiot takes a month nap, and then asks stupid ass questions while she can't get the fuck out of bed." Each word was stained with intense hatred.

Samar handed Adira a cup. "Drink that and calm down."

Adira took the cup. When she sipped whatever was in the cup, her face didn't mend. Her body didn't relax. She appeared ready to take on the gods, and Ashni pitied them.

"What's going on, Adira?" Ashni asked.

Adira didn't even bother to glance in her direction. "There's nothing you can do about it right now."

"Why not?" Ashni asked.

When was the last time she couldn't do something? Couldn't set something right? She thought back to Tau and Midnight Thunder. She hadn't been able to make things right with Tau, no matter how hard she still tried, but she had been able to do so with Midnight Thunder.

Adira sneered at the floor. "Because if I put this cup in your hand, you'd fall over."

Unfortunately, Ashni couldn't argue that. *Why is Adira so angry?* It had to do with the bruises on Nakia's face. There had to be a connection. Which meant they Ashni had failed the people she was meant to protect. Guilt twisted in her gut, turning her mouth sour.

She thought back to her vision of meeting Adira, riding with Adira. Was she great in Adira's eyes? Not at the moment, no. *What do I need to do to be great?* She needed to protect those who trusted her to do so and she failed. *Who am I if not a protector?*

***

Nakia had trouble sitting on the throne, beyond the ache of her body. It was a visual lie, but she needed to be strong for the people. Much of her was sore and tired. Her back was bruised. Her thighs ached. She couldn't even imagine what her ass looked like, having been beaten last night with a riding crop meant for a horse.

Asad had become particularly brutal. Everything hurt, down to the roots of her hair and even her fingernails. She finally understood why some people thought it shouldn't be acceptable to beat a slave to excess.

"You little bitch." Asad shot up the dais and shoved her out of the seat. "Did you think we wouldn't find out?" His voice boomed, and he pointed behind him where Jay strode in, holding Saniyah by the wrist. Jay was calm but gave off a vibe like he could tear the world apart if he decided to.

Nakia groaned. She shook away the ringing in her ears and glared at Asad. He glared right back.

"Find out about what?" Nakia asked.

"The army from your sister's spouse," Jay replied.

Wicus' army. Why did that catch their interest? Nakia arched an eyebrow and shook her head. "What about them?"

Asad grabbed her by her hair, yanking her face to his. "He's moving massive amounts of troops. Does he think he can attack us?"

These guys have no clue. "I don't know what the hell you're talking about. If anything, the troops are probably going north. He wants it to be secure, as goes his agreement with us. It has nothing to do with an attack. They're not close to the city, right?" Nakia replied.

"As if they can't be rerouted to attack us," Jay said. That was true, but they'd see an attack coming a mile away.

Nakia smirked. "Why would Wicus go to war with the Roshan Empire now? It doesn't make sense."

"He sees this as a chance to free himself from the Empire," Jay said. "He said so himself."

"You contacted him?" Nakia held in a gasp. Wicus had to have lied to the brothers...hopefully. And the brothers could be lying to her about any number of things. Why didn't Wicus say they got in touch with him? *He might have tried, but it's a little harder to get in touch with you since Asad is glued to your ass.*

"Of course." Jay inclined his chin, smug as hell. "We told him the Empire had no desire to control him or his territory. He agreed and will leave his troops in the north."

Well, the latter had already been the plan. The former was probably a lie. Wicus was a man of his word, yet he was also practical. Would he find advantages to Jay's offer? He might assume Jay's word was as good as Ashni's, and then all bets were off. She'd press on if he dared to believe the brothers. *I'll have Layla get in touch with him and find out what's going on with Wicus. At least Thia has Saffi.*

"You think you can outflank us, princess?" Asad sneered, using her title as if it was a curse.

"We've been to war," Jay said. "You've only played a game."

Asad released her hair and kicked her in the ribs. Pain rippled through her body. Coughing, she curled into a ball to protect herself. *If only I could laugh in their faces. I've played a game.* They hadn't figured what was going on yet.

"You shouldn't go behind our backs and try to do things. You're only here because we allow it," Asad said.

Liar. The moment they got rid of her; they'd be faced with consequences. Hell, even the way they wielded power through her now was illegal. Killing her, though, would start a revolution or create all sorts of other chaos. No matter how much Chandra might love her children, she'd need to do something about this nonsense.

"I'm here because you need me," she said.

"Nakia," Saniyah said, wide eyes locked on her. "Don't."

Nakia laughed. She couldn't *not*. The tension in Asad's face every time she said something was more than enough to keep her talking. For a brief second, it seemed that he recalled she hurt him, both physically and verbally.

Asad leaned down and grabbed her, fingers wrapping completely around her neck. "Do you like this?" he asked.

She stared him in the eye. "We both know if your big brother didn't have Saniyah, I'd have put my knife between your ribs that first time."

Asad blew a column of smoke through his nose. "You really like to get beaten, don't you?"

"You hit me because you can't hit Ashni," Nakia replied. She knew all of this happened because they couldn't touch Ashni.

He squeezed. "Because Ashni's dead. She's not coming back to avenge you."

She choked for a moment, gasping for air, and then he eased his grip just enough to let her respond. "I don't need her to avenge me. I can protect myself and my people."

Both brothers laughed. "You can't even protect your ribs," Jay said.

"Neither can he," Nakia snapped back. Jay gave her a solid punch to the ribs, causing her to grunt, and still she pushed on. "I can protect a legacy."

"What legacy? Ashni's filthy habit of bonding with barbarians?"

"Like your dad?"

Jay punched her in the shoulder, and pain burned through her. It felt like he shattered her entire body with one blow. The yell boiled up her throat. She couldn't keep it in.

"You leave our father out of this. Ashni's done nothing but tarnish his image since birth," Jay said.

The rage they felt for Ashni over rumors of her birth and relationships with "barbarians" was beyond Nakia. Did they think Ashni ruined their father, or did feel rejected by Ashni? She couldn't figure it out. *It's not something you need to figure out.* Still, Nakia couldn't let it go, her questions got under their skin. The brothers were upset that Ashni chose barbarians over them.

"Your father accepted Ashni. Why can't you?" Nakia asked.

"Ashni thought she was special because our father accepted her. Ashni thought the gods had chosen her because of her lightning. Hell, even Mom pretended Ashni was worth something because it made her feel better about being tricked into having the damn girl." Jay replied. "Ashni's nothing. That's why she's so attached to barbarians. They're not worthy and neither is she."

Okay. They felt slighted. Ashni seemed special to everyone important to the brothers, including the gods. That was why they hated her. They wanted that attention and never got over it.

"You speak as if you think she's still alive," Nakia said.

Jay hissed. "She's dead, like she should've been a long time ago. Ashni wasn't supposed to exist."

"Because your mother got tricked? Wouldn't it make more sense to just believe Ashni's your blood sister?" Nakia asked.

Jay wasn't moved. "Except she wasn't. She got things that weren't owed to her because Dad was easy to fool. He was too carefree. He didn't know how to protect himself."

"And you do?"

"I know how to protect myself, my brothers, and this empire. We don't even need this giant waste of land. Ashni's too stupid to even realize logistically this would be impossible to rule from Helli."

Nakia didn't believe him. Ashni didn't seem to have a problem staying connected to Helli, but it might be for the simple fact that the territory had a ruler now. What would happen when Chandra died and someone new was on the throne? It didn't matter. Ashni mattered. These people mattered.

"So, you care and she doesn't?" Nakia asked.

Jay threw his shoulders back. "I was trained for this. No one ever bothered to try to show Ashni how to lead. It would've been a waste."

Nakia had a feeling that was a lie, but maybe Jay believed it. She glanced at Asad. His jaw tensed, yet he didn't say anything. Maybe he was resigned to not inheriting the Empire, but she couldn't believe that either.

"Was Asad trained for this?" Nakia asked.

"Don't concern yourself over us," Jay replied, the conversation obviously over.

The day went on. When she got a chance, Nakia wrote to Wicus, if only to make sure he hadn't sold her out. She also had Adira look into it to make sure Wicus didn't lie to her. Then she checked on the troops going into Tariq. They had begun filtering people out, directing any non-fighters to Khenshu on Naren's orders. At least that was in order.

Unfortunately, it was taking a long time. Nearly three weeks already. They would have to hold on for weeks more, hoping the brothers didn't catch on to what was happening.

***

Ashni could drink medicine now. She could also sit up with no problem, and all that meant was that she had a clear view of Adira sharpening her sword in the corner. Preparing for war. With whom and where? Surely not in the palace.

Questions swirled in her mind. Why was she still in this room instead of in her bed? Why was Samar still treating her instead of advising Ashni's doctor? Ashni had her own royal physician, and Samar's time was better spent with her people or with soldiers. Yet, Samar was the only doctor ever there. Why was Varaza standing off to the side, quiet, poised, and baggy-eyed, and not with Nakia? What was happening in the palace? No one would answer even the simplest of things, but she decided to give inquiring another try.

"Is anyone dead?" Ashni asked.

"Not yet," Adira replied, eyeing Ashni over her blade.

"Who are we killing?"

Samar seemed to float over and put a cup to Ashni's mouth filled to the brim with clear liquid. "No one for you to concern yourself with."

Ashni drank the bitter concoction. *Sometimes, I miss not being able to taste things*. She fought against making a face. "Why is medicine never sweet?"

"To punish your stupid ass for getting injured," Adira replied.

It was like this whenever she was there, standing guard with Varaza, and neither Adira nor Layla ever explained. Adira was full of snark now, barely containing her rage. Sometimes, Adira stared at her like she wanted to stab Ashni in the chest. She searched her mind for how she might have wronged Adira, but nothing came to her.

"Adira, maybe you should deliver that potion to Saniyah," Samar said. It sounded like a pleasant suggestion, yet Ashni knew it was a hard command.

Adira scowled and sharpened her sword with more fury. Someone was possibly going to die by the end of the day. *I hope like hell it's not me. I probably couldn't fight her off if I tried right now*. Adira's energy was wild, and she probably could've yanked the sun from the sky if she desired to do so.

"What does Saniyah need a potion for?" Ashni asked, knowing what the answer would be already.

"None of your damn business!" Adira glared at her.

"Obviously, since you're so pissed at me."

Adira took a breath, taking in so much air that Ashni could see her chest move. "I'm not pissed with you. It's the whole situation."

Ashni sighed. "So, what the hell is the situation?"

Adira's nostrils flared, and it looked like she chewed on her tongue for a second. "When you can wave your swords around, I'll tell you."

Ashni would hold her friend to that. All she could do now was sit, take her medicine, eat, and wait for the few minutes she got each day with Nakia, the highlight of her day. Well, that and when Adira had to leave. She hated seeing Adira in obvious pain and not being able to do anything about it.

Of course, she hated seeing Nakia in pain, too. Nakia always had bruises and cuts. Samar almost always had to treat Nakia, no one offered an explanation for the injuries, and it agonized Ashni each time she saw her beloved. *Who dared put hands on my hellcat?* She couldn't imagine who could be so bold. Except maybe Amal and there was no way he was there.

Nakia came into her room and curled up at her side. She smiled and Nakia managed a smile back. Ashni had enough range of motion to turn and could lift her arm enough to caress Nakia's face. She was so careful.

"What happened to your face?" Ashni asked. Her beloved's beautiful visage was covered in old and fresh bruises. Both of her eyebrows had been stitched. There was a split in her top lip, an old cut at the bottom, and a gash at the corner of her mouth.

Tears slid down Nakia's cheek from an almost swollen shut, purple eye. "I don't want to lie to you."

Ashni brushed Nakia's hair back. "You could tell me."

Nakia gave her a sorrowful smile. "When you're stronger."

Did that mean physically, mentally, emotionally? She could be there for Nakia, for everyone in so many ways, even if she could barely move. Soon, she'd be able to be there for them physically as a warrior. She had gained weight. Faded dark lines still ran down her body, but her color had returned.

"Why won't you tell me?" Ashni asked.

Nakia put a hand on Ashni's hip. "Because we all need you to focus on you. We're holding things together."

"Is that why your face looks that way, and why there are days Adira looks ready to kill me?"

Nakia wrapped her arms around Ashni. "Adira's going through something right now. She's having trouble dealing with it."

"What happened?"

Nakia shook her head. "It's not my place to tell." They were silent for a moment. "Would you want children?"

Ashni blinked. "Huh?"

"Children. One of the things about being married is producing children. We can't do that."

Ashni shook her head. "What brought this on?" *Is it connected to Adira? To her anger?*

"I've been thinking about you and your childhood a lot.''

"Oh." Okay, so nothing with Adira. "That's funny. I had...visions about my childhood."

Nakia's brow wrinkled. "What were your visions about?"

"Relationships with my parents, my horse, and my siblings. I think it was to set me on a path, and I'm not sure about the path yet." Maybe it was to help her work through whatever this mess was. "You mentioned us producing children and we can't do that. You've been thinking about me not being my father's, but him raising me anyway?"

Nakia nodded. "You are his, aren't you?"

"Completely. He raised me. That's Roshan culture," Ashni said. Nakia's library was packed with knowledge about Roshan culture. Nakia was fascinated with it, wanted to know what she married into, and Ashni loved to indulge her. Nakia could probably teach her about the Roshan at this point.

"It is Roshan culture, and it makes so much sense for the Roshan's beginnings," Nakia replied slowly, as if choosing her words carefully. "Times were uncertain. Raise who would take care of you when you were older. Raise who you could trust to carry on your name. Put yourself into a child to live on through that child. Why didn't your brothers accept that?"

Ashni shrugged. "I just assumed it was all the talk."

"Why do you think the nobles talked about you?"

Ashni shook her head. "I was an easy target. The only girl. I had lighter skin. Lightning. Dad loved us, raised us all."

"Gave you all the same attention?"

"Yeah. He was always happy to be included in anything we did, and in turn, we liked when he included us. The nobles wanted to sow discontent to take over the Empire through us. It worked in the sense that it divided us," Ashni said.

Nakia's face scrunched up a bit. "Divided or just split you from the older brothers?"

Ashni stared at her beloved, wondering why she was so curious about her brothers. "I think they split, too, even if they pretended, they didn't. Asad spent a lot of time with Jay instead of Amal, and Asad also spent a lot of time on his own. I'm sure they were all looking to stab each other in the back at some point, but they've focused on me first."

Nakia chewed on her lip. "So, they'd just as soon kill each other as they, would you?"

"I don't know if they'd kill each other, although they'd do anything to be the one to get the throne. They've had poison dripped into their ears for a long time."

"They'd kill you."

"Because they don't think I'm family. My mother raised us to love your family, but only Fahim, Kek, and Kiran accept me as their sister."

Nakia sighed. "So, if we were to have children, how would that work?"

Ashni's cheeks burned. "We could adopt, or one of us could get pregnant if you'd like."

Nakia flinched at that, pain in her usually vibrant green eyes. Ashni kissed the end of Nakia's nose.

"What's wrong, kitten? Tell me," Ashni said, her voice a begging whisper.

"As long as we raise the child, the child is ours?" Nakia asked with a wobble in her throat. Tears welled up in her eyes.

"Of course. Why? Do you want children now? We can start looking."

Nakia sobbed in reply, and the sound cut through Ashni. *What did I miss?* Adira was hurting. Nakia was hurting. It was like the world was crumbling, and no one wanted to tell her why. She had never felt so useless and beaten in her entire life.

When Nakia's sobs quieted down, she fell asleep. Ashni gazed at her beloved. Nakia managed to look larger than life, carrying a weight she didn't deserve. Not alone anyway. As her spouse, Ashni should share the load. *So, I do have to get stronger.*

Chapter Thirteen

EVERYDAY ASAD AND JAY forced Nakia and Saniyah to take at least two meals with them. Nakia had to sit across from Saniyah, her friend and mentor, be able to free her from this hell. As the reigning monarch, she should be able to stop this sort of terror.

"Soon," Nakia said under breath, a promise to herself, to everyone. Her plan might be slow, but it was working.

"Soon what? You'll find you actually do like being hit?" Asad slapped Nakia in the mouth.

After many weeks of abuse, Nakia thought she'd get used to being hit. Her ears rang as her mouth throbbed. Still, she remained patient. According to Naren and Hafiz, things were slow, but going well. They hadn't aroused any suspicions yet, and they were almost done.

"It's almost boring," Asad said.

Jay ate a dumpling. "Of course, the West is boring."

"And when do you plan to leave?" Saniyah asked, rubbing the marks on her neck. Jay got a sick joy out of choking Saniyah to the point his fingerprints might be etched in her flesh for all eternity. Not that it mattered, as he had left a much more permanent mark on her, changed her life forever.

"You're coming with me." Jay reached for Saniyah's abdomen.

Saniyah slapped his hand away, glowering. "Never!"

Jay's hand went right for her throat, and she gagged. "Who the hell do you think you are?"

Saniyah showed no fear, glared at him with all the fire and hatred in her belly. "I am Saniyah Gyan. I am a noble of the Roshan Empire. My family legacy is as old as yours."

He curled his lip in disgust. "You threw your status away when you married that barbarian fisherwoman."

"You can't pull my rank by your whim or jealousy. You'll never be half the warrior or leader my damn fisherwoman is, and your father fucking knew it."

Jay's grip tightened, and Saniyah's face turned red. She clawed at his beefy hand, but he didn't budge. Her eyes glazed over. Nakia threw hot cereal at Jay. The slush splashed on his face, but he barely winced.

"You're going to kill her!" Nakia sought something else to hit him with, curling her fingers around a glass.

"Control your bitch, Asad!" Jay snarled.

Asad put his hands up. "Control yourself. You're going to kill her. Mom won't look kindly on that, nor would any noble families in support of us. The Gyan name goes back just as far as Akshay and is just as prestigious."

Jay's face remained twisted, but he loosened his grip some. Saniyah gasped for air, his hand still on her throat. She dug her nails into his fingers, trying to get him off of her.

Murdering Saniyah was up there with murdering a royal. There was no way either of them would inherit the Empire if Jay killed Saniyah with Asad sitting there and doing nothing to stop it. They could get away with a lot, but not that.

They were able to get away with this for months by claiming they were helping Nakia understand how to rule a piece of the Empire without Ashni. Chandra was busy mourning Ashni. It would've been humane to let Chandra know Ashni, but they couldn't risk the communication. No one knew who touched Chandra's missives before they got to her. The last thing they needed was someone in Helli to tell the brothers Ashni was still alive. Jay and Asad assumed she was lying every time she said it, but if she told the empress, then things would be different. They'd know she wasn't lying because no one in their right mind would lie to Chandra. They'd hunt Ashni down before their mother could find her.

"Do you want to murder your child?" Asad asked his brother.

Jay blinked, coming back to himself. His eyes softened along with his grip. Saniyah dropped to the floor, gasping for air. Her face was near blue, her neck the color of watered-down wine.

Jay glowered at his brother. "Worry about your own child. Or lack thereof."

Nakia swallowed down vomit. Asad yanked Nakia close. He squeezed her around the middle.

"She hasn't bled since I've bedded her and her servants said she has sickness in the morning," Asad said.

Until recently, these had been lies her servants told, but now she was late and had been sick several mornings in a row. *Don't think about it.* She didn't understand why he was so interested, yet now she got it. It was just to hurt Ashni even more. He would do what Ashni couldn't. He put his permanent mark on Nakia. Jay did the same with Saniyah. They were demented.

"You two boast about things that'll get you killed," Nakia said.

Jay was on borrowed time. Adira planned to slay him, and Nakia might kill Asad with her bare hands, especially if her condition was true. He might be the better fighter, but Nakia had raw rage on her side.

"Do you think the Amir would approve of this? Of how you've treated me? He blessed my relationship with Adira, which means we were blessed by the divine. You can't deny that," Saniyah said.

Jay went silent. He had trespassed on the divine, something sacred. And the same could be said of Asad. Her marriage had been blessed by the empress, the daughter of a god in her own right. These two were tempting the gods.

"You know you'll pay for this," Saniyah said, staring Jay down. Nakia had to admire her courage and her faith.

Jay rolled his shoulders. "You forget, we are also divine."

Saniyah scoffed. "You think you're above the Amir?"

"The Amir is dead," Jay said.

Saniyah scowled. "He still hears and sees. The Empress still hears and sees. You might've lied to the empress. You might've changed my life, but you haven't changed me, and you can't keep this hidden forever."

"I have no reason to hide," Jay said. "You two fail to understand, we're well within our rights to do this."

"No one's going to save you." Asad patted Nakia's knee. "You need to eat. Wouldn't want my child to be underdeveloped."

Asad passed a plate of cooked vegetables under Nakia's nose and she was hit with a wave of nausea. She gagged, slapping her hand over her mouth. Her stomach twisted. Bile burned her throat. Asad laughed and shoved the dish closer. Nakia pushed the plate away and took off running. She needed privacy if she was going to be sick.

She barely made it to a different room before her body erupted and she spewed the little bit of food she had eaten all over the floor. Servants fell upon her almost immediately.

"Highness, forgive us!" They cleaned her and the floor as best they could.

Nakia groaned. "It's not your fault."

This is the price. It had to be worth it. They saved thousands of lives, but that didn't mean she didn't want to break down in tears. She wanted to throw herself in Ashni's arms and beg her to make everything better, yet Ashni still wasn't in any shape to take on her brothers. Jay and Asad were deadly. Ashni wasn't ready for deadly.

One servant rubbed her back, trying to soothe her. It wouldn't work. Only one thing would ease her ache. "The medicine doesn't work with them."

Tears stung Nakia's eyes. Every single time she was with Asad, her servants made sure that after, she took a potion to prevent pregnancy. It was usually very effective. She and Saniyah weren't so fortunate. Even potions prepared by Samar did nothing. It was like the gods were on the brothers' side. The gods were often cruel.

"Highness, please don't cry."

Nakia didn't realize she was weeping until she saw the droplets splash on the floor. It hurt so much that it overflowed. *Pull it together, damn it. Do you think Ashni is fucking crying over what happened to her?* A dark chuckle rippled inside of her mind.

You're not Ashni and you're not divine. You've got nothing working for you.

Nakia took a deep breath. No, she had things working for her. She was about to completely flank the brothers and win this whole thing. She had nobles on her side and the military. All she needed was for Layla's people to be safe. There were sacrifices she needed to deal with, like Saniyah. Saniyah wasn't crying. *So, suck it up and carry on.*

Sniffling, she wiped her face. There were people who would have much worse than she did if she didn't keep it together. Taking several deep breaths, she managed to calm her nerves. Her stomach, however, felt like it was wringing itself out.

"We can try other items, Highness."

Nakia shook her head. "Samar made the last few. And before her, the royal physician. The gods seem determined for me to carry the spawn of a demon."

Why, though? What have I done? She couldn't understand why she'd be punished this way. She'd take the beatings. Cuts would mend and bones would heal. A child was forever. She'd have to take care of the child of a man who had forced himself on her countless times, violated her because it was fun. She'd have to look at his child for the rest of her life and live with it. And knowing Ashni...Ashni would accept and love this fucking abomination.

A servant clutched her biceps. "No, Highness, you mustn't look at it that way. This child's yours, not his."

Nakia snorted. Nothing felt like hers anymore, not even her body. Asad possessed every bit of her. Well, he could have her, but not everything Ashni built.

The servants helped Nakia to her feet and took her to her room to bathe and change. Her stomach didn't settle, even after all of that. She went to see Samar, even though it meant seeing Ashni.

Ashni's convalescence was going well, according to Samar. She could hold down meals and had a steady appetite. She could move, do little workouts, and complain with the best of them.

Right now, though, she was asleep. She still slept more than she ever did. Nakia couldn't help staring at Ashni, trying to will her better.

"You just missed her being awake," Layla said from her spot by Ashni's bed.

Nakia brushed Ashni's hair from her face. "That's fine. How was she?"

"Up and moving," Layla answered.

"They tried to spar." Samar rolled her eyes.

Nakia gasped. "You didn't let them, did you?"

Samar arched an eyebrow. "Of course I didn't."

Nakia breathed a sigh of relief. Samar wouldn't allow them to be so reckless. She sat down next to Samar, who was mixing potions, for Ashni, for Nakia, for Saniyah. The only one the potions seemed to work for was Ashni.

"What do you need?" Samar asked.

"I feel sick. It's lasted almost an hour and it hasn't gone away." *Please have something to make this better. Please.*

Samar glanced at Nakia's abdomen. Nakia squirmed. She hated that people knew. It was like she had a festering sore and Samar, the brothers, and the servants scratched at the wound with their eyes. She wrapped her arms around herself, as if trying to block their view, like that would make it all go away.

"It might be best to let it resolve itself. This situation is like nothing I've ever combated. It's like the Darkness itself is against us," Samar said.

"But why?" Nakia's voice cracked.

Things were bleak if Samar thought the Darkness was against them. That was like saying everything was against them. There was no way to regain her body, no way to regain control of herself.

Samar wrapped her arms around Nakia. "We could live a thousand years and not understand the gods. We cannot comprehend the Darkness, so it will always be beyond us."

That wasn't what Nakia wanted to hear, and she wept. She couldn't be strong anymore, not when it felt like she was decaying inside. She felt Layla's arms around her, and she crumbled against Layla. She stayed like that for a few minutes, only coming back to herself as Adira showed up with a message from Naren. *Please be good news.* Wiping away her tears, Nakia unsealed the letter.

"Is it Tariq? Tiq?" Layla asked.

Nakia felt like she could breathe. "He's gotten almost everyone out who needs to be out."

"Ready to make a move," Adira said.

"He says in a week at the least. He's setting up a defense."

Adira nodded. "Smart move. He actually learned while he was out on campaign."

Layla smiled. "Told you he was more than a pretty face."

"I promise you none of us thought he was a pretty face," Nakia said. Layla chuckled and gave Nakia a squeeze. Hope dared to blossom in her chest. Then it faded as another wave of nausea hit. Ashni's dream and everyone else might be fine, but she was done for, the price too high to pay without tears.

***

Ashni moved with Adira, going through the paces with their swords in the hall right outside of Ashni's tiny convalescing room. She figured out they were in a part of the palace that was under construction, yet now it seemed abandoned. There was no bustle, no servants. It was quiet, only the sounds of her grunting and their swords clashing echoed through the place.

It felt like forever since Ashni held her weapons, and they were still like extensions of herself. Weakness pulled her to the floor, made her motions slow like honey.

Adira took it easy on Ashni, on Samar's orders, but it felt good to move, good to hold her weapons. She pushed against Adira and found herself on her ass moments later. Adira sneered.

"For all of Samar's potions and balms, you're still worthless," Adira said.

Ashni coughed, biting down the agony that hummed through her. It shouldn't have been so easy for Adira. "Say that to Samar's face."

"I'm saying it to yours. You're weak as a kitten while your hellcat is trying to hold your damn empire together with spit and fire!"

"Adira," Samar's calm voice carried out from her corner.

Adira sucked her teeth and turned away. Ashni climbed to her feet, then Adira cracked her across the face with the hilt of her sword and she was down again. Samar didn't say anything about that one. Ashni was appreciative of her silence, even though she couldn't do anything against Adira. She was down many more times before Adira left.

Layla arrived with a hearty meal of stew. Ashni went back into her room and ate while Samar gave her a tart potion and soothed her wounds with sweet-smelling salves and medicated linens.

"Mom, maybe you shouldn't let Adira spar with her," Layla said.

"They both need it and since they bruise each other, I've learned more about making medicines for her biology," Samar replied.

Ashni twisted her mouth up. "I've become an experiment?"

"You've been an experiment, my dear. Do you have any idea what it's like coming up with any sort of medicine for you? Your body fights the strangest things. Poison, you push out like grapes. Antidote, your body decides it doesn't need it. And when I make something that should fortify your body, your body completely rejects it. I don't even know if anything I've done is the reason you're still standing," Samar said.

Ashni scratched her head. "Witchcraft usually works when conventional medicine doesn't."

"Your mother's witchcraft?"

"Yes."

Samar shook her head. "No, that wouldn't work at all."

"You handle everyone else like magic. And whenever I have a normal wound, you're fine with that."

"Yes, thank you for not being poisoned constantly, especially with something of unknown origins. It would've been a huge blow to my self-esteem."

Ashni chuckled. She was improving. If not Samar's medicine, what was healing her? *You're the daughter of two demi-gods and the Chosen One. You better be damn hard to kill.*

Despite complaining, Samar continued her work. Even if Samar was frustrated, her work might still be helping Ashni get back on her feet. "I do want to thank you for your hard work," Ashni said.

Samar gave her a smile. "You don't have to thank me. You know I view you as a daughter. I don't want you to die. I don't want you to be permanently out of commission."

"Why?" Ashni found herself asking. "I mean, I get because of Layla, but why accept me as a daughter?" Months had passed, and she was still troubled by her visions from the poison. Samar wasn't one of the relationships she got to experience a second time.

Samar studied her. "Beyond the fact that Layla attached herself to you like a weird leech, your father impressed me. He never made me feel conquered. He made me feel like I was a part of something, and he opened his arms to Layla when you started saying she was your sister. You remind me of him in that sense. One day, you'll get there."

"I'm not there yet?" Ashni blinked. "I make people feel conquered?"

"No, you don't pause long enough for that to happen. Your mother said your father used to be the same way. You treat people like they're people. Your father did that. Your mother does that. I think it's one of your greatest strengths."

Ashni nodded. That felt good to know. "An injury can take away from my ability to lead, though."

"I don't think that's true. It could take away your ability to ride along on conquest, but conquering isn't leading."

That sounded vaguely familiar. *I charge you with leading the world*. Her father told her to lead. Adira hadn't been impressed with conquest, hadn't considered it great.

"You should rest," Samar said.

Sleep seemed to be the best medicine, so Ashni didn't argue. She collapsed into bed, feeling the effect of Adira's workout as soon as she was down. Sleep came easy, and she always woke up feeling more like herself. Except that was usually when she woke up on her own. Waking up because someone crawled into bed with her was another matter.

Her instincts were on high alert, her mind ready to react when she realized she wasn't alone. Her heart felt like it might explode for the second, so startled by the sudden intrusion in her bed. She jolted up, but then recognized the feel of the body next to her. Gathering Nakia in her arms, she settled back down. Nakia curled into her.

"Are you all right?" Ashni asked, surprised her beloved had climbed into bed.

Nakia visited her often, although never like this. She tended to keep her distance, almost like Ashni was poisonous. Ashni was pleased she seemed to be over that.

"Fine," Nakia whimpered. "Finding out a lot about myself without you around."

"I am around, and I'm fit enough to help around the kingdom. Maybe I can't do any heavy lifting, but I'm more than just my fancy muscles." Ashni smiled in the dark, even though Nakia probably couldn't see. The smile didn't stop the bleed in her heart. Her spouse should be able to rely on her, lean on her, share the burden.

Nakia sniffled. "I have everything handled. Just...please get better soon."

"I am, which is why I'm taking all of Samar's medicines and sparring with Adira, even though I'm almost certain she's trying to kill me."

She wasn't joking this time, sure the only reason she wasn't dead was because Samar never left the room. It wasn't like Varaza could stop Adira. Varaza was an amazing warrior, but Adira was gifted in ways Ashni couldn't explain.

Nakia stroked her back. "Don't be upset with Adira. She's dealing with a lot."

That wasn't the point. None of them seemed to understand she wasn't upset with their behavior. "I need to help her. And you. I'm on my feet. My mind is clear. Let me help."

Nakia was quiet for a long time. The silence burned a hole in Ashni's soul. She itched to be there for all of them, punish whoever dared to hurt them, and take all of their pain away.

"What are your thoughts on children?" Nakia asked in a small voice.

Ashni rolled her neck and shoulders. *This question again?* It had to mean something.

"Children in general, children of people close to us, or children of our own?" Ashni asked. *Is she worried about securing our legacy? There's so much more to do. Are we ready for a child?* Still, Nakia was from a culture where married women were expected to have children, so maybe that was nagging at her now.

"Our own?" Nakia's voice cracked and cut through Ashni, but she wasn't sure why. Having their own children should've made her happy. Instead, it was harder to breathe.

Eventually, Ashni found her voice. "Of course. If I have a child, then you have one as well, and vice versa."

"If you have a child?" Nakia sounded on the verge of tears.

"It could happen." It wasn't in her plan, but they hadn't really talked about how they'd go about starting their family. "I always figured I'd adopt a child, like I adopted a sister."

"That would be enough for you? You wouldn't need to carry a baby to have it be yours?"

Ashni kissed Nakia's forehead. "The child would be mine, through raising the kid and passing on my legacy. Come on, kitten, we've gone through this. Passing on your legacy's the important thing in the Roshan. Your legacy is in behavior, not blood."

"True."

"Layla's more a sibling to me than my three older brothers. And you know the history, possibly better than I do."

Nakia nodded against her. "Family was built through emotional bonds because life was hard on the plains and people died, especially children. To keep tribes going, you have to keep the children thriving, so no child could be left orphaned."

"We didn't even have a word for orphans until we started to interact with other communities. So, I'm fine with adopting."

Nakia sighed. The sound made Ashni's stomach drop. It was like she had made this worse somehow. She wanted to give Nakia the world, but the way Nakia sounded, it felt like the world had fallen away from her.

"Are you sure?" Nakia asked.

"Yes." Ashni licked her lips. "Do you want to carry a baby? That's fine, too. There are women couples who do that. We could even pick a man who'd help."

Nakia went stiff. "I don't know. I never thought about it."

"Isn't that a big part of your culture?" Ashni thought that was what this whole thing was about. Nakia wanted to and was being shy about it since Ashni planned to adopt or was hesitant because Ashni had been injured.

"It is."

"If you want to have a baby, we can figure it out. There are so many options for us." Ashni thought she was being helpful and understanding, but Nakia started sobbing against her. It seemed like she couldn't be more wrong. She wrapped her arms around Nakia and held her tight. Each sound hacked through her like a blunt sword, taking chunks of her soul. Ashni didn't know what to do, what to say. Her voice took on a pleading tone. "Talk to me, kitten. What happened? What can I do?"

"Hold me." The whimper that escaped Nakia made Ashni believe that was the best thing for right now.

"Now and always." Ashni kissed the top of her head, needing to take Nakia's pain away. "Share your burden with me. You'd scold me if this was the other way around."

Nakia shook her head. "I can't."

Ashni looked into the darkness of her room. "I'm stronger than you think." *And if I'm not, I'm going to get my ass there now.*

"You're the strongest person I know, but I have to let you heal, just as you would let me."

Ashni sighed, feeling weary down to her bones. "I'm not sure what brought this on, but I'd love and cherish any child between us. It doesn't matter how we got the child. I'd teach the child how to rule, how to be a warrior, and how to play chess."

Tears poured from Nakia's eyes, dampening the blankets, Ashni's shirt, her skin, yet Ashni still couldn't understand why. The only thing that came to mind was that Nakia was pregnant and didn't think Ashni would approve, but that was ridiculous. Nakia would never...unless the gods had stepped in.

Still lost, Ashni whispered, "I'm always here for you, kitten."

She held Nakia until sleep took her. Ashni's thoughts spun in the darkness. *What the fuck is going on? A leader would know and act. A leader would make things better.*

Chapter Fourteen

NAKIA SAT ON HER throne and went through her usual paperwork while trying to keep down the rumble in her belly. Her stomach twisted. She wanted to vomit but refused. She was sick all the time now. She wasn't sure if it was the abomination growing inside of her or waiting for word from Naren. Word should be coming any day now.

What if the feeling actually came from Ashni being so supportive? It haunted her, the truth stalking her. Ashni would support her, accept this demon, raise and love it as her own...while Nakia wished it dead. *What does that say about me?* She didn't deserve Ashni, especially since she could hardly hold what Ashni built for her together. Ashni had done so much for her and she had failed Ashni.

The back of Nakia's throat burned and tears were close; she swallowed them. The pregnancy made her emotional. She needed focus. Control. And she needed Naren to tell her Tariq and Tiq were safe!

Layla came up from a shadow with a scroll in hand, and Nakia couldn't help but smile. It ached with hope. Layla smirked. That was all Nakia needed. More confirmation came from a bellow as Asad charged into the room.

"You dare fuck with me!" Asad flung a fireball at Nakia's face.

Layla leaped in front of Nakia and opened a void, vanishing the fire. "You want to play? I'm game now."

Nakia gasped at the gaping hole of blackness in front of them that had eaten the flame so readily. When Layla snapped her fingers, the void vanished.

Asad chuckled. "So, you actually think building an army to take me will work out?"

"That army is to protect the people of Tariq and Tiq," Nakia replied.

Asad shook his head. "The second your troops engaged mine, you started a rebellion against the throne. My mother will use the might of the Empire against you and yours."

Nakia inclined her chin. "I don't care. You won't massacre Layla's people."

She didn't know what Chandra would do, yet something inside of her said it would be the right thing, even if she was fighting Jay and Asad.

Snarling, Asad's fists flickered to life, flames dancing on each one like a hot promise. Layla put her hands up as well, black smoke flickering over her knuckles. He tossed flames at the base of the throne, igniting it. A burst of hot air washed over Nakia, singeing her eyebrows, blackening the edges of her robes. The fire shot up higher, so she raised her hands to cover her face.

Layla grabbed Nakia's arm and together they fell into a shadow. For a brief moment, Nakia feared they were running. *To hell with that!* It was time to take a stand now that thousands of lives weren't on the line.

They emerged from a shadow in the throne room, a few paces away from the throne. The throne still crackled, flames licking the sides, cinders sparking to the ceiling. Servants rushed away, darting into the hallways and closing the doors. Smoke billowed toward them.

Asad threw a column of fire at them. Layla shoved Nakia out of the way and then put her hands up, trapping the fire in a void. The void extinguished the flaming column.

"Light will always be overcome by Darkness," Layla said.

"You savage Shadow Beasts and your obsession with evil," Asad sneered. "The Sun always banishes the Dark."

Twin pillars of fire swirled around Asad up to the ceiling. Layla didn't flinch as the temperature in the room climbed higher than the fire. Black fumes wafted from Layla, growing with every passing second. Layla's eyes went black, and the right side of her face was hidden in a shadow. Glowing red spots popped up in the onyx aura, and the aura growled. This was nothing like when Layla sparred with Ashni. This was her true power, raw, unrestrained, and hungry. The walls shook.

Nakia was so invested in their display that she crumpled when something hit her from behind. Her knees slammed into the floor, aching from the impact, and her very bones shook. White-hot pain burned through her body, licking under her skin. It felt like she had been thrown off of a cliff. She coughed. A long line of drool hit the floor.

Nakia glanced up at the imposing visage of Jay towering over her with Saniyah just a step behind him. She blocked out a high-pitched ringing in her ears and gritted her teeth. *Get up.* Not that she'd be able to stop whatever he was about to do on her feet either, but she wouldn't take anything on the floor again.

"We can easily subject you to the same punishment Amal has to live with," Jay said, staring at her as if she was an ant.

"Fuck Amal," Nakia managed to breathe the response out.

Jay went to grab Nakia, and Saniyah grabbed his wrist. He backhanded her and Saniyah went down in a heap. Darkness engulfed Nakia. Back in a shadow. When she emerged, she was in a room with Layla and Saniyah. *Okay, living to fight another day might be the right move here*. It wasn't like she could help Layla do anything when she couldn't move.

"Wait here. I have to get my mother," Layla said.

Nakia wasn't sure where "here" was. Layla vanished. *Why does she need to get her mother?*

Saniyah put a hand on Nakia's shoulder. "Are you all right?" Saniyah asked, her voice soft, calm.

Nakia schooled her features to be as composed as Saniyah. "Yes, of course."

It wasn't like that was the first time a brute hit her, though it felt like everything inside of her turned to dust. How did Saniyah put up with such blows?

"You're bleeding."

Nakia arched an eyebrow. "What?"

Saniyah pointed at her and she followed the finger down. The front of her robe was streaked with blood from her waist down. She gasped.

"What the hell?" Nakia said.

Shadows spread from the corner of the room, and Layla and Samar appeared.

Samar's eyes went directly to Nakia. "Shit, this is not good."

Nakia wasn't sure what that meant, but Samar began ordering her about. Something was wrong. Cramps started in her stomach. Something was wrong with the baby.

***

Ashni found herself on her ass again in the hall. She snarled, as Adira stood over her, brown eye hard as an off-color diamond. This wasn't a sparring match. None of them ever were. They were all lessons in restraint for Adira to not slaughter her.

"You're still so damn weak," Adira said.

"Says you." Ashni took a breath before climbing to her feet. She put her fists up. They had been banned from using weapons after Adira almost decapitated her not too long ago.

"Yes, me, the woman who's about to put you on your ass again. When was the last time you downed me?"

That was a good question. Ashni felt the most like herself as she had in weeks and she could barely touch Adira. *She's not this good, so I must still be weak.* Yet she could move fluidly, she got regular amounts of sleep now, and she wasn't constantly being rubbed down with ointments. She felt like herself. She should be able to at least touch Adira.

"You know, maybe you're as pathetic as Jay. He faced me once and learned never to do it again. Maybe you're scared of me," Adira said, the taunt as clear as the curl of her lips.

"Like hell I am!" Ashni advanced, guard up. "I didn't even fear the Amir when he was alive. I'd never be afraid of you."

Lips pursed, Adira stood in her fighting position. "Then what else could it be? Maybe I've been holding back."

A horrifying possibility. Ashni had beaten Adira many times since taking command of the Roshan military. *What if Adira had been letting her win?* It would help her confidence and help her gain the respect of the soldiers. *What if it was all a lie?*

Adira was one of the greatest warriors she had ever met, especially without a talent or magic or witchcraft. Adira had her wits and her body and used both with masterful precision. Maybe Ashni never could defeat Adira.

A sharp pain in her jaw snapped Ashni out of her thoughts. She stumbled from the hit to the mouth, and she dodged the next blow. She dipped, evaded, ducked, and then ended up kicked in the chest. On the floor again.

Adira yelled, frustrated. "Seriously? It's like I haven't taught you anything! You're so fucking useless now!"

Ashni gritted her teeth and sucked up all the pain in her chest. "I'm not useless. I'm the leader."

Adira scoffed. "To think the Amir chose you. He chose wrong. Then again, so did I since I chose to ride with you."

It was like lightning struck Ashni in her belly. She rushed Adira, which she knew only proved Adira so right. *You thought you were a leader, but you're not. You thought you were a good spouse, but your kitten cries in your arms. Your best friend wants to kill you.* So, who was she?

"Stop daydreaming!" Adira's knuckles were on her cheek again and she was on the floor.

The tang of iron on her tongue jolted part of Ashni's brain, pushing her off of the floor. Her body moved like she knew it could, how it should. And then Adira was finally the one on the floor. They boxed until they were both panting, sprawled out on the floor.

That was much more natural, even if it wasn't the desired outcome. Just being able to go at Adira until they both were exhausted felt good to Ashni. Showing that she was back to her old self—for the most part—was even better. Next time they sparred, she needed to win and then she'd force them to tell her what the hell was going on.

Ashni wiped sweat from her brow, her long hair plastered to her forehead and frazzled out in all directions. It was so much longer than she usually kept it. It needed braids. She leaned against the wall, her hair acting as a decent pillow.

She took a deep breath and gathered her courage. "Why do you hate me?"

Adira blew out a long breath as she sat up as well. "I don't hate you. I don't do this because I hate you."

"You look at me with an intense hatred all the time, like an enemy. Sometimes, I can feel it." Ashni pressed a hand to her gut.

"Oh." Adira turned away and seemed to chew on her words, like she wasn't sure if she should say it. She spoke low, like Ashni wasn't meant to hear, but she couldn't stop herself from saying it. "You look like them."

"Like who?" Ashni cocked an eyebrow.

Adira sighed. "You're still not ready."

Ashni growled. She was sick of hearing that. "What if that's it?"

"What?" Adira's head snapped back to look at her.

"What if I'm not ready because you all keep telling me I'm not?" That was what she heard every single day. It was a self-fulfilling prophecy. "I feel like myself. Hell, maybe even better. But Nakia won't let me help, you're ready to kill me, and Samar is telling me my body is weird."

"I'm trying to prepare you." Adira rubbed her neck, looking uncomfortable.

"I feel good, ready. How am I supposed to feel when the best people I know tell me I'm not enough?"

Adira hung her head. "Maybe we are holding you back."

It seemed like she got through to Adira, so might as well continue on. "Want to tell me what's going on?"

Adira gave Ashni a smirk. "So your hellcat can devour me? Please."

"Since when are you scared of Nakia?" Ashni asked.

Adira pulled her legs up to rest her arms against her knees. She smiled. Actually smiled. It had been ages since she'd done that in Ashni's presence. "You're going to be so proud of her when you find out about this. So proud."

She was proud of her spouse regardless. "Then why are you so angry? Who do I look like?"

Adira shook her head. The story would remain a mystery. It took away the high Ashni had at fighting Adira to a stalemate, and her stomach sank into a pit. Change the world...how had her mother read her so wrong? *How did I ever think I could become great in the sense Adira meant?* How could she do that when she became the worst version of herself? It seemed the poison had worked.

"I should get us something to eat," Adira said.

"Food would be nice, although Samar usually makes me take something with the food. Wherever she is today." Curious, Ashni poked her head into the room and gazed around, but she didn't see Samar anywhere. Ashni couldn't remember a time since she had woken up that Samar wasn't in her corner putting together some type of treatment.

Adira let out a pitiful laugh. "I know."

"Yeah, so Samar can blame you if I eat without whatever medicine she'd want me to take."

Adira chuckled, sounding a little more genuine now. "And she'll be pissed if I don't feed you if she's gone for a while."

"Where'd she go, anyway?"

Adira didn't answer. Ashni scowled. This wouldn't do. Something had to give. Maybe she was a burden. "Would it be...easier if I had died?"

Adira rushed to Ashni's seated form. "Never fucking say that!" She grabbed Ashni's biceps and squeezed. "How dare you? You're so fucking selfish. You're not so special that everything happens because of you."

Ashni didn't mean to, but she yelled, "Because I'm not special, not great? Because you chose wrong? Because my father chose wrong?"

Adira growled. "Shut up."

Ashni rose. "First, I just want to help. Second, look me in the face and tell me that your pain and suffering isn't my fault."

In silence, Adira walked away, the movement beyond a gut punch. Like Ashni wasn't even worth her time, wasn't worth her fury anymore. Ashni's world had collapsed around her, and she hadn't even been allowed to see it. *She told you she chose wrong.*

Ashni resisted the urge to punch the wall, not wanting to risk damaging her hand. Taking some time alone to freshen up, she then ignored Varaza staring at the floor in her room and crawled in the bed. What was the point in living if she let everyone she loved down? The gods chose wrong. *All this time I thought I was Chosen for greatness and all I've done is let my people down. I've ruined it all, just like nobles used to whisper about me. I've ruined his legacy.*

"Hey, stop your pity party and eat," Adira said, putting a tray full of food on her bed. When did she get back?

Ashni grunted in response. Her stomach wouldn't hold much food.

Adira popped her hard on the thigh. "Stop being a little bitch and eat."

"You can leave it and then you can leave," Ashni replied.

"Eat."

Ashni growled, ready to tell Adira to shove it up her ass, but what good would that do? She sat up and accepted the meal tray. She ate the vegetables, beans, and bread and drank the honeyed tea. Silence settled in the room.

After some time, Adira took a breath. "It's not your fault."

Yeah, that was why Adira was trying to hurt her. That was why everyone shut her out. She scowled. "You've already made it known."

Pulling up a chair, Adira rubbed her palms together. "It's easier to hurt you than to face the fact that I'm the one at fault. I'm the one who can't protect the right people. If you go down, I should be able to hold it together until you can get back up."

"Why? You're not me."

Adira glowered at her. "No shit!"

Ashni held up a hand. "I don't mean that as an insult. If I go down, I expect you to back up Nakia and Layla, like you do me. You're the voice of reason. You keep us grounded as we get caught up in lofty ambitions. I'm sure you did that."

"I'm supposed to keep you safe when we're out."

"What?" Ashni looked at Adira like she had eight heads. "I'm not a little kid anymore, Adira. You're supposed to save me from me being me, nothing more."

Adira shook her head. "And I didn't. You got poisoned."

Ashni snorted. Almost dying didn't usually throw them off balance like this. They did it too often. "I've been poisoned before."

"You didn't see what this poison did to you. It was like nothing I've ever seen, and I hadn't protected you from it. You almost died. I wasn't there for you."

Ashni sucked her teeth. "You gonna throw yourself in front of me?" She'd never stand for that. That wasn't Adira's job.

Adira nodded. "Like you'd do."

Ashni narrowed her eyes. "This wasn't your fault. You did what you were supposed to do."

"And so did you. You didn't do anything wrong."

Ashni laughed. "You tried to seriously hurt me on multiple occasions. Samar took our blades away."

Adira's shoulders dropped. "I'm taking it out on you."

I look like them. But...who? "I'm sure you're right to. You're not one to fly off the handle at me unless I deserve it. Even when it brought you the wrath of the biggest jackasses in the kingdom. There's never been a reason for you to back me."

Adira slapped Ashni in the back of the head. "Are you really this much of an idiot? Of course there's a reason to back you. I believe in your dumb ass."

Ashni sputtered. "You just said you chose wrong."

"I was angry! But I still believe in you. I've believed in you since that first battle. Hell, before that, I heard whispers of the Amir's daughter, possibly chosen by the gods because she wielded lightning. Or maybe even the daughter of a god herself and they said this like it was a bad thing. Instead, Khalid presented you proudly. You were his. You were his chosen, and he was the first person to ever see the real me."

"So?"

"He entrusted you to me and you took to me. You were humble enough for instruction, unlike your older brothers. And when I met your mother, I could see why she chose you. You truly are the best mix of them. I've been proud to teach you and stand by you."

Ashni groaned as she finally realized what Adira was to her, even when she tried her damnedest to fight it. "How the fuck am I the middle child even in my emotional family?"

Adira chuckled. "I've been a poor older sister if that's the case."

"I've always thought of you like an aunt. You seem so much wiser than I am and more put together and mature, but nope. I forget you're only a few years older than I am, yet I'd give up almost anything for you. If you're upset with me, I'd let you take your anger out on me with the hopes it would make things better for you. You're my sister."

A small, soft smile settled on Adira's face. "It might not seem like it right now, but I'm honored. Shit is hard. Harder than it's ever been, and no, I can't tell you. Your kitten will beat my ass, and I know she's tough enough to make it work."

"She's a force." Ashni laughed again. It was one of the reasons she loved Nakia.

"That she is."

Silence fell over the room, and Ashni stared into her plate for a long moment. She should feel better, yet she didn't. She was pressed, crumbled up. Adira was another sister she let down then. And that force Ashni loved so much still couldn't count on her. Adira might have been upset when she said it, but she seemed to be right. She chose wrong.

Ashni finished her food. She went back to bed. Adira sat in the corner, guarding her until Ashni fell into her usual fitful sleep.

***

Nakia wailed the whole time she was with Samar and didn't stop when Samar was done trying to heal her. The demon spawn inside her had died. Her baby had died. When Jay had hit her, it had traumatized her body so hard, she miscarried.

She was both broken and relieved. She didn't want that baby and still, it was part of her and now it was gone. She had worked so hard to outmaneuver the brothers, and it all came crashing down in the end. Yes, she saved Layla's people, but she lost Ashni's kingdom and dream. At least she was free of Asad's poison inside of her.

She was fractured, and the pieces were coming back together in pure agony, like each piece had to cut the one it fit with. She curled into a ball on the bed, falling into herself.

"We can't leave her," Saniyah said, but her voice sounded far away.

"We have to take her to Ashni," Layla replied.

Nakia should object, yet she wanted Ashni. She wanted Ashni's arms around her, her sweet kisses and reassuring words. *I need to feel whole again.* Ashni would make her feel like herself or at least keep her safe until she did.

Nakia wasn't sure who moved her, but she knew immediately when she was with Ashni. The familiar scent of berries and honey surrounded her. Whimpering, she curled into Ashni. Arms wrapped around her, and it was like warm water poured over her. She felt better and burst into tears once more.

"Kitten, what's wrong?" Ashni asked, her voice low and gruff.

Nakia didn't answer. Couldn't. Ashni pulled her close. Nakia wanted to share skin with Ashni, if only to feel secure and untouchable. She wanted to rebuild herself with Ashni's care, but how could she ask anything of Ashni after all of this?

"Talk to me, my love. Who hurt you?" Ashni asked.

"I'm not hurt!" That was both a lie and the truth. Everything hurt, yet somehow her soul felt eased as well. There was so much anguish but hope as well. She had part of herself back and it was bizarre that a piece of her had to die for that to happen. It just hadn't felt like a piece of her.

"My dear hellcat, you're bawling."

"Because I'm happy! I could be like Saniyah and still carrying that demon." It was out of her. It was out of her body. It was Asad and it was gone, so she could recover who she was. She could heal from some of the damage.

Ashni made a strangled noise. "Demon?"

The words flowed without thought, without meaning. "The demon that was inside of me, stealing my energy, my will to live! The baby. It took me and it would've taken you."

"A baby?" Ashni choked out. "You could never lose me or yourself. You're too strong. Remember, you're the woman who looked me in the face while you were decorated in chains and told me you should be in charge."

Nakia shook her head. "No, I was stupid then, as I am stupid now. I wasn't meant to be in charge. I'm not made for it."

"That's not true. You grew into a mighty visionary of a ruler. This city, this region wouldn't function without you." Ashni took a deep breath, her voice cracking. "You're the backbone. The heart and soul. My own closest follow you over me."

Nakia whimpered, clutching Ashni's waist, curling tighter into her. "I've only led them into pain and suffering. I ruined Adira and Saniyah's marriage. I ruined us!"

"Never."

"You would've accepted this child, loved her as your own. You would've been proud to raise her, but I'm happy she's dead," Nakia wailed. Ashni would never love her now, knowing she was happy her child—their child—had perished.

Chapter Fifteen

ASHNI'S CHEST HURT AS though Nakia's weight crushed her, causing her ribs to stab her in the heart. Everything seemed to have drained out of her and she wasn't sure how she didn't flatten out against the bed. Nakia was pregnant? Nakia had a baby, and now that baby was dead?

Her questions weren't important right now. Not when the love of her life had absolutely fallen apart in her arms. More than that, Nakia had admitted she was happy she lost the baby, yet she was bawling like every bone in her body was broken. Nakia sounded broken. Ashni needed to put her back together.

"Shh," Ashni said and rocked Nakia. She kissed the top of Nakia's head. "It's okay."

Nakia tugged at her, clutching her with such agonized fervor. "You would've loved her no matter what, and I would've hated her with all parts of me because I'd always see him!"

Ashni caressed Nakia's side and kissed the top of her head once more. Nakia didn't seem to notice. She wept harder, each sound pounding into Ashni, grinding her bones to dust. It was worse than when she first woke up from being poisoned. Who dared trespass against her beloved? The other part of her soul? She'd make him feel Nakia's pain times ten.

"I'm so happy, but I can't stop crying. It doesn't make sense. I won! I won in Tariq. And then they found out and it hurts. I lost everything you worked for but saved so many people and I just feel so awful!" Nakia soaked Ashni's shirt in tears.

Ashni could hardly keep up. Nakia was happy and felt awful? And what about Tariq? They didn't have any enemies there. *Oh, don't we? No.* That was why everyone was being so damn hush-hush around her. Asad was the one doing this. He had threatened to destroy Layla's people countless times as a means to control them. Well, it sounded like he had tried again, and Nakia stopped him. Good on her, but Asad wasn't one to just lie down and accept a loss. He hurt Nakia and Adira.

The second Ashni fell, the door was open for Asad to destroy everything she built. Her family, included. *He'll pay for this.*

Nakia had a death grip on her, fingers tearing into her shirt. "I'm so sorry!"

Ashni took a deep breath before she spoke. Every bit of her insides trembled. Her skin sparked and her talent vibrated through her. It took every piece of her self-control to keep from causing a storm over the city. She wanted to throw up. More than that, she wanted to put her hand in Asad's chest and personally rip his heart out, like he did to everyone she cared about.

"You have nothing to be sorry for. You didn't do anything wrong." Ashni stroked Nakia's hair.

Nakia cried out as if she had been stabbed in the gut. "I shouldn't be happy. I shouldn't!" Now, the sobs sounded almost like laughter. "I shouldn't be happy, but I am."

Nakia coughed some as she cried on. Soon, she had worn herself out. She fell asleep in Ashni's arms.

Ashni looked at Adira, who Nakia probably didn't know was in the room. Adira's face was like stone.

"Asad," Ashni said.

"And Jay," Adira replied.

"Because they're rarely far from each other." Ashni felt an odd calm. Almost like peace. Even as she knew what Adira would likely do. *Forgive me, Mom and Dad, but they brought this on themselves.* She needed to know exactly what she was punishing them for beyond harming Nakia so thoroughly. "Tell me everything."

Adira let it go, every single horror. It was clear they had come merely to torture those she loved. They were worse than Amal. At least he wanted her territory. They only wanted to pollute and taint everyone she held dear.

"And Saniyah is...?" Ashni gritted her teeth.

"Jay is mine," Adira growled.

"I would never deny you." This was beyond the pale. "After, take what you need from me." It made so much sense now. Adira had more than a right to hate her, to hurt her, to want her dead. She had failed them spectacularly with her own carelessness. She opened the door for this to happen the moment she was poisoned.

Adira scoffed. "Idiot. I've been taking it out on you and that was wrong. It wasn't your fault. It's not your fault. Their actions are their own."

"They did this because of me! They did this because I wasn't here. You were right."

"I wasn't. I was angry."

Ashni couldn't accept that. She was supposed to be the leader. She wanted to be great in the eyes of this woman. "They were able to do this because I wasn't there."

Adira held up a stern finger. "No. They did this because they're assholes. I've been an asshole abusing you over their actions, behaving just as they would. This isn't your fault, except they hate that you're better than they are. You always have been."

Ashni shook her head, seething. How dare her brothers do this? "How did they pull this off? What made them think I was dead?"

"They have spies in the north and in our military. I looked into it but didn't get far because Saniyah got attacked. Beyond revenge, why do you think they did this?"

Ashni shook her head. "The throne. Jay wants the throne and he'll want all the support he can get when the time comes."

"How does this get Jay the throne?"

"It keeps Asad from challenging him. That's probably the deal. Asad's the type of bastard who'd rather burn it all to the ground than concede the fight. Besides, it'd look really good for Jay to have all the support of his brothers when he ascends the throne. So, he makes a trade and supports Asad's revenge."

Adira nodded. "That makes sense."

"They've become poison."

"I'm glad you and the little ones are different."

Ashni smiled a little. It was nice to have Adira forgive her, although it didn't stop the burning under her skin. It felt like she was about to split apart. The snakes that were her older brothers bit yet again. Amal had wanted her, and he had hurt children and others. Jay and Asad made this more personal than just taking her city, though. If she didn't do something about her brothers, she was certain she'd turn to dust and blow away in the breeze, forgotten.

"This wasn't your fault," Adira said again.

Ashni shook her head. She was the leader, so it was her fault. She was supposed to take care of this, protect everyone. *That's why Dad spoke to you after all that nonsense. He knew you were going astray. That's why you needed to see those relationships. You have to remember who has been there for you, who made you the Chosen One. You have responsibilities to these people, not some adventure out in the world. You owe these people.* Doing right by her people would put her on the path of greatness.

Ashni glanced down at Nakia, snoring softly in her arms. Nakia needed the sleep. Ashni needed it, too, yet it refused to come. Her mind filled with what she would do to her brothers. No, not her brothers. Her enemies. They never wanted to be family. Well, message finally received.

After some time, Samar and Layla appeared with food and medicine. Nakia awoke to share in both. There was a loud, long silence between all of them. Ashni could see the weariness on their faces. What really caught her attention was Saniyah, tucked in close to Adira. So, unlike the confident woman Ashni had grown to admire. Time to end this crap.

"I'm going to assume they haven't burned the palace to the ground yet," Ashni said. Samar and Layla stared at her with wide eyes

"No, they took a break to eat lunch," Layla replied. Samar glared at her, but Layla didn't flinch.

"Where are my swords?" Ashni asked, eyes locked on Samar.

Samar arched an eyebrow. "Excuse me?"

Nakia's brow wrinkled. "Swords?"

"Yes. I need to do something. Now." If she didn't start being a leader right now, the acidic hole festering inside of her would eat her alive. It was bad enough they had been dealing with Hell while she was asleep, lying in bed, and being fed. No more.

"Ashni!" Nakia clutched her arm.

"I can't stand by as any more of this happens." Ashni wasn't sure about who she was right now, but she wasn't the type of person who could let anyone hurt everyone she cared about.

Adira stood. "Let's go."

"No! She's not in any shape to fight those animals." Nakia held Ashni tighter.

"It's time to put some dogs down. She's more than ready," Adira replied.

Her confidence made Ashni want to puff out her chest. Adira's faith subdued some of the gnawing in her stomach, although it wasn't nearly enough. Only blood would calm her blood.

Ashni pulled Nakia close and kissed her cheek. "Kitten, knowing how bad they hurt you, all of you, I can't go on living unless I do something about it as soon as possible. You won the war, even if you don't think you did. You did better than I ever could but let me have this last fight."

Nakia looked at her with wide eyes, tears gathering at the corners. "When does it end, though? It'll just make them come back."

"They won't." Ashni got out of the bed and gave Nakia a soft kiss on her lips. The cycle stopped here. Adira handed her the twin swords, and Ashni turned to her sister. "Layla."

Layla opened a void, and they were gone. They reappeared in the throne room. Ashni took in the sight. Bodies of servants littered the floor. Blood slicked the once-polished marble. The walls had scorch marks and gore on them. The throne had been burned, flames still licked the pillows and rugs and curtains. Black smoke lingered, an acrid haze in the room.

Ashni shouldered her weapons. "They're not in here."

"Well, this is where I last saw them." Layla looked around.

A gasp caught their attention and they all turned to see a servant peering around a nearby column. His robes had been ripped and blood dribbled from a cut on his neck. "Highness, you're alive!"

"Never mind that. Where are the fuckers who did this?" Ashni asked.

The servant pointed to the doors. "Tearing through the main garden."

They wasted no time going there and found Jay and Asad. The garden was in shambles. The smell of smoke choked the air and burned Ashni's eyes. Trees were toppled and charred, some still burning. Bushes had been set ablaze. Statues bent, broken, pushed in the dirt, and melted in various places. Swords had been taken to things, cutting them away at sharp angles. It would be a long time coming before Nakia and her sisters could have lunch there again.

"Do your tantrums ever stop?" Ashni said loud enough for Jay and Asad to hear her.

Both men paused and turned to the sound of her voice. Their faces pinched. Ashni would have smirked at them, though that seemed too playful for the situation. Nothing about this was a game.

Asad's upper lip curled. "Ashni? You're like some bug that won't go away. How the hell are you here?"

"The same way Tariq and Tiq are still here—Nakia," Ashni said.

A demented grin overtook Asad's visage. "Did she tell you how I beat her? She cried for you every time."

His words pounded every bit of Ashni. The thought of Nakia calling out for her, scratched deep into Ashni's being. She had been weak and helpless and couldn't protect Nakia as Nakia protected her. She couldn't save Nakia from Asad then, and now she'd make sure he never touched her again.

"My princess thwarted you at every turn," Ashni said, raising her swords.

Asad chuckled. "She's pregnant with my baby, you know."

She scoffed. "No, your ape of an older brother took that victory from you. Thank you for that, Jay. So kind of you."

Asad glowered at Jay. "You hit her in the stomach?"

Jay curled his lip. "Of course I wouldn't do that. She's lying. Ashni's trying to get in your head."

Ashni rolled her shoulders. "I'm already in your heads. I've been there for years. You can't stand the fact that Dad accepted me, and the people called me Chosen."

"You've always thought too highly of yourself," Jay said.

"Yet here you are. I understand now. That's what you really hate," Ashni replied. It was beyond them wanting what she had or wanting to be her. They couldn't turn away from her, couldn't stop thinking about her. It was the insane, sick side of love and admiration. They wanted her to notice. She was their Sun. "You worship me."

"Never!" Jay scowled. "Gods would never bow down to some bastard in a sick robe."

"You're nothing," Asad said. "All you have belongs to the Empire, which will eventually belong to us."

"Then why do you think of me so often? I can't believe I never saw it until now. You'll never be me and it kills you." Ashni shook her head.

"Tell yourself whatever lies you want, Ashni. You don't have anything. It's all ours." Asad motioned between himself and Jay.

Ashni shook her head. "Who's giving you anything? You're the one who doesn't have anything, not even your twin. You're nothing but a shared form of the fuck up on house arrest. Jay didn't promise to share anything with you. There's no reason for him to do that."

Asad was delusional. The best he could do was make a nuisance of himself when Jay tried to take over and Jay probably already had plans for Asad when the time came for him to ascend the throne, but they wouldn't make it that far. Ashni raised her swords.

"You dare pull your swords on us?" Jay pointed his massive double-edged straight blade at her. His sword was taller than she was.

"Enough talk." Adira snarled as she unsheathed her sword.

Jay laughed. "Really? Fine. And when we end you, I'm taking Saniyah with me. She can enjoy a proper marriage befitting a sterling noble whose family is almost on par with mine."

"No, you stop here." Adira rushed Jay.

Asad was in Ashni's face moments after, blade aiming for her face. Ashni put her sword up just in time. The swords clashed together, and Asad blew fire at her. She moved in time to avoid being burned. Heat washed over her cheek, singed the tips of her hair. She might have new burn scars to join the ones Amal left her.

Calling up her talent, she forced Asad back with a heavy wind. He dug his heels in to fight against the gale and tried to breath more fire. Ashni's wind went right through his flames. The blaze snuffed out. He snarled, sending a wave of fire at her. She cut through it with the *Golden Feather*. Her blade cleaved the flames in two. He rushed her, but Ashni aimed lightning at his feet.

"Your talent's weak," Asad said, skidding to a stop.

"You're weak," Ashni said, swinging at him with her blade. He blocked with his own sword and raised his other hand to use his fire. She wasted no time swinging her other sword and he lost a couple of fingertips.

"You fucking bitch!" Asad let loose several darts, blood droplets flying as well from his wounded hand.

Ashni hit most of the projectiles with her lightning. Two hit her in the abdomen. She growled from the sharp pain. Knowing Asad, the damn things were poisoned. Asad smirked. *Fuck, Samar's going to be so damn pissed with me.*

"When you die, I'll put another baby in your barbarian," he said.

Echoes of Nakia's cries drummed in Ashni's mind, pumping her blood and possessing her. She couldn't process the fury inside of her. She was ready to erupt.

The feeling went from her heart to her blood to her body to her soul and then flared outward. It was like each erupted beyond her. It was inside of her and outside of her. The energy was her, and it was also the universe.

A cascade of lightning tore down from the heavens. Thunder boomed like it was the planet tearing itself apart. Asad called forth a wall of fire to protect himself, but the bolts went through the fire with ease. The bolts struck Asad, the force blowing him out of his boots. Wind doused his flames. He landed on a patch of blackened, burnt earth. She marched over to him, her sword tight in her grip.

Asad coughed. His body smoked, white and grey. He raised his head up enough to look at her. "You'll never be one of us." He managed to wave his hand spraying flames, but he didn't come close to her.

"I don't want to be. I haven't for a long time," Ashni replied.

"Liar. It's always burned you up not to be in our inner circle."

Ashni snorted. "Never. After all, I am Chosen and you're nothing. You didn't even realize how much Amal wanted to be part of your inner circle. You abandoned your own twin." In some demented way Amal had tried to fill the void of missing his twin by engaging Ashni in all the wrong ways.

Pains shot through Ashni's abdomen. She coughed and flecks of green liquid came from her mouth along with blood. Damn. The darts were definitely poisoned.

Asad climbed to his feet, panting. He was still smoking, clothing torn and burned away. "You don't talk about my brother. You don't dare speak his name."

She sneered. "Amal, the brother you cared so much about that you didn't bother to find him after he killed his wolf-brother in the circus." She would never forget Amal's shrieks after he became a member of the Wolf Guild. Their father standing by him was probably the only thing that kept him from completely falling apart.

"He was too attached to the beast," Asad said. "It was a means to an end."

Ashni shook her head, groaning as it felt like her guts were inflamed. "If that was all your pup was to you, then you misunderstood the purpose."

Jay hadn't been bothered when he killed his bear cub, so Asad mimicked him. Following Jay got him exactly where anyone would've predicted—second.

Asad's chest heaved. "Stop acting like you know so much more than us! You know what I know? Not even a week ago, your bitch was swollen with my seed. And she will be again soon."

Ashni gnashed her teeth, blood dripping from her mouth. She could feel her blood boiling again, nerves popping with energy.

"You'll never touch Nakia again. Never threaten Layla again," Ashni said. It wasn't a promise. It was the truth.

Asad chuckled and raised his charred hand. He called up more fire between them, a curtain of flames.

Ashni waved it off, wind cutting through it, giving her enough space to get to Asad. He had brought enough time to grab his sword again. He slashed at her, and she sparked lightning from her fingers, making him back away. She hit him with lightning again, the bright strands of power clinging to his sword and traveling down to his hand, arm, and chest. He was blown back once more. He tossed his sword away, realizing she was using it as a lightning rod. Ashni kicked him square in the chest.

Asad cried out as he hit the dirt. To keep her away, he threw more darts. A burst of wind handled them. She buried the *Ivory Claw* into his knee. He screamed, blood gushing from the wound.

Asad held up both hands, pointing singed palms at her. "Ashni, wait." Tiny cinders jumped from his fingers but died before doing anything.

She sucked her teeth. "Never again."

Asad tried to reach for a dagger, but she twisted her sword and halted all motion. He hollered again. Ashni felt his ache in hollowed out sections of her being, places put there by him and Jay. His distress vibrated through her, pulsing, and she savored it like a sweet treat. *I hope my hellcat can feel his agony.*

"Ashni," Asad said, panting rhythmically to alleviate his pain.

"Now you say my name as if it's something to be respected. Too late."

He pressed his palms together. "You've won."

How dare he! He said that like it was supposed to make up for everything that happened, like she was supposed to just stop. "When I cut off your head, I've won."

"You can't kill me," he said with a forced laugh.

She leaned hard on her sword and he screamed. "Why can't I?"

"Mom would never forgive you."

It was possible. No matter what, their mother always loved them all and never liked to see one of them hurt the other. Their mother wanted so badly for them all to be the best of friends. Yet she had seen her mother punish people who betrayed her. It was never pretty.

"I'll take my chances," Ashni said and brought the *Golden Feather* down through his throat, severing his head.

Feeling relief, Ashni turned to Adira and Jay's battle. Jay looked like a mountain compared to Adira, but Adira's sword cut deep into his arm.

Jay's fire jumped from his fingers in short bursts, but he couldn't control it. Adira had cut specific points on his body, making it hard for him to use his Fire. Ashni laughed.

"I'm going to crush you!" Jay roared, trying to force fire from his mouth. A pitiful column spewed out, and Adira had no trouble dipping away from it.

"What are you without your Fire? You couldn't even beat me with it when we sparred. What have you ever had to actually fight for? That's why your father, hell the world, preferred Ashni!" Adira sidestepped his slow flame pillar and blocked his sword with her own.

"The world won't put that bitch on a throne any more than Dad meant for you to actually take Saniyah. She deserves better than you, just as the Empire deserves better than Ashni."

"We've all made our choices. Now, live with them."

Jay charged Adira. Not the wisest decision for a warrior his size, but he was furious and that clouded his judgment. Adira moved out of the way and brought her sword down on his leg, cut through the tendons of his right leg. Jay yelled and fell to his knees.

"You think you own the world, and you think it entitles you to whatever the hell you want." Adira circled him as he tried to get up. She shoved her sword through his thigh. "Stay."

Jay blew fire at her, and she put her arm up to block the licking flames. He took a deep breath, managed to get himself under enough control to focus his talent. More fire formed from his lips, fanning it out to keep Adira at bay.

Adira moved to the side, taking out Jay's other knee. She swiveled behind him, sword to his neck.

Jay clamped down on his Fire, sealing the flames away with his lips. "You can't kill me," Jay said, smoke curling from his mouth as he said the words.

"I have witnesses," Adira replied. "And you violated my blessed marriage."

Jay smirked. "That's right. You'll always remember that, and my child will live on, even if you kill me."

Ashni shook her head. Jay was an idiot and, for all of his talk of being a sterling, he bucked one of the greatest Roshan traditions. Saniyah wouldn't have his child. She was never having his child. No one thought Saniyah was weak or tainted for what he did. He was the one who was weak and tainted. But that baby was about to be blessed with the best mothers ever.

Adira chuckled. "Killing you would be much too easy. No, you get to live with being beaten by this barbarian fisherwoman in a serious fight, where I could've killed you if I felt like it, who will raise that child with my customs and values. We'll even teach the baby how to fish. Yeah, she'll be the best fisherwoman, just like her mother."

He paled, sweat and blood pooling beneath him. "That's my child!"

"It was never yours, rather always mine and Saniyah's." Adira smirked. "And you'll live powerless because everyone will know I defeated you in battle. Everyone will know what you dared to do to Saniyah Gyan, a member of one of the highest houses in the Empire. They'll know of your treachery along with Asad. They'll remember you were involved in a matter that cost your brother his life and you were outmaneuvered by a little barbarian hellcat." Adira patted him on the shoulder with the sword. "Live with that."

Jay's eyes went wide, his dream of ruling the Empire gone. His future was as dead as Asad. Ashni couldn't have been prouder of her friend, her mentor, her sister.

Chapter Sixteen

NAKIA BIT HER LIP. The nightmare was supposedly over. Ashni showed Nakia Asad's body, proof that he couldn't hurt her ever again. But at what cost? Ashni had killed her brother, a prince of the Empire. How did they come back from that? Hell, Nakia had used the Roshan army to fight itself.

"Ashni," Nakia said, leaning against her as they sat on the throne, issuing edicts to try to smooth this over. Servants milled around them, straightening up what they could. A few days after the attack, it was nearly impossible to tell there had been a massacre in the area.

"Yes, Nakia?" Ashni held her tight.

"How do we fix this?" Try as she might, she couldn't think of how they came out of this all right.

Ashni sighed. "I don't think we can."

It wasn't what Nakia wanted to hear, wishing to cling to the idea that Ashni could make everything better. So Ashni was out of miracles. That was fine. They'd come up with something together. Things would be all right as long as they were together.

Nakia swallowed. "So, what do we do?"

"What's best for all of us."

There was only one thing that could mean. A break from the Empire they rebelled against. That wasn't an easy decision for Ashni to make and Nakia's guts twisted. Things shouldn't have come to this. She wanted to save Ashni's dream.

"Are you sure? Your dream. Your father's dream. The army's dream."

Ashni nodded. "Sometimes a harsh reality pokes you awake, and your dreams vanish into glaring daylight. Time to wake up."

Nakia wrapped her arms around Ashni's waist. She nuzzled Ashni and felt reassured in Ashni's presence. Ashni was alive, even though her fight with Asad left her bloody and poisoned. She had vomited several times the past couple of days, but Samar took care of her. This poison they were familiar with, and thankfully, it wasn't debilitating.

"Wake up to what, though?" Nakia peered off to the end of the throne room, past the open doors, the carpeted hallway, staring well beyond it.

Layla marched in. They had sent her out to assess the damage. They weren't sure if Jay and Asad's people had made it into the city or beyond. For once, Layla didn't whine about that not being her job.

"What're we working with?" Ashni asked.

"The city's fine. The north's still being fortified. Everything's still running smoothly," Layla said with a grin and she motioned to Nakia. "Nakia had it."

Nakia blew out a breath. She wanted to crawl in bed with Ashni and never leave. Everything about her was an open, deteriorating, throbbing wound.

"Naren?" Nakia asked.

"Returning with my father and Hafiz. They won the battle against Asad's troops. Now, they're trying to organize refugees, from both Tariq and Khenshu. Word's already traveled."

"What're people saying?" Ashni asked.

"They think Nakia's trying to steal the Empire. Nobles in Jay's and Asad's territories are calling the battle an act of war and they still swear you're dead. Shit's going to hit the fan when they realize you're alive and Asad's dead. The nobles will be screaming for justice."

Ashni rolled her eyes. "Justice. This was justice."

Layla shook her head. "They won't believe it."

Ashni rubbed her chin. No, the nobles wouldn't believe it. They'd make the battle, the princes' defeat, and even moving people from Tariq, Tiq, and now Khenshu so much worse. They'd say it was more than a rebellion.

"Everyone knows what we have to do," Nakia said, her voice small. It wasn't fair. Ashni worked so hard, had done nothing wrong, and she lost everything. "I'm so sorry."

Layla scoffed. "Sorry for what? Do you have any clue how many lives you saved? You really stepped up and did an amazing job. Every Shadow Walker will always be indebted to you, as well as any person from Tariq and Tiq. So, don't apologize."

It would take some time to get used to Layla's praise, but it did help to ease the sense of failure. Hundreds, maybe thousands, of people were alive thanks to her.

"You are an amazing queen," Ashni said as she gave Nakia a little squeeze. Pain lanced through her with that small pressure, yet the kind words, again, helped. Ashni wasn't upset with her over the accidental rebellion and the probable break from the Empire.

"I think we all had an inkling of what would happen once we crossed the waters into the West, anyway," Layla said.

Nakia glanced at Ashni. There was a slight tremble in her chin and bottom lip. Her eyes were wet. She looked haunted. It was quite clear Ashni had never envisioned this. Ashni had always meant to have the world be called Roshan. Instead, her world was falling apart in front of her.

"Are you okay?" Nakia asked Ashni.

"We've all made sacrifices." Ashni blew out a breath. "Mine might be the easiest."

"Don't you dare think that. You've lost just as much as any of us." Maybe even more. Ashni might have lost who she was. Her brothers were certainly gone with her killing Asad. Her mother might be gone—they hadn't heard from her yet. She'd lost her home, her people, and her entire cultural identity. She was no longer a princess of the Empire.

Asad and Jay had even robbed Ashni of the security that she could protect her spouse. The mental scars might never heal. Nakia wasn't sure how Ashni hadn't broken down weeping yet.

Despite that, Nakia was eternally grateful for her spouse. To know what Ashni would do for her would always be etched in her soul. Ashni proved time and time again she'd go above and beyond for Nakia. Nakia couldn't put a name to the emotions she felt toward Ashni now.

"You've lost more than any of us could imagine," Layla said, approaching the throne and settling at her feet, laying her head on Ashni's lap.

Ashni shook her head and opened her mouth to say something. She closed her mouth just as quickly. There was something there. Ashni just needed a moment to get it out. Nakia ached for her beloved, trying to be so strong and hold things together for them, even as adrift as they were. *As long as we have each other, we'll help each other through.*

"Is this what it's like to be conquered?" Ashni finally asked, her voice tiny, fragmented, like the distant look in her eyes.

Yes. Nakia looked to Layla. Yet they hadn't lost all of themselves in the Roshan conquest. Layla still had her people with her, her parents. Nakia had regained her sisters. There was a give and take for them. There had to be a give for Ashni. Nakia realized exactly what it was.

"This is freedom, my love," Nakia said.

Ashni could now do whatever she wished with her territory. She could shape her nation into whatever she saw fit rather than handing it over to someone who might dismantle it or take it in a direction Ashni didn't desire. And she wouldn't have to worry about backstabbing while she worked. It might be less stress on her. They might be happy being separated from the Empire.

Ashni arched an eyebrow. "How so?"

"You were adding to an Empire you weren't sure you'd inherit. An Empire packed with people who were vipers and wanted to see you gone. You'd have had people you couldn't trust around you. Now, you can build an empire of your own and cement your own legacy. You can build your own vision and create something so beautiful it would put the Roshan Empire to shame."

Ashni took a deep breath and looked at Nakia, then at Layla. "No, we can build our vision. Together. We'll work to make this the best place it can be. I want to truly unite the people and never hear the word sterling again."

"That's the spirit." Layla grinned.

Ashni still looked adrift in uncharted waters, so Nakia took her hand. Everything would be all right, even if it didn't seem quite right at the moment. Nakia squeezed Ashni's hand, a silent promise to help Ashni through any doubt. Ashni offered her a small smile, although it didn't reach her eyes.

"My darling, you're not alone," Nakia said.

"I know," she whispered. The look didn't fade from her gaze, though.

Ashni didn't appear better as the day pressed on, despite the fact that their kingdom was in good shape. Jay and Asad had done all their damage on a much more local level.

To help the healing process, Nakia invited Adira, Saniyah, and Bashira to sit with them. Samar also came along. They sat for a meal in one of the smaller rooms that had survived Jay and Asad's tantrum.

The meal was presented well, even though Ashni released every servant after the attack. Everyone waiting on them now was there voluntarily, and Nakia was grateful for their strength. The servants had been through just as much as anyone else.

"Is your sister going to come back?" Bashira asked, eyes on the table. She moved to eat something, and then pulled her hand back.

A twinge went through Nakia's heart. "I'm not sure. I wrote to her, but I haven't heard back."

To be fair, it had only been a few days, yet she suspected Saffi wouldn't return any time soon. Maybe not at all. She was supposed to keep Saffi safe, and she had put Saffi right in harm's way. Maybe Saffi shouldn't come back. Thia could keep and care for their sister.

Bashira nodded, a twinkle in her eyes. "I hope she returns. We agreed to see so many shows together."

Saffi had been quite interested in Bashira's dancing and entertainment in general. It brought joy, as Bashira tended to do. Hopefully Thia would be able to build on that.

"She'll be back. She liked it here," Adira said. Nakia hoped that was true.

Adira had one hand on Saniyah's back, and the other on her abdomen. Saniyah rested comfortably against Adira like she hadn't spent months being tormented by Jay. His bruises still marred her delicate neck.

Nakia admired Saniyah's ability to bounce back, at least in front of them. It was amazing how both Saniyah and Adira accepted her pregnancy. Culture was a powerful thing. There was no way Nakia would've been so comfortable or confident in herself. There were times she wanted to hide from servants who knew what happened, yet Saniyah threw her shoulders back and stood strong.

Saniyah put her chin up. "We'll get back to normal."

"No, we won't," Ashni said, drawing all eyes to her.

It wasn't something anyone else wanted to say aloud, but there was no way to go back to normal. Normal was done when they engaged the Roshan army. Then again, Jay and Asad had already stolen their normal. Their normal was as dead as Asad. *Not that I'm sad he's gone.*

Ashni took a breath and smiled. "We're at a point where we have to create a new normal. I've killed Asad. There's no getting around that. Naren has led my army against the Roshan army in Roshan territory. And what happened to you." Ashni's eyes drifted to Saniyah.

"What's to be done?" Saniyah asked as she put her hand on her belly, twining her fingers with Adira's. While tradition dictated that the baby was Adira's and Saniyah's, there was always a chance for some idiot who supported Jay would show up and cause more trouble. Of course, that wouldn't end well for the idiot, but they didn't need any more issues with the Empire.

Ashni opened her mouth, and nothing came out. Nakia stroked Ashni's hand with her thumb. Ashni leaned into her. The motion made Nakia feel light inside. She was giving Ashni strength and that helped fortify her.

Nakia picked up the conversation for her beloved. "We're going to break from the Empire. We're already in rebellion thanks to the orders I gave. Depending on how Chandra reacts, Asad's death could be viewed as treason and an act of war."

"It didn't help that I cut Jay's tongue out," Adira said.

Nakia wanted to applaud the move, yet that wasn't appropriate. It didn't help, although it certainly was satisfying. Jay lost his tongue, so he couldn't spin lies on what happened between him and Saniyah nor about his battle with Adira. He couldn't pretend to be better than they were anymore. And he got to go back home, unlike his little brother.

Ashni scowled. "He deserved worse."

Layla nodded. "Much worse."

He definitely got off lightly, even though humiliation was a punishment worse than death for him. Maybe it was hard to balance the scales here. She wasn't sure what justice could look like for them, yet Asad's death and Jay's destruction didn't feel like enough.

"No one's arguing otherwise, but these are the options before us. Build our own nation or wait for Chandra's judgment with dozens of nobles demanding our blood," Nakia said. None of them would miss the damn scheming Roshan nobles.

"The nobles can bark all they want, but no one knows how Chandra will take the death and maiming of her sons," Saniyah said.

"Does it matter that the stupid sons started this?" Bashira folded her arms. It was idiotic that Jay and Asad got to escape blame free, especially when there was evidence of their crime.

"It should matter. They made her think Ashni was dead." Adira motioned to Ashni.

Saniyah nodded. "That sounds like it should count for something."

It should. Then again, Chandra was unpredictable when it came to her children. And thinking Ashni was dead wasn't the same as Asad actually being dead. Nakia wasn't sure how any parent would react to that.

"Maybe, maybe not," Ashni said, shrugging. "We don't want to be around for the maybe not."

It was easy to think of Chandra as the motherly figure dressed in white, forever mourning her husband. However, she also fought off a horde of nobles to become empress of the mightiest nation on the planet. They should bow out gracefully while they had the chance, *if* they had the chance.

"She could come for us even if we withdraw, then we lose all the trade we promised Wicus. This could end up as two wars for us on opposite fronts," Adira said.

"I'm not worried about Wicus. He's been an honorable ally. He has my respect and trust right now," Ashni replied. "Is a split the best thing for us? As Samar said, we might lose almost all of our trade once we step away."

"I think we should. There is no guarantee you would inherit the Empire and we've all worked hard for this," Saniyah replied.

"No, you're definitely not getting the throne now, so time to start something new," Layla said, and she nodded toward Nakia. Nakia smiled, returning the nod.

Bashira frowned. "I don't see why this takes her out of the running with the Empire."

Nakia could agree with Bashira logically. Ashni hadn't done anything worse than her older brothers, except she didn't have the same support as the brothers. It wasn't Chandra, but the nobles who hated Ashni. And even if they didn't control the Empress, they still had some power. It wasn't fair, but politics rarely were.

"You can't reward me for killing my brother if you're the empress. I took away my chance as much as Amal did and Jay did," Ashni replied. She didn't sound upset about that.

Nakia shook her head. Was this something they had considered before all this happened? It seemed like a forgone conclusion that Ashni wouldn't inherit the Roshan Empire. It was strange that Ashni didn't consider she'd get the throne, yet never considered she might have to break her territory away from the Empire. Maybe it didn't matter. What mattered now was saving what they had built over the years.

***

Ashni sat at her desk, staring at a parchment. She wanted to write to her mother, explaining why her son was dead and Ashni's decision to break with the Roshan Empire. The words wouldn't come though, so she went to bed. *There might never be words.*

"Are you alright?" Nakia asked, already under their blankets and ready for sleep as she hadn't slept in days. Ashni wasn't sure how to help that beyond giving her time.

"I am." *Not.* She wasn't sure if she ever would be again. She killed her mother's son and so she might lose her mother. She was one announcement away from not being Roshan anymore. She lost her father's dream, her dream. Who the hell was she if she wasn't Roshan? *I thought I knew, but now it's just a mess.*

Nakia cuddled into Ashni, as she did every night, except now Nakia held her as if begging for her to take the pain away. Yet Ashni didn't know how.

"Don't lie to me, my love," Nakia said.

Maybe Nakia could help Ashni figure out who she was now. She was still Nakia's spouse, even if she wasn't sure how to help Nakia. That was a start. *You're still Layla's sister and you're still a leader. There are pieces of you there.*

Ashni sighed. "How do you apologize for killing your brother? I don't feel sorry for it. I'm sorrier he was her son."

"You don't need to apologize. Speak your heart, your truth, and leave her to decide if that deserves an apology."

Ashni chewed on her words as she caressed Nakia's back, wanting to relax her. Nakia fell asleep. She gripped and tugged at Ashni, whimpering and begging in nonsense words. Asad was dead, but alive in Nakia's mind. Ashni didn't owe her mother an apology. An explanation maybe, but nothing more, and she did owe the people who protected her when she was down. So, she cuddled Nakia until she calmed and then returned to her desk.

To my mother,

I address this as such because you will always be my mother, even if I can no longer accept you as my empress. Please understand this has nothing to do with your leadership or my conquest. I've always been grateful that you allowed me to press on and pursue my dream, Dad's dream. You always applied the law fairly and evenly, except in one instance. You are the mother of five others and that's affected us both my entire life.

By now, you know much of what happened here. I've sent you Asad's body for you to properly mourn and bury him. If he were anyone else, I'd have fed his body to stray, dying dogs and then used those dogs to fertilize farmland. What he did to my beloved cannot be put into words. He could not be punished enough, but I dislike that I've punished you, my mother, in the process. You don't deserve that.

Asad committed a trespass against me and mine. I took justice into my own hands and I do not regret it. I also stand by the use of my section of the Roshan army to battle against the troops in Asad's region. And, if those were the only issues, I would probably beg your forgiveness. I would probably throw myself on your wisdom and mercy, yet there is so much more.

I have to separate from the Roshan Empire because it's harmful for my family and my people to remain. The Empire gave authority to people who came through and wreaked havoc on those I love and threatened people I'm meant to protect. I will be respectful to your position and make only one request. The Roshan Empire can release the West into my custody. Allow any people in my territory in the East to depart if they wish, and then give my territory to Fahim. I trust he will care for Khenshu with my same affections. Regardless of your decision, for the mental health of my family and the safety of any who follow me, we will not return.

I understand this could lead to dire consequences. You could cut off trade or invade us. Yet I rely on you as the balanced empress you tend to be. I would also like to thank you, both for being my empress and my mother.

I know I couldn't ask for a better mother even though you didn't come to grieve my death and comfort my wife. I only hope that I can fulfill the words you once said to me. I hope to be destined for those great things. I wish to carry on your legacy, and Dad's as well. I want to be the person you both believe me to be. I want to be worthy of being Chosen. I want to be worthy of being the daughter of Khalid and Chandra Akshay.

Once done, Ashni felt like the letter captured the essence of the matter. She went back to bed and gathered Nakia into her arms. Nakia nuzzled her in her sleep. It should've made Ashni feel better, that Nakia still sought her out for comfort. But all it made her think about was how she had failed her beloved.

"I promise you nothing like this will ever happen again," Ashni whispered into her hair.

Ashni would devote all of her energy to maintain her family and their nation. It was time for her to take care of the things she collected. Time to take care of what and who she adored.

* * *

Dearest daughter,

I write to you as a grieving mother who has to admit her failures at her greatest task. I am fully aware of your brothers' crimes against you, both past and present. I had hoped as they matured, your brothers would come to understand you were one of them, but perhaps they saw what I missed. You are not one of them, for all the right reasons.

With Amal, I could always write his troubles off as an extension of your childhood relationship, though I never realized how damaged the relationship was. The attempts on your life were always serious, and I couldn't accept that. I couldn't fathom why my child would want to slay my other child. I still can't understand why my children wish to hurt each other. I love you all so deeply to the point where my love for you all should have poured into you, and you could feel each other through me. We know that is not what happened, and sorrow has swallowed my heart because of it.

I have to face what Jay and Asad have done as much as anyone else. I will personally write Adira and Saniyah, as Jay had no right to do what he did. Adira punished him accordingly, and the Empire will not seek revenge.

Jay's behavior hurts more as he was the one to tell me you were dead. There was no proof, yet he still saw fit to tell me I lost my daughter. It ripped me apart, a wound that still aches, even as I know you're alive. Nothing will assuage this agony I feel for you or for them. I don't hold what you did to Asad against you, but my heart still aches, for both of you.

Asad's actions were unforgivable, and I beg Nakia's forgiveness as well as your own. Asad thought he was seeking justice, but he was obviously out for revenge. Revenge he didn't deserve. And the path of revenge ended as it often does. The fact that he saw nothing wrong with violating a queen and his sister's spouse means that he was clearly lost.

I am saddened, but he was dealt justice. I will not seek any actions against you, either. It was a fair match. I deem what happened legal. The same with Jay.

I'm sorry you had to be the one to deal this justice. No one should have to make the decision you made. And you had to do it twice. The first time, I was blind, but my eyes are open now.

As for breaking from the Empire, I understand that too, and expected it for a long time. Why wait to inherit an Empire and spend your valuable time fighting snakes for the rest of your life when you could build your own? You have my blessing. You will not lose trade with the Empire while I'm alive. Fahim will care for Khenshu. The twins are old enough, so they can have Asad and Jay's territories. I hope our nations can be allies for many generations.

Do know I will always be your mother, no matter what happens. I hope we can continue to be in each other's lives. I love you, now, then, and always. I love Nakia as my own. Any family you claim as your own will also be mine, and I will do my best to protect them. There will be no more blind eyes. I wish you all the best. Please, may you all find it in your hearts to forgive me.

Your mother and ally,
Chandra Akshay

Ashni clutched the letter to her chest and cried, while Nakia held her. This was who she was. Nakia's spouse. Chandra's daughter. Layla's and Adira's sister. A woman learning to lead people who stood by her as they moved into the unknown. She wouldn't let them down.

***

Nakia woke up from a fitful sleep, nightmares fading as consciousness took over. She tried to squeeze Ashni but found herself wrapped around a pillow instead. Sitting up, she scanned the bedroom in a panic. *No, no, no! Where's Ashni?*

Thoughts of Ashni being dead flooded Nakia's mind until she noticed someone sitting on their balcony. The puffy hair was unmistakable. She rushed to the balcony and found Ashni tucked into a sitting pillow, staring off into the night sky. *She's okay. She's alive.*

"Come." Ashni held out her hand for Nakia, who didn't need to be asked twice.

Nakia eased against Ashni's side and curled into her. Ashni wrapped her arms around Nakia and Nakia did the same. She laid her head on Ashni's chest to listen to Ashni's heartbeat.

"You okay?" Nakia asked.

"Yeah. Sorry I left you. I just..." Ashni shook her head. "I needed air or something. I dunno. Not a fan of being in bed just yet."

"Understood. Something on your mind?" Even though they got away with rebellion and revolt and Ashni hadn't lost her mother in the process, there was still so much hanging over them. "We should talk."

"You're right. We should." Ashni ran her fingers through Nakia's hair. "Layla knew eventually we'd have to split from the Empire, which means Adira definitely knew. Why is it that I never saw that?"

Nakia stared into Ashni's eyes. "Do you feel silly for not seeing it?"

"Maybe a little blind. What did I think would happen? I just thought my mother would live forever, and I should know better."

"No one faults you for not considering your mother would one day die. No one wants to think about that."

"It was irresponsible, and I don't want to be like that anymore. I need to have foresight. Like you."

Nakia arched an eyebrow. "Like me?"

"Yes, because you saw it, too. And you had the patience to get entire towns to safety without engaging Jay and Asad. I never would've been able to do that. Hell, you saw the moment I could get up, I got up. I didn't wait. I didn't plan. I moved. I can plan a battle, but I can't stand a siege. You dug in for a siege."

Nakia shrugged. "What else could I do? I couldn't let Layla's people be slaughtered."

"And you put them before yourself. You sacrificed yourself." Ashni's hand drifted close to Nakia's abdomen before moving to her hip.

"You taught me to lead from the front."

Ashni chuckled, but it sounded hollow. "Look at what that got me. Poisoned over land I don't even care about. Away from you."

"It's not your fault." Nakia kissed her cheek.

"You have to know, you're a hero. Nothing Asad did changes that. You have everyone's utmost respect. Hell, I hear you and Layla are even sisters now." Ashni grinned, though her eyes didn't shine the way they used to.

"Yeah. But you also have everyone's utmost respect. No one's looking down on you because you got hurt. No one's saying you weren't there. No one's blaming you." Ashni needed to know those things. She was still herself.

Ashni nodded. "It'll take time."

Nakia sighed and settled against Ashni again. "For both of us." There was a long silence. "Although, maybe one day, we could adopt."

"I look forward to raising a family with you. We can practice with Saniyah and Adira's kid." Ashni gave her a squeeze. "It's okay for you to feel the way you do. He didn't have a right to touch you, hurt you, force you."

Nakia inhaled sharply and expected to feel a cut inside of herself, but instead felt some ease. She needed to hear Ashni didn't blame her for any of this.

"In my culture, I'd have been forced to marry Asad," Nakia said.

Ashni winced. "I know. We're not like that and you don't even have to think about it. You're not wrong for feeling the way you do about that baby, just like Adira and Saniyah aren't wrong for feeling the way they do. You're entitled to your emotions. You're entitled to relief."

Nakia smiled at her. "You're actually pretty wise."

Ashni scoffed. "Not how I'd usually describe myself but thank you."

"You're not alone in this, beloved. You might not describe yourself in a lot of ways, yet you are those things. And maybe you're not in the Roshan Empire anymore, but that doesn't mean you have to leave behind the cultural bits that make you who you are. You're a strong and special person. We're lucky to have you."

"You're a strong and special person, too. Thank you for gracing me with your presence and for being by my side through so much." Ashni kissed the top of her head.

"Thank you for the same." Nakia sighed as weariness settled into her bones. She was tired, but she was safe, so she could rest. Ashni had her, and she had Ashni.

***

Naren was back and Ashni was happy to see him. She treated him to a return usually reserved for Adira—a grand feast and a party—because he had gone above and beyond. *He is worthy of Layla, and she married well.* Yet there was a somber air as they celebrated. Ashni assembled her closest at breakfast to discuss their current situation.

"As of this moment, we, the West, are our own independent nation. The Roshan Empire will continue to be trade partners, although we're not part of the Empire," Ashni said, expecting to feel the words in the pit of her stomach. She felt light instead. Hopeful. Maybe it was Nakia's hand in her own.

"And our people?" Layla asked. She sat in Naren's lap and rubbed her nose in his cheek. It had to be trying times for her to be so openly affectionate.

"Anyone who didn't come with Naren will be allowed to leave if they desire to do so. We will also allow anyone who wants to return to the Empire to do so. From this moment on, we're on our own. We have to govern the people. There's no more empress, no Roshan courts, no Roshan laws," Ashni replied. "It's us."

"We'll be fine," Nakia said.

Ashni couldn't resist kissing Nakia. It was good to hear Nakia so confident. "We will."

There was silence for a long moment, winding around each of them. They ate as a way to explain away the silence. Yet the quiet pressed on them. They needed to talk.

"The empress wrote to us." Saniyah motioned to herself and Adira.

Ashni nodded. "She said she would."

"She welcomed us as family. Tell me it's because she knows you see Adira as a sister now and not because she has some misguided notions on our child." Saniyah rubbed her baby bump.

"I believe it's the sister thing, but we'll make it clear. Nobody's coming for my niece or nephew in the name of Jay," Ashni replied.

"This is my child." Adira put her arms around Saniyah.

"And since you have a child to worry about, it might be time to retire from the field. You've been fighting most of your life. Time to pass it on. Hafiz is ready. You trained him well," Ashni said.

Hafiz wasn't there. She wasn't sure, but there was a possibility they might lose him to the Empire. But if he stayed on, Adira had put enough into him that he could step into her shoes. He proved that.

Adira's shoulders dropped, and she pulled Saniyah close to her. Saniyah would need help from her spouse to raise a baby; they all knew that.

"This is my legacy now," Adira said, smiling.

Ashni nodded. Adira and Saniyah had served not only her, but her father. They deserved so many things. Things Ashni might never be able to give, although she could start. A governance if they desired it. Anything to make sure they lived their lives in contentment.

"And the people of Tariq and Tiq?" Layla asked.

"I'm granting land to your people to start over," Ashni replied. There was space in the West, plenty of it. They could welcome new people and keep them safe.

"We'll help settle them." Naren pointed to himself and Layla, who nodded.

The reality hit Ashni when she and Nakia were sitting on the throne. Nothing looked different or felt different or smelled different. Yet everything was different. It was now the Throne, not an extension of power. They were a true Queen and her Queen. She grinned at Nakia.

"I wouldn't be able to do this without you," Ashni said. Nakia had proved that she was a fit leader. Ashni would try to follow her example.

"I will always be by your side, my love. Nothing will ever drive me away," Nakia replied. And there they began their legacy, a new life together in a blossoming empire.

The End

About S. L. Kassidy

What is there to know about me? Not much. I was born, bred, and raised in New York and I have no desire to live anywhere else. One day, I would like to travel to a few places, but for now I am content where I am.

I started out writing poetry in junior high and continued to do so for ten years. I wrote short stories, usually fantasy and romance stories, for my own entertainment throughout high school and college. Back then, I wrote strictly for me and those stories remain locked in the back of my closet in little notebooks, written in my almost unreadable, tiny handwriting. In between writing those stories and poetry, I managed to get a college degree in history.

After graduating college, I had a semester off before graduate school and I didn't really have anything to do with my time. So, I took a chance and wrote a fanfic and dared to upload it to the Internet. I was surprised that other people enjoyed my work and I've been posting ever since. I had quite a bit of fun with fan fiction and eventually decided to try my hand in original fiction. I suppose it was sort of like coming back around to what I had been doing in high school and college, except this time the stories were for whoever wanted to read them. I uploaded my first original story a few years ago and haven't looked back. I plan to continue writing as long as I continue getting ideas for stories and it continues to be fun.

Contact Information

Email: slkassidy@gmail.com
Facebook: S.L. Kassidy

Note to Readers:

Thank you for reading a book from Desert Palm Press. We appreciate you as a reader and want to ensure you enjoy the reading process. We would like you to consider posting a review on your preferred media sites and/or your blog or website.

For more information on upcoming releases, author interviews, contest, giveaways and more, please sign up for our newsletter and visit us as at Desert Palm Press: www.desertpalmpress.com and "Like" us on Facebook: Desert Palm Press.

Bright Blessings

www.ingramcontent.com/pod-product-compliance
Lightning Source LLC
Chambersburg PA
CBHW052029020726
47501CB00004B/1326